WHO NEEDS ENEMIES

KERI ARTHUR

KA PUBLISHING PTY LTD

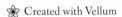

With thanks to:

My agent, Miriam; the fabulous Lulus—best buds and great writers, one and all; and finally, my lovely daughter, Kasey.

AUSSIE SLANG ~ AMERICAN TRANSLATION

Apartment block ~ apartment building

Barracked for ~ rooted for

Barrow ~ wheel barrow

Bins/rubbish bins ~ trash cans

Bitumen ~ concrete/paving material/asphalt

Bottle shop ~ liquor store (In Australia, drive-through bottle shops are often a key part of hotels)

Car boot ~ car trunk

Car park ~ parking lot

Council rates ~ property taxes

Cupboards ~ cabinets

Drink driving ~Drunk driving

Front up ~ show up

Glove box ~ glove compartment

Lane ~ alley

Lash out ~ spend big/ hit someone

Lift ~ elevator

Lolly ~ candy

Magistrate ~ judge

On the outer with ~ not speaking to

Pissed off ~ angry or left the area

Ring/rang ~ call/called

Rostered on ~ scheduled to work

Rubbish ~ trash

Runners ~ sneakers

Shadow Minister ~ opposition politician

(Westminster system of government)

Singlet ~ sleeveless shirt

Squiz ~ look around

Suss ~ suspicious

Takeaway ~ take-out

Tattier ~ more run down

The tip ~ landfill site

Underclothing ~ undergarments

Weatherboard ~ clapboard/wooden cladding

White with one ~ Milk and one lump of sugar in
coffee or tea

A NOTE FROM THE AUTHOR

This novel, unlike most of my Australian-set novels, uses a lot of Australian terms and slang. While Australia is an English speaking country, we tend to use words just a little differently to the rest of you—and words can often have several different meanings. For example, old chook—a chook is a chicken, and therefore an old chook is an old chicken, but it often also used when referring to an old woman. Yes, we Aussies are a strange lot. If you come across a word or term you don't understand, feel free to email me. I'll endeavor to explain.

Also, it might be worth noting that while dragon shifters can talk when in dragon form, it's very hard for them to do so. As a result, their words come out rather garbled. This is reflected in the text; it is not spelling/formatting errors.

Oh, and while this is set in Australia, I've used US English.

CHAPTER ONE

T he sense of trouble slipped across my skin like a teasing caress, making the hairs on my arms stand on end and my heart race.

I paused and studied the street ahead. Though the sun had yet to rise, Berren was waking and her streets echoed with the growing sounds of life. A tram rattled down nearby Collins Street, car lights speared the shadows as they sped past, and joggers pounded the pavement, the sting of their sweat lingering in the air.

There was absolutely nothing that remotely resembled a threat, but I'd learned long ago to trust that niggly sixth sense of mine. It had gotten me out of a whole lot of trouble in the past.

Of course, it had also gotten me *into* trouble, and I was never entirely sure which side of fate's coin my luck would fall.

I glanced at my watch. It was nearly five, which meant I was a few minutes late for my meeting with the one and only relative I had much to do with these days. But that wasn't unusual, and the old elf was certainly used to my tardiness.

So why did I suddenly feel that *this* time, my tardiness had landed him in hot water?

Frowning, I turned into Little Collins Street and jogged down the hill towards Charles Street. Buildings loomed overhead, their rooftops lost to the shadows of a day not yet risen. A light breeze stirred the rubbish left in the wake of garbage trucks, and a rainbow assortment of plastic bags pirouetted limply down the center of the road. Rodents scurried through the deeper shadows closer to the buildings, and the scent of urine and unwashed flesh mingled with the waking groans of the drunks who'd spent the night passed out in doorways. They were no threat, but something here definitely was.

I suddenly wished I'd bought something more than a camera with me. I had a basic understanding of fighting techniques thanks to a former boyfriend's instance that all women should be able to protect themselves, but, right now, with the sensation of danger getting ever stronger, that didn't seem quite enough.

Of course, I generally *could* sweet talk my way out of sticky situations thanks to the fact I was also part siren, but there were definitely some occasions where being armed made much more sense. It was a sad truth that a silver tongued woman wasn't half as respected as a loaded gun, although anyone who knew anything about sirens had a clear under-standing of which was more dangerous.

I jogged on. Abnormal sounds began to leach through the

gloom—the scrape of a heel against concrete, the smack of flesh against flesh. Grunts of pain.

And it was coming from the very place where Lyle and I were supposed to meet.

I thought briefly about calling the cops, then swore softly and sprinted forward. Whatever trouble Lyle had gotten himself into, he sure as hell wouldn't appreciate me bringing the law into it. Not that the cops would make it here in time to save the situation, anyway.

The sounds were becoming more aggressive, but I nevertheless slowed as I neared the lane that ran between Little Collins and Collins Street. Over the years it had become something of a haven for the drunk and drug addicted and, to some extent, Lyle was both. Or as much as an elf could be given they really didn't have addictive tendencies when it came to alcohol and drugs.

The lane itself was narrow, and filled with bins that had yet to be emptied. Their contents spewed over the bitumen and the stench of rotting food rode the air. A solitary light gleamed down the far end of the lane, but it did little to lift the majority of shadows. Not that I really needed light—I could see as well at night as I could by day. A gift of the Elven part of me, and one of the few I was thankful for.

In the shadows, three large forms were beating a fourth, much smaller, and all too familiar one.

Shit, I thought. Shit, shit, *shit*!

Lyle wasn't being beaten up by your every day, run-of-the-mill muggers. His assailants were *trolls*. Which in itself suggested a professional hit, because trolls didn't touch anyone unless they were paid first. They claimed it went against their pacifist natures to do otherwise.

Lyle had obviously pissed someone off again.

But the troll factor was a major problem, because trolls were immune to the song of a siren. And fighting was *definitely* out. No matter how capable I was of defending myself, it was one half-breed female against three fucking large trolls. Not great odds at the best of times. Hell, even a *baby* troll was probably beyond my capabilities.

I bit my bottom lip, still torn between the need to call the cops and the knowledge that Lyle would be furious if I did. Then I sighed and swung my camera around. When all else failed, lie through your teeth. Or so one of my brothers was known to say, and it seemed to work well enough for him. He was a successful politician, after all.

I switched the camera to infrared, took several shots, then removed the memory card and replaced it with another. After switching it back to normal flash, I took a deep breath that didn't do a whole lot to calm the butterflies doing cart-wheels in my stomach, and then strode forward, taking several quick shots as I did so. The flash's light bit through the darkness and, as one, the three trolls turned. Lyle slapped back to the bitumen like a piece of raw meat.

"Hey, that's not, you know, cool," the biggest of the three said. There was enough gold hanging off his ear to fill a barrow and it clanged when he moved, sounding like a symphony of ill-tuned bells. "We're gonna have to take that off you now."

I stopped and raised the camera. Their gazes didn't follow the movement, but then, I hadn't really expected them too.

Trolls weren't fools, despite appearances. "If you take one step in my direction, I'll press this little bitty button marked sat-link, and your smiling faces will be splashed all over the morning news."

Which was something of a fabrication given I'd lost the sat-link when I'd given up my job as a photographer for the newspaper several months ago. But trolls didn't have the sharpest eyes, and they weren't likely to spot that the button was inactive from this distance.

The troll wiped a hand the size of a spade across his bulbous nose. "A fucking reporter. Just our luck."

"Yeah, it is. And that's my uncle laying at your feet." I glanced at Lyle. He wasn't moving or making any sound, but he was at least breathing. "You want to tell me just why you're beating him up?"

The troll grinned, revealing uneven rows of yellow-green enamel. I was suddenly grateful that I wasn't close enough to smell his breath.

"We were just discussing the weather. Nothing serious."

"I don't suppose you'd like to tell me who sent you here to discuss the weather?" I didn't hold much hope of getting an answer, because trolls considered it a matter of honor to uphold all deals made. Of course, they were also opportunists, and would certainly weather honor's loss if a greater amount of money was offered, or their life was threatened. I couldn't exactly do either.

The troll sniffed. "Now you know I can't do that."

"Then step away from my uncle." I hesitated, and then added, "Please."

5

It didn't hurt to be polite. They might be pacifists, but I preferred not to take a chance.

The three of them glanced at each other, and then took one step back. Doing what I asked, nothing more. I wasn't about to push my luck.

"Lyle, get up."

He didn't respond. The trolls shared another glance. Deciding whether to risk the early morning publicity or not, I thought with a shiver. I had to get Lyle out of here, and quickly. Yet I didn't dare step any closer in case they realized my lie about the sat-link.

"Lyle, get your lazy carcass into gear." My voice was curt. "Move, *now*."

The old elf groaned in response then, finally, he moved—with all the speed of a snail—into a sitting position. "That you, Harriet?"

I rolled my eyes. Lyle was the only one who ever used my god-awful first name, and nothing I ever said could persuade him to do otherwise. Elves tended to be sticklers when it came to that sort of stuff—it was one of the many reasons I was more than happy to be a half-breed reject.

"Yes, it's me." My gaze went back to the trolls. Most races signaled their intention to attack with their eyes. With trolls, you watched their hands. Their sheer size meant they had to swing their arms into action before the rest of them caught up. "Get off your butt and over here."

Lyle scrubbed a hand across his face, smearing blood. It looked like wet war paint in the predawn darkness. Then he climbed slowly to his feet and staggered forward. I caught him before he could collapse, suddenly grateful the old fool didn't weigh much.

The hands moved. Only fractionally, but it was warning enough. I flashed the camera again. The trolls clenched their fists but otherwise remained still.

"Let's make a deal, boys. You let us go, and I'll give you the memory card."

They shared another glance. "You ain't no stinking reporter," the troll with all the gold said. "No reporter is ever willing to give up a good story."

"You're right," I said, my voice calm despite the fact the butterflies were now tying stomach into knots. "I'm not a reporter. But I *am* a photographer working for the Herald-Sun. Trust me, I have the contacts to make your life a misery."

The troll contemplated me for a moment, and then held up his hands. "The missus will kill me if I land another jail term right now. We accept the deal."

"I have your word that you'll let us go?"

He sighed. "Yes."

I relaxed, but only a little. Few trolls ever broke a promise, but I still wasn't about to turn my back on them, all the same.

I retreated, dragging Lyle with me. At the corner of the lane, I thrust the old elf against the wall, leaned a shoulder against his chest to keep him upright, and then removed the memory card from the camera. I held it up so the trolls could see it, then placed it on top of the nearest bin. Once

I'd swung the camera back out of the way, I wrapped my arm around Lyle again and got the hell out of there.

Once we'd reached the relative safety of busier Charles Street, I glanced over my shoulder. The trolls had kept their promise. They weren't following us.

Relieved, I turned left and headed for Matthews Street. The few people who were out and about barely looked at us. It was far too early—and far too cold—for people to stop and stare.

Lyle groaned again, and I glanced at him. His face really *did* resemble freshly tenderized meat. One eye was closed and puffy, his cheeks were bruised and battered, and a raw looking cut ran from his temple to the back of his head, the oozing blood caking his thick black hair. His shirt hung in tatters from his thin frame, revealing pale flesh that was covered in welts and cuts.

Trolls took their work seriously, and they were both fast and meticulous. If someone had wanted Lyle dead, he would have been so long before I'd gotten there. As it was, he didn't even have any broken bones. Either this was a warning, or the trolls had wanted something from him before they'd gotten down to the serious stuff.

Maybe, I thought with a chill, it was about whatever he'd wanted me to do. And if it was bad enough for trolls to get involved in, then maybe *I* shouldn't be.

Yeah, a sarcastic inner voice said, *how has that gone for you in the past?*

Up ahead, Matthews Street Station glowed brightly in the shadows of the morning and, like the rest of the city, was beginning to come to life. People hurried down the steps and joined the small crowd waiting for the pedestrian lights to change. A faun in a brightly colored caftan stood on the steps and idly played his flute. The happy sound of his music slid through the early morning murk like sunshine through rain, and people smiled and threw money in the cap at his feet as they passed him by.

I turned into Matthews Street and headed for the old Banana Alley vaults. Maggie Tremaine had her store down there, dispensing both new age medicine and ancient wisdom from the old bluestone shop. Despite the early hour, I knew the old witch would be getting ready for the day's trading.

I half-dragged Lyle down the steps then kicked the old wooden door with the toe of my boot.

"Piss off," came the reply. "I ain't open 'till seven."

Polite and to the point, as ever. "Maggie, it's Harri. I need some help out here."

"Harri? What the hell are you doing out this early, girl?" Chains rattled, then the door swung open. Maggie's matronly form filled the doorway, her gray eyes widening as she studied the two of us. "What happened to Lyle? He had a run-in with a tram or something?"

"Worse," I muttered, wishing she'd step aside so I could get in. Lyle might be little more than a bag of bones, but he was beginning to get heavy. "He was set upon by three trolls. You were the closest medical help I could think of."

"And one of the few specialists of Elven anatomy who will help a couple of outcasts," she noted, voice dry. She finally

9

stepped to one side. "Well, bring him in and I'll see what I can do."

I entered carefully. Her store was literally bursting at the seams and the unwary could really hurt themselves. Herbs and dried animal bits hung from the ceiling, some low enough to brush skeletal fingers across the top of my head. Baskets and boxes spilled across the floor, their contents overflowing into each other, creating a riot of texture and color. Weird-shaped bottles crowded the shelves that lined the four walls, mingling easily with an unusual array of pots, brooms, and other witchy paraphernalia. The smell was incredible—a heady concoction of cinnamon, orange, eucalyptus and sage, all mixed with other, less definable but no less pleasant scents.

"Head on through to the back, Harri. I'll grab some medicinals."

I zigzagged through the store and pushed past the heavy curtain. I might as well have entered another world. Everything here was orderly, all the bits and pieces stacked in neat little piles on the shelves, with nothing overflowing or creating hazards on the floor. People expected witch stores to be untidy, Maggie had once explained. Give them what they want, and they'll keep coming back. She obviously knew her market—she'd been in this store for close to fifty years now, and was still one of the most sought-after witches when it came to alternative medicines.

I placed Lyle on the worn sofa, and then rolled my shoulders in relief. Maggie bustled in, arms full of bottles and bandages.

I got out of her way and walked across to the kitchenette to help myself to her coffee. Lyle's face looked no better with the blood and grime washed away, and with the brightly colored salves Maggie was currently plastering all over him, rather resembled someone who'd been attacked by a squadron of kids armed with finger paints.

"He's lucky," she said eventually. "No broken bones, no internal damage that I can sense. His face is pretty bad, but then, it was never much to look at anyway."

I grinned. "I'm sure he'll be thrilled to hear you say that."

Maggie waved a gnarled finger in my direction. "Mention one word," she said, voice sharp but gray eyes twinkling with merriment, "and I'll curse your sex life for the next year."

I snorted. "Curse away. It can't get any worse."

She shook her head. "How can a siren have such a pathetic love life?"

"Because I'm a siren who can't actually sing, remember?" And the ability to sweet-talk didn't achieve much when all prospective dates wanted to do was inspect your ears and talk about Elven society. Elves may have been around for as long as anyone could remember, but they were an aloof race at the best of times, and there were whole chunks of society that knew next to nothing about them. I'd come to the rather sad conclusion that it was my lot in life to attract the persons who would rather chat to an elf than bed them.

Maggie raised an eyebrow. "Have I mentioned Nicolas, the very nice—and very eligible—son of a good friend?"

"Probably." In fact, over the last few years I'd met every eligible male in her immediate *and* extended family, and she was now doing the run through her friends' families. Unlike myself, she hadn't yet realized it was a lost cause. I motioned towards Lyle. "Is he going to wake up any time soon?"

She grunted and shoved a vial under the old elf's nose. Reaction was immediate. He jerked away from the scent and coughed harshly for several minutes before glaring at her with his one good eye.

"What the hell are you doing, woman? Trying to kill me?"

"Got your attention, didn't it? How are you feeling?"

"Surprisingly, like I've just been set upon by a trio of trolls." He hesitated, his gaze sliding across to me. "That was a pretty brave thing you did."

Brave or stupid—and I'd bet most people would vote for the latter option. "I could hardly let them beat you up, even if you are a worthless bag of bones."

"Takes one to know one, half-breed."

I smiled. His quick retort at least proved his brain wasn't rattled. "So who did you annoy this time?"

Lyle snorted. "You got ten hours?"

My smile grew. At one time, Lyle had towed the family line, becoming first a lawyer, then a magistrate. He'd even looked likely to replace his brother—not my father, but Marquane, the oldest of the three—on the high court bench. Then, to the despair of his family and the horror of his wife, he'd given it all up to work with legal aid down in Sandridge. Said wife had long since departed in disgust, but the family still retained hope, alternating between trying to persuade him to return to his former—and to their eyes, at least—more acceptable lifestyle, or attempting to get him declared insane. Which never went well simply because he was a damn fine lawyer when he put his mind to it.

Right now, his kin were in the middle phase—ignoring him. How long it would last was anyone's guess.

I took a drink of coffee and sighed in pleasure. Maggie, like most witches, only bought top shelf—at least when it came to her own supplies. The free stuff in the main store stunk—literally *and* figuratively.

"I can't imagine anyone in the oh-so-proper Phillecky clan deigning to mingle with the likes of trolls," Maggie commented. "Even in an attempt to rein in a rogue brother."

"You'd be surprised," Lyle said, voice weary and still edged with pain. "There're more than a few skeletons stuffed in the family closets."

"Yeah, and not all of them are dead, I'll wager." Maggie climbed to her feet with a grunt of effort. "But I've seen your brothers work a few people over in their time, and they certainly don't need troll assistance."

"No," Lyle agreed heavily. "They don't. And I wouldn't mind one of them coffees, Harriet."

I filled two mugs, handed them across, and then topped up my own. "So what have you been up to in the last week that warrants trolls being unleashed upon you?"

"I don't know." Lyle scrubbed a hand across his face, smearing the bright dabs of salve. "The only thing I've been doing is working a case in the siren district."

"Which one?" There were three main districts—Sandridge

was the biggest and oldest, but both the Barport and Frankston areas were growing fast.

As a general rule, the sirens were a well-behaved, peaceable lot, and so were the men caught by their song. They had to be, because sirens had no tolerance for the drug or alcohol affected, and tended to preclude those types from entering their area. How they did this no one was really sure—other than the fact it had something to do with their aural shield—but it generally made them a welcome addition to any neighborhood, despite the risk of the occasional husband straying.

Maggie dragged in a chair from the other room and plopped down. "You after anyone we know?"

Lyle shrugged. "Doubt it. A man by the name of Reg Turner has gone missing before his trial, and I just wanted to make sure he was okay. He'll be thrown in jail if he doesn't front up to court this time."

"You think he's been caught by a siren's call?" I asked.

"Maybe. He was shacked up with one the last time this happened."

Having been raised by a siren, I had to wonder why the hell anyone would be willing to live with one. As much as I loved my mother, I'd realized at a very early age that a siren's song and heady sex did *not* equate to happy, long-term relationships—if only because very few sirens were willing to give up their song for the love of just one man.

"So you didn't find him?" I asked.

Another shrug. "Your lot can be rather closed-mouthed when they want to be."

That they could, especially when it came to outsiders—of which I was one, these days.

"You chasing down a possible runner doesn't exactly explain why trolls were set onto you." I hesitated, frowning. "Did they say anything? Want anything?"

Lyle gingerly scratched his chin. "Yeah, they kept saying 'da photos, man' like I knew what they were talking about."

"So have you taken photos lately?" Maggie asked, before I could.

"No. Well, not case related, anyway. I did take some a few days ago at a niece's birthday party."

And *that* was his first lie—a thought confirmed by the sudden evasiveness of his sapphire gaze. I glanced thoughtfully at Maggie, who was as lovely a person as you could ever get, but who couldn't keep a secret to save a life. Whatever had gotten Lyle beaten up, he wasn't about to mention it with her in the room.

"Maybe it has something to do with the niece," she commented.

Lyle snorted. "Trolls have better sense than to take a job that has *anything* to do with a Phillecky child."

Because full-blooded Elven children were rare and precious things. Us half-breeds were even rarer, but they preferred for us to be neither seen nor heard. Lyle was the only Elven family member I had contact with, and only because he was also an outcast. I guess in his eyes, an unwanted member of the family was better than no family.

A doorbell chimed in the other room. Maggie glanced at her

watch, then cursed softly and rose. "That'll be Jamie Green. The old bastard is always here early on Saturdays to get his pipe weed."

"You're selling tobacco these days?" Lyle raised an eyebrow. "I thought you witches were against it?"

Maggie swatted his knee. "I said pipe weed, you old fool. Need your ears cleaned out, do you?"

"No, but I didn't know there was a damn difference."

Neither had I, but I didn't bother saying so.

"The difference, elf, is the fact that Jamie is a manic depressive. The weed is a special blend that helps him maintain the status quo."

"Oh."

"For such bright people, you elves know jack-shit." She turned and began to walk out.

"Maggie," I said. "Haven't you forgotten something?"

She turned, one bushy brow raised in query. "I haven't got time for games, girl. Spit it out."

I tapped my nose. She gasped and rushed to the fridge. After pulling out a tray of what looked like hairy black peas, she carefully selected one and pressed it on.

"There," she said, putting the tray back. "How does that look?"

The wart now sitting on the end of her sharp nose looked bigger, blacker, and definitely more hairy than it had in the tray. I grinned. "You are the perfect image of an old hag."

"You always say the nicest things." She patted my arm briefly then walked out.

I finished the rest of my coffee, then placed it down on the counter and crossed my arms. "So, uncle dearest, how about you tell me the truth?"

Lyle raised a dark eyebrow. "What makes you think I wasn't?"

"Because you couldn't lie straight in bed, old man."

Amusement lurked around his battered lips. "A trait not usually associated with lawyers, I admit."

"Which is why you're such a damn good lawyer. You're shockingly honest." I hesitated, and then added dryly, "At least when it comes to dealing with the law, anyway."

He chuckled softly. "Ah Harriet, it's a shame there aren't more like you in the Phillecky clan."

If I'd been in the Phillecky clan, I'd probably be married off to some nasty old fart by now. Arranged marriages were the norm, even in this day and age. "What were the trolls after?"

"Photos. Just not of the niece."

"Then who?"

"*That* I'm not sure about. When I was hunting for Turner, I happened upon a government car parked within the siren zone. The number plates had been smeared with mud so they couldn't be read easily, and the windows were tinted, so I couldn't see who was inside."

I frowned. "Then how did you know it was an official vehicle?"

"The driver happened to be leaning against the bonnet, having a ciggy. He was wearing the official grays."

A government car in a siren zone—*that* was a photo more than a few newspaper editors would be happy to get their hands on. Sirens might be an accepted part of society these days, but they were, after all, still prostitutes. No government official who valued his career could afford to be caught visiting one. "And have these photos got anything to do with you wanting to meet with me in that goddamn awful alley?"

He nodded. "I needed to meet you somewhere safe."

I raised my eyebrows. "And you couldn't think of anywhere more suitable in the entire city?"

He frowned. "It's not a place you'd normally expect to find an elf. I didn't know damn trolls were going to jump me."

"Which begs another question—how did *they* know about the photos? How many people have you told about them?"

"No one. I'm not stupid."

"Did the driver spot you taking them?"

"Not that I'm aware of."

"Then why were the trolls sent to retrieve them?"

"I don fucking *know*." Irritation ran through his voice. "And, right now, I don't care. I just want you to develop them for me."

"Lyle, you've got a digital camera. All you have to do is take out the card and shove it in the nearest computer. It's not hard."

He waved a hand. "You know I suck at that sort of stuff."

I did, but I still kept hoping that one of these days he'd step into the digital age—although that could be said about most of the elder elves. "If the trolls were after the memory card, someone pretty special must have been in that car."

"Yeah, that's what I figured." He crossed one leg over the other and began taking off his shoe.

"If the trolls didn't get the camera's card, where the hell is it? They would have done a thorough search, I presume."

"But not thorough enough." He pulled off his sock and peeled a small black object from the arch of his foot. "We both know it would take a brave soul to venture anywhere near my feet."

That was certainly true. I could smell them from here, and it was turning me off the thought of more coffee. I took the offered card somewhat gingerly—not because there was any danger of damaging it, but because it had a definite sweaty foot odor.

"That isn't the only reason I wanted to meet you this morning, though," he said, thankfully containing the smell with his sock and shoe again.

I tucked the card into a pocket. "It isn't?"

He shook his head and leaned back. Just for a moment, exhaustion deepened the crevices in his face, and it made him looked both older and gaunter. "Are you and Ceri busy right now?"

Ceri—which was short for Cerite—Wells wasn't only a retired cop and a good friend, but now my partner in *Sui Generis*, our fledgling PI agency. "I'd love to say yes, but the only thing we have on the books at the moment is gathering evidence against a cheating husband."

Lyle sniffed—a disparaging sound if I ever heard one. But then, Elven society had a more open view of marriage vows, which tended to be made for political reasons rather than emotional ones. "Then you can accept a job from me?"

We'd accept a job from Satan himself if it meant being able to pay the overheads, but surprise still slithered through me. He'd asked for my help a number of times over the years, but this was the first time he'd asked for Ceri as well. She was basically human—and while Lyle might be an Elven outcast, he still held Elven views when it came to allowing humanity *any* sort of insight into Elven society. "Why do you want her involved?"

"She's an ex-cop. She has contacts you haven't, and they may come in handy."

Ever the pragmatist. "You want it to be official or off the books?"

"Off the books, cash in hand. I can't risk anyone uncovering what I'm doing."

Which meant the proposed job was the *real* reason for the meeting location that had almost gotten him killed. "That's not a problem."

"Good." He paused. "That car I photographed was parked outside a friend's place. She was reported missing two days ago."

I raised an eyebrow. If the slight crack in his voice was anything to go by, the siren had been more than a friend. Which was unusual, to say the least. Elves were generally immune to the call of a siren—and to such a degree that most were physically sickened by the mere thought of coupling with one. But there *were* occasions when the song was stronger than revulsion—my presence in this world was proof enough of that.

"So you think the attack on you, and the siren's sudden absence, are connected?"

"Well, it's a bit suspicious that both happened not long after I spotted the government car at her place, isn't it?"

It was. I studied my uncle for several minutes, seeing the anxiety in his bright eyes. Seeing the shadows and truths not yet spoken. "I take it you want us to track her down?"

"Yes. I can't risk doing it myself at the moment. Adelia's having me followed. She wants a divorce and is looking for a reason."

And the fact they hadn't lived together for thirty years wouldn't give her that reason—at least when it came to the Elven council, who still officiated in such matters. But Lyle having an affair with a siren would not only provide that justification, it would also bring shame onto the Phillecky name. And hell, they'd only *just* recovered from the embarrassment of *my* existence.

"When do you want us to start?"

"Now." Lyle dug into his coat pocket. "Here's the address. The cops had a brief squiz, but I'd like you to have a look too."

21

I glanced at the address and realized it wasn't actually that far from where I'd grown up. "I'm not likely to uncover anything the cops haven't."

"You lived with sirens for nearly twenty years, Harriet. You're one of them."

I was *never* one of them, and that was half the reason I'd left. "That doesn't mean they'll talk to me, Lyle."

"Everyone talks to you. It's your gift." He pulled a photo out of his pocket, then handed it across. "Her name is Mona Delmare. No family, and not many friends, even within the community."

That was unusual, as sirens were generally a tight-knit bunch. I frowned down at the photo. Looks wise, Mona was all siren—she was busty, with an hour-glass figure, platinum hair that fell in ringlets to her waist, and big, sea-green eyes. I'd always been thankful I'd taken after the Elven side of my heritage—black hair and sapphire eyes—although there had been some times in my life where I wouldn't have minded either platinum ringlets or big boobs. Usually when I was with some male who was too busy talking to take the hints that I actually wanted more.

I pushed away from the bench. "Are you going to be okay?"

"Yeah, I'll catch a cab home and rest up for a while." He hesitated. "I really need to know what's happened to her, Harriet."

"I'll do my best."

"Good. Just be careful."

Given what had happened to him, it was a somewhat superfluous warning. I walked through the curtain into the next room. A man sat huddled on a stool near the door, looking like little more than a bundle of rags. Maggie was measuring what looked like yellow grass into a small sack, but looked up as I entered.

"Off so soon?"

I nodded. "Yeah, got stuff to do."

"You up for dinner later this week?"

I smiled. What was the betting the very single son of a good friend was going to be there? Still, the old witch had been good to me over the years, and it never hurt to humor her now and then. "Sure. Give me a call."

Maggie got back to her sacking, her smile cheerful. I left the shop, but hesitated on the steps and looked skyward. The sun was on the verge of breaking night's grip, spreading pink and red fingers across the sky. As mornings went, it was quite magical, but the nagging sensation that something was wrong stole stirred anew. If it wasn't Lyle, then what the hell was it?

In the distance came the soft whir of rotor blades—a helicopter flying low through the city, probably heading for the helipad down near the old World Trade Center building.

Beyond that, almost lost in the growing symphony of the waking city, came the sweeping sigh of wind, the creak of leather. A sound I knew all too well. It was a dragon, but one flying in restricted airspace, and beyond officially approved times.

And *that* really did mean trouble if it went anywhere near the helicopter. Dragons didn't have great sight at the best of times, but in the half-light of the early morning their problems with identifying smaller objects increased tenfold.

I stepped onto the pavement and headed back to the railway station. I'd left my car up near the Berren Cricket Ground this morning so that I could enjoy the walk through the parks that surrounded the city, but I'd catch a train back. The parks, like the city itself, would be filling with people taking the shortest route from one point to the other. The serenity offered by the century old elms and oaks would now be lost to the rush of everyday life.

I glanced skyward again. If the sighing of the wind was anything to go by, the dragon was drawing closer. So, too, was the helicopter. Most of them were fitted with equipment specifically designed to deal with the occasional misdirected dragon or griffin, although even witches had been known to cause the odd problem for aircraft.

The pilot *had* to be aware of the dragon's presence. There would be all sorts of warnings going off.

A sudden gust of wind hit, knocking me several steps sideways. I caught my balance and quickly looked up. Like an illusion coming to life, a fire-colored dragon swooped out of the shadows, leathery wings outstretched and gleaming molten gold in the pale morning light.

I quickly shoved a memory card into the camera and took several shots of the creature against the barely visible mirrored sides of the Rialto towers. I might not work for the paper any more, but my former editor loved shots like this, and he'd pay good money for it if no staff photographer had managed to capture it. If nothing else, it would give us decent coffee for the next few weeks.

The dragon suddenly dropped several meters. One wingtip brushed against the closest building, scraping a trench in the concrete as it soared skyward again. Its tail flicked and smashed into radio antennas, sending them crashing downward.

This was more than an inability to see, I realized suddenly. The damn dragon was *drunk*.

From my right, the helicopter swooped into sight, a gleaming silver insect compared to the size of the dragon. For a moment it appeared they would avoid each other, then the dragon did an abrupt, half turning rise just as the sun broke over the horizon and spread her brightness across the sky.

Whether the sudden shift into light blinded the dragon, I have no idea, but he flew straight into the path of the helicopter.

I raised my camera as the two collided in a fiery explosion of metal, heat, and flesh.

CHAPTER TWO

D ragon and helicopter plummeted to earth, hitting Princess Bridge with enough force to crack asphalt. The dragon somersaulted, went nose first over the railings, and plunged toward the riverbank below. What was left of the helicopter exploded again, firing bits of metal and god knows what else into the air. The smell of burning fuel and flesh churned my stomach, but the instinct to grab photos was stronger than horror.

I pushed my way through the crowd that had gathered and threw up an arm against the heat. The helicopter lay on its side like some giant's ill-used toy. The tail boom hung over the same railing the dragon had flipped over, the metal twisted and the rotor blade dipping toward the Yarra River. Flames crackled fiercely as they devoured the remains of the cabin area. There was very little chance of anyone being left alive inside.

I couldn't see the dragon from where I stood, but if the slurred abuse currently staining the air was anything to go by, it was very obviously alive.

Only trouble was, it was a voice that sounded horribly familiar.

I took some shots, then put my camera away and edged around the crowd, heading for the steps that led down to the riverbank. Fire crews hadn't yet arrived, but the cops were currently pushing everyone back. They were creating the same sort of space around the fallen dragon, too, and it was just as well. He was on his back, thrashing about like a turtle trying to get right side up. One wing—battered and bleeding, but otherwise whole—flapped about, creating a wind strong enough to knock the unwary over.

The other one was broken. A dragon's wing, while fragile looking, actually wasn't. They were formed by a tough membrane of skin, muscle, and other tissues that stretched from their small back legs to a dramatically lengthened fourth finger. It took a lot to break a wing, but they were relatively quick to heal. There were advantages to being able to shift shape, and one of them was the fact that your body healed wounds in the process.

Not that I could shift shape. That was another siren gift I'd missed out on—although I wasn't really all that sad about not being able to become a fish. I did have an affinity with the ocean, but not so much that I wanted to be forced to spend a part of every month in it.

Black liquid oozed from under the dragon's back, staining the ground and stinking to high heaven. Dragon blood was highly toxic, though in an open area like this it was doubtful it would do anything more than pollute the air. But the cops were erring on the side of caution and pushing the gawkers back even further. I headed for the most senior cop there.

"Officer, that dragon is a friend of mine." I stopped in front of him and gave him what I hoped was a winning smile. "If you'd let me get closer, I might be able to calm him down."

The cop looked me up and down, no doubt seeing a tall, somewhat slender individual with Elven features. He didn't look impressed. "Sorry, lady, but we have orders to keep everyone away until the tow trucks arrive."

"They won't get him on the truck unless he's calm, trust me. You need to let me—"

"Lady, you really need to step back a safe distance."

He looked over the top of my head and made a come-here motion. Obviously calling in backup. So much for common sense and charm. Time to bring in the siren. I hit him with every ounce of siren magic I had in me. His eyes went wide and, for several seconds, he did nothing more than blink. I hastily toned it down. He was obviously a more susceptible to sirens than most if he was *that* affected by one who couldn't even sing.

"Officer, with the way he's thrashing about, he could cause serious damage to the bridge. I really need to get in there to calm him down."

"Uh, sure," he said and waved me in.

"Thanks, officer."

I lowered the wattage another notch and he blinked again. His gaze burned a hole in my back, but he didn't attempt to stop me.

The dragon's one good wing still thrashed on the ground,

and trenches deep enough to lose a person in were beginning to scar the riverbank. I stopped just beyond reach.

"Keale," I said, raising my voice to be heard above all the noise he was making. "You really need to calm down."

The dragon stilled, and his head snaked around. Black eyes regarded me owlishly. "S'arri?"

A dragon's mouth wasn't really designed for speech, and everything came out sounding a little garbled. "Yeah. The shit has really hit the fan this time, I'm afraid."

"No 'rink, s'romise. With 'umar."

Numar was an old school friend of Keale's who'd been in Berren the past fortnight for training purposes. I frowned. "I thought he flew back to Brisbane yesterday?"

"No. Was 'rinking with him."

My confusion increased. "But didn't you have a date with Rebecca last night?"

Rebecca was both a dragon and his current girlfriend. She was also fiercely opposed to any sort of drinking. Given Keale was in the midst of his mating cycle, it really *was* doubtful he'd risk a drink and jeopardize his chances with Rebecca—especially given a dragon's mating cycle only came around once every couple of years. He wouldn't have left her until he had to, and he certainly wouldn't have left just to grab a drink with Numar. Friendship stood no chance against the possibility of sex.

"No 'ecca. With 'umar at 'arrandyte pub."

Warrandyte was a long way from the city. This was really weird. "So where were you going, Keale?"

"S'raight 'ome. Do nots 'ass go, do nots-"

"Yeah, yeah, I get the idea." I frowned and scrubbed a hand across my nose. The blood stink was getting worse. Keale must have cut his back up pretty badly when he'd hit the helicopter. But he wasn't likely to get any real medical attention until he changed form. It was too costly —and a dragon's hide too tough—to be practical. "If you were going home, what the hell were you doing over the city?"

"S'old ya. Going 'ome."

Keale lived in Research, which was a stone's throw away from Warrandyte. He actually had to fly *away* from his house to get anywhere near the city. None of this made any sense.

"How long have you been in dragon form?"

"Six 'ours."

Like all magic, a dragon's shape shifting had strict time limitations. No matter what form he took—dragon or human— he had to stay in that form for a minimum of twelve hours. Which meant there wasn't much point in discussing the matter any further—better to wait out the remaining six hours and give Keale time to sober up.

"They've called in a tow truck to haul you away."

"S'all not gets me on no s'uking s'uck."

I sighed. "They have to. You can't stay here bleeding all over the landscaping."

"S'uck the 'scaping."

I smiled. "Keale, you're in enough trouble as it is. Be a good dragon and do as they ask."

The black eyes regarded me somewhat unsteadily for several seconds, scaly brows drawn down. He doesn't know what he's done, I realized. This really *was* something more than drunkenness.

"S'rouble?" he said eventually.

"Yeah. Listen, I'm going to call Lyle in. Don't talk—don't say anything until he gets there.

"S'wy?"

I glanced across as a tow truck pulled up. It was a big mother, the size of a double semi, at least. But then, so was Keale. "Just trust me, and do as I ask."

"S'kay."

Three men cautiously approached, two of them hauling cables as thick as my wrist, the third a medical kit. All three looked ready to bolt if Keale so much as breathed the wrong way. Keale behaved himself though, watching thoughtfully as one man immobilized then splintered his broken wing, and the other two attached the cables to his body. Mind you, it was the sort of look a spider might give its prey before devouring it—not that many dragons ate humans these days. Too gristly, according to Keale.

I'd never been brave enough to ask *how* he actually knew that.

The man with the medical kit ran back to the truck. The other two did a final check on the position of the cables, and then waved a go-ahead. The winch roared into action and

Keale was hauled unceremoniously—and swearing all the way—onto the back of the semi. He was quickly secured and then driven away, two police vans acting as escort.

I dragged out my cell phone and dialed my uncle. "Lyle," I said, when he answered. "I need a favor. Urgently."

Lyle sighed. "Who in your heterogeneous group of friends is in trouble this time?"

I smiled. Though I rarely called on Lyle's skills as a lawyer, it was a somewhat sad fact that my friends were a somewhat motley—and certainly very different—collection. "It's Keale again."

"That pisspot? There's nothing much I can do to stop them taking his flight license away this time. I told him that the last time."

"It's more than that. He's downed a helicopter."

Lyle was silent for several seconds. "Anyone killed?"

"A pilot, at least. It's only just happened."

"So *that* was the crash we heard." He swore softly. "They'll charge him with manslaughter, for sure."

And with Keale's record, they'd lock the door and throw away the key. "If you're feeling up to it, could you head over and see that he gets a blood test?"

"Why?" Confusion ran through the old elf's voice. "They'll do that as a matter of course."

"Yeah, but I want you to make sure they look for Prevoron."

"That can be deadly to dragons if they take too much. Why

the hell would he risk it?"

Because if the correct dose was taken, it had the same sort of effect on dragons as catnip did on many cats. They loved the stuff. Of course, it also gave the same sort of high to humans, but added the whammy of killing their inhibitions, with often hilarious results. I'd taken some truly funny photos of humans up to all manner of mischief when the paper had run a two-page spread on the drug and the problems it was causing a few years ago.

"He mightn't know he's been taking it. Given it can be either injected or ingested, maybe someone added it to his booze." Although I couldn't imagine Numar clandestinely drugging his friend, even as a prank. I *could* imagine the two of them deliberately tempting fate to get the high it provided, but if that had been the case, why had Keale been so insistent they'd been doing nothing more than drinking?

"Why would anyone bother drugging someone like Keale?" Lyle commented. "Feed him enough booze and he'd sell his mother. And throw his sister in as a bonus."

Having met both, I could understand why. "I don't know, Lyle, but it's better to be safe than sorry given what he's done. They'll be taking him to the Melbourne Assessment Prison—it's the only place with a cell big enough to cater for a dragon Keale's size."

"I've just called a taxi, so I'll swing past and get things moving."

"Thanks, Lyle. I'll talk to you later.

He grunted and hung up. I hesitated, and then called Ceri. I knew she'd be in the office at this hour. While she *was* technically human, her grandfather had been a gargoyle, and she'd inherited his sensitivity to sunlight. She didn't turn to stone like most of those with gargoyle blood, but her eyesight was severely restricted in sunlight and her pale skinned blistered in even the coldest winter morning. Which is why as a cop she'd worked the graveyard shift and why our business was open twenty-four hours. She ran the night shift, I ran the day, although we did sometimes cross over.

"Hey," she said, her deep voice warm and cheerful. "What the hell you doing up this early? I thought it went against your religion to be out and about before seven?"

"Lyle called me."

She made a disparaging sound. "I have no idea why you associate with that drunken old fart. He has no respect for you, you know that, don't you?"

"Elves don't respect anyone," I replied easily. It was an argument we'd had more than once, and I was more than aware of her views on not just Lyle, but the rest of those I called kin.

"That's certainly true. So what did he want this time?"

"Actually, he's given us a job."

She snorted. "What's the catch?"

"It's cash in hand, and off the books."

"Illegal, in other words. You know how I feel about-"

"Ceri, it's not like that." I gave her a brief rundown of what he wanted, and then added, "In any case, we can't afford to be turning down work, and you know it."

34

I might own the house in which we'd set up our business, but electricity, water, council rates, and license fees still had to be paid, and right now we were behind in payments on all four.

"Yeah, I know." She sighed. "So I gather you're off to this woman's house to see what you can uncover?"

"Yes. But I want you to check something else for me."

"Sure. What?"

"Keale just crashed into a helicopter over Princess Bridge. I want to know who was in it."

She swore vehemently. Ceri had known Keale a lot longer than I had—they'd grown up in the same neighborhood. "I can tell you that now—it's been all over the news. There were four people—two press, the pilot, and Logan's brother."

"Frank Logan? The Federal treasurer?"

"The same. Apparently, he was also supposed to be on it, but was called away at the last moment."

I frowned. "Why would Logan be hiring a private helicopter to come down to Berren? As a politician, he gets free flights."

"But the others don't, so he often hires private planes or 'copters to ferry him and friends about."

"Then why does he come down here? His family is up in Sydney, aren't they?"

"Yes, but he has several businesses down here. The word is that they're in trouble."

"That doesn't explain why his brother was on the helicopter in his stead."

"They're business partners."

"They are? Since when?" The last I'd heard, the two men had had a rather violent falling out over James's excessive gambling.

"You really need to start watching the news more," Ceri commented dryly. "They patched up their differences a few weeks ago."

"I have enough drama happening in my life—I don't need to watch the news to find more of it." I paused. "Do you know what sort of business the Logans are running?"

"They're importers, as far as I know. But I can find out, if you want."

"I do. I have no idea how knowing will help Keale, but I just have this itchy feeling something is very wrong."

"Another itchy feeling," she muttered. "God help us all."

I grinned. "And if he won't, your police friends surely will."

"I wouldn't count on that." Her voice was dry. "Anything else you want me to do?"

I hesitated, and then said, "Keale mentioned drinking with Numar last night, but I was under the impression he'd gone back to Brisbane. You know his mom, don't you?"

"Yeah. I take it you want me to ring and see if he actually made it home?"

"If you could. If Keale's in this bad a state, I hate to think what Numar might be like."

Ceri snorted. "Having seen the two of them drinking before, he probably ended up in Western Australia rather than Brisbane."

That's what had me worried. "How'd the stake out go last night?"

"The husband is an idiot. I don't think he's even trying to cover his tracks."

"Meaning lots of lovely evidence?"

"Yes. The wife is coming in this morning. I'll hang around in case you don't get back in time to take care of her."

"Thanks. And good luck. Have a box of tissues handy."

"God, I hope there's not tears," she muttered, and hung up.

I shoved the phone away and made my way back through the crowds into Matthews Street station. After a short trip through the underground loop, I was in my car and on my way to Sandridge.

Mona lived in an apartment just off the main strip, which meant she wasn't a very high profile siren. The prime spots were actually along the outer ring, a position that gave those sirens the pick of incoming customers. The sirens living on or near the main strip had far less choice. Mom had been middle rung, so our apartment had been situated closer to the outer ring than inner.

I found parking just off Fitzroy Street and walked back. Once upon a time, this street had been the trendiest of places to hang out, a place that was a mix of restaurants, live music venues, and strip clubs. All that had changed once the sirens moved in, simply because the sirens brooked no competition. By day, the place was so deserted and uninteresting that even the seagulls looked bored. The neon signs and gaudy lights that had once blazed so brightly were dead, and the old posters that hawked the wares of lap dancers long gone flapped forlornly in the breeze. Under the harsh glare of sunlight, the place looked, and felt, like some sleazy sideshow trinket cast aside for brighter cousins.

Of course, the sirens—the area's biggest attraction—needed no lights or signs. They had their songs.

I found Lock Street easily enough and headed down, looking for number seven. It turned out to be a three-story brick affair that had been painted hot pink, with lavender trim. I shuddered. I still had nightmares about living in a house like this, having grown up only a couple of blocks away on Burnett Street. If Mona had the same tastes as most sirens, it wouldn't only be the outside of the building that was pink, but the interior walls, the furniture, even her clothing.

I climbed the steps. The door wasn't locked—siren apartments rarely were. I'd never been able to figure out why they were so trusting, and had certainly never believed my mother's explanation that the aural shield kept away the worst elements of crime. It might have kept away the drunks and drug addicted, but it seemed to have had little effect on anyone else. It had certainly never stopped our apartment from being robbed more than a dozen times.

I shoved open the glass door and entered the building. According to Lyle's directions, Mona's apartment was on the second floor. I climbed up, the steps creaking softly under my boots. The air was warm, and thick with the mixed scents of orange and sage.

The scents of my childhood.

The scents of my mother.

I paused and looked up. Surely she wasn't back in town? When last we'd talked, she'd been adamant about remaining on the Gold Coast, despite the fact she had no family up there. She claimed the constant sunshine was far better for her arthritis than the often chilly Berren air.

I grimaced and walked on. It wasn't like my mother had a patent on those scents—lots of other sirens used them. Maybe Mona was one of them.

I hit the second floor landing and paused again. The corridor was shadowed, and the grime and cobwebs gathering in the corners suggested there were few who actually cared about this place, let alone lived here. Only three doors led off the hall—Mona's was on the left, down near the end. As I reached for the door handle, one of the two doors behind me opened.

"Well, strap my ass to a flagpole and hoist it skyward," an all too familiar voice declared. "Harri!"

I closed my eyes in resignation. The scent I'd smelled hadn't belonged to my long absent mother, but rather one Valentine Prytoria—my long avoided, and generally annoying—younger brother.

I slowly turned around. Standing in the doorway of the apartment closest to the stairs was what could only be described as a thin streak of colorful humanity. His sharp features were framed by platinum curls that flounced to his shoulders, and he wore a bright pink smock and purple pants, which were artfully torn at the knees and splattered with blobs of blue and gold paint. His feet were bare, but his toenails were rainbow painted.

It was a rather tame outfit by his standards.

"You told me you bought a house, Val, not a fucking apartment block."

"It's almost the same thing, darls. And you know I've always loved this area." He waved a hand around, fingernails glittering. "Isn't the place delish?"

I glanced at the grimy, pink painted walls. Delicious was one way to describe it. Fucking awful was another. "Why the hell would you want to live in a place like this again? In a building filled with sirens, for god's sake?"

Val raised silvery eyebrows. "My, don't we have some deep-seated resentments still hanging about in our subconscious cupboard?"

"Yeah, don't we," I muttered. I opened Mona's door and stepped inside. There was no escaping Val, however. Not that I thought there would be.

"And to what do we owe the honor of your presence?" he said, trailing into Mona's apartment after me.

"You mean it isn't your birthday?" I stopped in the center of the small living room and looked around. As it turned out, Mona wasn't like most sirens. Her walls were a deep, almost purple black, and her furniture bore the same tonal tendencies. The door frames, skirting boards, and cornices were pink, however. The same hot pink as my brother's smock, in fact. It was a deadly combination.

"Oh, funny." Sarcasm edged Val's voice. "But speaking of birthdays, I meant to thank you for the wand you sent. It was an inspired choice given I broke my other one only the day before."

"I know." We might be somewhat estranged when it came to daily—even monthly—interaction, but we shared the same siren blood, and that meant I sometimes caught echoes of his sharper emotions. "I'm not a complete bitch all the time, Val."

"I know." He patted my arm gently. "Just most of the time."

I snorted softly and walked across to the desk. Fingerprint dust decorated both the top and the drawer handles, so the cops had obviously already been through it. But Lyle was paying me to look, so look I did. I found exactly what I'd expected—nothing.

"I gather you have a good reason for being in this apartment and going through Mona's drawers?" Val said.

"I do indeed." I turned and studied the room. Other than the garish paintwork and odd blobs of fingerprinting dust, nothing seemed out of place. Not that I'd actually *see* anything out of place given I knew nothing about Mona.

This was useless.

"Well?" Val said, voice impatient. "What is it? I do *own* the building, remember. I'm not sure I should be allowing you in here."

My gaze came to a halt on what looked to be the bedroom doorway. Where would a siren keep stuff she didn't want anyone to find? In my mother's case, it *hadn't* been the bedroom—with all the traffic, it would have been nowhere near private enough.

Neither was the bathroom. Mom's answer to keeping her 'treasures' safe had been the laundry—usually at the bottom of a laundry basket filled with stinking socks. But her friends had always kept their treasures in the kitchen. I headed that way.

"Are you even listening to me?" Val asked.

"Do I ever?"

A tissue box came sailing at my head. I caught it with a half grin, then handed it back as I walked past him. I found the kitchen and hunted through the cabinets, searching for something—anything—out of the ordinary. Her fridge provided the first revelation—a dozen cans of beer were neatly stacked on the bottom shelf.

Lyle was a champagne and spirit drinker from way back, and hated beer almost as much as he hated having to deal with the occasional human. The beer *had* to belong to someone else, because sirens rarely drank. Mona had obviously liked someone enough to allow them access to her fridge.

Lyle had competition.

I slammed the door shut then glanced across at my brother. He stood in the doorway, arms crossed and one brightly painted foot tapping. He rather looked like a garishly colored flamingo. "What do you know about Mona?"

"Oh, so now you want to talk to me?"

I didn't really, but he did own the building and he certainly knew Mona better than me. "She's disappeared. I've been asked to find her."

"Mona's always disappearing. Sometimes for days, sometimes for weeks. I told the cops that, when they were here yesterday."

"Was it just the usual need to be in the sea, or something more?"

"More." Val pursed his lips. "I mean, she did the minimum three day stretch in the ocean, but she was away at least once a month apart from that."

"Was she married or engaged?"

"Are any of them? Was Mother?" Val snorted softly. "Get real, darls."

"Yeah, I guess it was a stupid question." I squeezed past him and headed for the laundry. "What about customers? What sort of men did her song attract?"

"All sorts, though she seemed to have a preference for uniformed men."

"So, firemen, policemen, that sort?"

"More the army type."

No wonder Val had bought the apartment block. He probably sat in his doorway all night, eating popcorn and watching the beefcake walk by.

I paused in the next doorway. Even by my standards, the laundry room was small. "Any trouble recently?"

Val shrugged. "Nothing I couldn't handle."

I picked up the laundry basket and tipped it upside down. A rainbow of wispy undergarments fell around my feet. "Then there *was* trouble?"

43

"Five nights ago. Nothing major, just—" He hesitated. "If I tell you, you have to promise not to tell your client. I could be in serious trouble with the Wizard Guild if it gets out."

I glanced up at him. "What the hell did you do?"

"Promise me, Harri."

"Okay, okay, I promise." I frowned at him. Tension rode his shoulders and he was practically wringing his hands. Whatever he'd done, it had to be *bad*.

He sighed. "Two customers answered her song at the same time. Neither was exactly pleased to see the other."

"Did you recognize either of them?"

He shrugged. "I've seen them both at one time or another, but I couldn't tell you who they actually were. If they don't swing my way, I don't pay them much attention, I'm afraid."

"I gather they got into a fight."

"They did."

"And?" God, it would be easier to get information from a stone.

"And I...er...changed the pair of them."

My eyebrows shot up. "You *changed* them?"

Val waved his hands. "It was only a little change, and only very temporary."

All wizard magic was temporary, with only the strongest of spells lasting, at the most, a week. That's why many wizards tended to have sidelines in other occupations. In Val's case, it was interior decoration, but there were also wizards in policing, emergency services, hell, even in medicine. Anywhere where a little temporary magic could make the difference between life and death basically—although interior design could hardly be considered that. But there were plenty of people who wanted to gussy up their house for a special occasion, and who were more than ready to lash out on temporary spells in an effort to impress family and friends.

"What did you change them into?"

"Butterflies. They don't fight, you see. They're such gentle creatures."

I didn't quite manage to restrain my laugh, and he scowled. "It's not funny, Harri. If anyone reports me, I could lose my license. Then what would I do?"

"Well, you could always go into the family business." Val—like most half-breeds—could sing, though few of us got the added bonus of being able to shape-shift.

Although, to be honest, there weren't that many half-breeds around. Sirens tended to be very careful about reproducing with clients, and it generally only happened when there was a long-term relationship involved.

Val picked up a bar of soap and threw it at me. I ducked. It sailed over my head and hit the front of the old washing machine with enough force to dent it.

"What happened after you changed them?"

"Oh, they saw the error of their ways and left."

Scared shitless, no doubt. But it was odd that neither of the two men had reported Val's breach of etiquette. The guild really did have strict rules when it came to altering human forms, and the first and foremost of those rules was that it had to be consensual. Val *would* lose his license if word got out.

I bent and carefully sorted through Mona's undergarments. "How long would the spell have lasted?"

"Half an hour, max."

As I picked up several flimsy body suits and dumped them back into the basket, a weird sense of déjà vu hit. Suddenly I was ten years old again, sorting through the mountain of washing while my brother chatted inanely from the laundry doorway. "And they didn't come back?"

"Not that night."

I paused and looked up at him. "But they *did* come back?"

He hesitated. "Someone did, but I can't be entirely sure it was either of them. All I heard was the shouting, but he left before I could do anything."

"Did you notice what type of car, by any chance?"

Val frowned. "Why would I? He left. I didn't peek outside to watch him walk away. Not my style."

But he would have, had the visitor been his *type*. I went back to sorting through the washing. "Did you see Mona at all that day?"

"No, nor have I seen her since. But as I said, that's not unusual."

I tossed more garments into the basket. One thing was sure;

Mona had a liking for designer brands. "These two men you saw—were they both human?"

"One human, one elf."

Tension slithered through me. God, if Lyle hadn't been entirely honest with me, he was going to cop an earful. "Young or old?"

"Young, both of them. Probably no more than the late thirties, early forties."

Which put my uncle out of the picture. I relaxed a little. "Would you be able to work up a sketch of the two men?"

"I could, but it'll cost you."

"Val, this is serious-"

"So is family." He crossed his arms, his expression determined. "A fact you seemed to have forgotten lately. I intend to remedy that."

"Val, you and I walk in very different-"

"I don't *care*. You're my goddamn sister, and I won't have you being such a stranger."

I sighed. When he used *that* tone of voice, there was no dissuading him—even if we both knew it could only end in tears. Hell, the last time we'd tried the whole happy family thing, he ended up leaving the state and declaring he never wanted to see me again—a fact he'd obviously forgotten. I loved my brother to death, but it was a sad truth that we just rubbed each other the wrong way. Sometimes, less was definitely more.

"What do you want?"

"A dinner party. At your place. Your friends and mine." He hesitated, an almost contented smile touching his lips. "And don't try that I-can't-cook crap. I may be a bit scatter-brained at times, but I can remember who did most of the cooking when we were both young."

Someone had to. Mom often forgot she had offspring. How we'd actually survived babyhood I had no idea. I tossed another handful of silk into the basket.

"Just one dinner party?"

"To start with, yes. We can see where things go from there."

Things would no doubt go downhill from there, but I guess I had no choice. Besides, I did miss Val. On occasion. When I was in a weird mood.

"Okay, deal," I muttered. Then I frowned and flicked aside a fluffy white thong. Sitting nestled in the bosom of a purple bodysuit was a little black book.

"Excellent." Satisfaction practically oozed from his pores. Emotional restraint and Val were not often companions. After a pause, he added, "What's wrong?"

"It seems Mona was hiding a little black book." I bent and picked it up.

Val sucked in a breath. "But that's considered a huge no-no in siren culture."

"Maybe, but that hasn't stopped her." I leafed through it, and discovered it didn't actually contain phone numbers and addresses, but rather memory cards. Each one was taped to a page, with a name carefully written in siren hiero-glyphics underneath.

Mona had been taking photos and, given the fact that all the names underneath were male, it suggested that she'd been cataloging her clients—an action far worse than jotting down contact details ever could be.

And if one of her clients had become aware of her penchant for collecting their images, what would they do? Especially if that person had been a government official?

Quite possibly, murder.

What I had in my hands was a ticking time bomb.

"What are you going to do?" Val asked.

"I don't know yet." I gave the rest of the underclothing a shake to ensure there was nothing else, then scooped them all back into the basket and put it back on top of the washer.

Val's expression was concerned. "If Mona's missing because of that book, why didn't they take it with them?"

"Maybe they simply couldn't find it without tearing the place apart. Maybe that's why they've snatched her—they want a little privacy in which to make her talk."

Val shuddered. "God, I hope not. She really is a sweet woman."

Most sirens were. "I need that sketch as soon as you can get it to me."

"I'll get onto it right away." He stepped to one side, giving me room to pass.

"Thanks." I hesitated, and then touched his arm lightly. "Be careful, little brother. Those two men might not be involved in Mona's disappearance, but if they are, and if they come back, they'll be ready for your tricks."

He nodded, expression sober. "Trust me, if I spot them, I'll run."

"Good."

He trailed after me as I headed for the door. "Do you really think something has happened to her?"

"Honestly? I don't know. But my client is pretty certain something has and, you have to admit, the existence of this book makes it seem more likely." I glanced over my shoulder as I stepped out into the hall. "Please be careful."

His smile was sudden and warm. "Anyone would think you actually cared."

"Of course I *care*." Amusement bubbled through me. "I haven't got enough money to buy myself a decent coffee, let alone a funeral for you."

He snorted softly. "You, Harriet Phillecky, are a lost cause."

"Totally," I agreed cheerfully, and waved goodbye as I headed down the stairs.

Fine rain had begun to fall outside, dusting the rubbish-lined street with silver. Overhead, seagulls surfed the breeze, looking for the next scrap to squabble over. But as I watched them wheel around, it suddenly struck me that there were an awful lot of birds up there. Usually you didn't get a flock *that* size unless something big had washed up on the beach.

It couldn't be a whale. Not in Port Phillip, not these days. And the bay's dolphins didn't usually hunt this close to the city's shoreline. The attraction could be dead fish washed up on the beach—it had happened in the past, when foreign tankers had accidentally spilled oil in the middle of the bay. Or it could be something else entirely.

Like a body.

I flicked up the collar of my coat then shoved my hands into my pockets and headed down to check it out. It might not be anything more than a busload of school kids armed with hot chips that was causing all the seagull fuss, but it would only take a few minutes to find out.

It soon became apparent that it *wasn't* school kids. Not with the crowd that had gathered on the foreshore.

I slipped through to the front of the throng, but was stopped from going any further by blue and white police tape. Ahead, on the beach proper, waves whispered up the yellow sand, their foamy fingers playing with the toes of the woman who lay there, tickling but not quite touching the tiny tattoo of a dolphin that leaped across her calf. It was a tattoo that was siren specific. God, I thought, no. My gaze darted upwards. A plastic sheet covered the majority of her torso, but the wind was fierce this close to the sea and the ends flapped unrestrained, revealing not only chilling glimpses of what had been done to her, but wet platinum curls.

The dead woman *was* a siren.

And *I* had no doubt it was Mona.

CHAPTER THREE

—————————

Fuck, I thought. How the hell was I going to tell Lyle? He obviously cared deeply for this woman if he'd been willing to pay me *and* Ceri to find her, and I really didn't want to be the one who told him the news. Not when it was likely to send him into yet another spiral of alcohol abuse. He'd only just come out of one.

Maybe I should wait until I knew for sure it was Mona. And maybe *that* was just cowardice speaking.

I sighed and let my gaze wander the immediate area. There were a number police officers standing around, either keeping the crowd back or taking statements, but it was the one who *wasn't* wearing a uniform who caught my attention. Not because he was tall and well-built—which he was —but because there was something very familiar about the set of his shoulders and the way his brown hair curled at the nape of his neck.

I dropped my gaze to his waist, and my breath caught somewhere in my throat and refused to budge. Strapped to the officer's right side was a plain black knife sheath, but the protruding hilt was anything but. The ebony stone of the grip was embossed with silver leaves and ornate swirls, the workmanship intricate and beautiful. I'd only seen it's like once before—in the workshop of the dark fae who'd been making it.

Dark fae were far different to the small, winged humanoid creatures who bore a similar name and who could found in both fiction and in life. They were also mostly human in appearance, and were smiths by nature, gifted with the ability to bend any sort of metal to their will. Like their smaller, fairer kin, they were also capable of magic and mayhem, and—despite their smithing skills—were at one with nature. Once upon a time it had been unusual to see dark fae in the city—like most fae and fairy folk, they preferred the shadowed safety of trees and wilderness—but their metalworking skills meant they were in great demand as both artists and as builders, and, over time, they'd developed a greater tolerance of humanities concrete jungles. That same tolerance had gradually seen them filter into other professions.

The dark fae I'd known had left the city ten years ago, and had sworn there was nothing on earth that could ever make him come back.

This *couldn't* be him. It simply couldn't.

He shifted slightly, revealing the sharp but beautiful angles of his face.

It was.

Panic surged, but I clenched my fists and forced myself to

stand still, to not make any sudden movements lest it catch his attention.

Kaij was back.

He was the boyfriend who'd taught me to fight. The man who'd made me feel more alive than any person ever had, before or since. Someone I thought I'd have a home and family with.

But he was also the man who'd taken my heart, smashed it to the ground, and stomped all over the shattered pieces.

I wasn't ready to face him again. Wasn't ready to see the rise of contempt and loathing in his eyes.

Checking whether the dead siren was indeed Mona could wait until later. If Kaij still worked with PIT—the acronym for the Preternatural Investigations Team—he'd leave the grunt work to the local police and get on with the business of tracking who she was and why she was murdered. Which meant he wouldn't be here long and I could come back and question whatever bystanders remained later. Hell, for that matter, I still had plenty of contacts at the paper, and if they couldn't confirm the dead siren's identity, they'd know someone who would.

I stepped back, but just as I did, he turned. His gaze—which I knew from long ago was the green of a shaded forest with flecks of gold floating in the deeper depths—skimmed the crowd, brushing past me without concern then coming back with force. For a moment, he simply stared, as if he couldn't quite believe who he was seeing.

Then his expression closed over and he began to walk in my direction.

I turned and fled. I wasn't by nature a coward, but when it came to this man I had no defenses. Not when I'd come upon him so unexpectedly. Given time and enough booze, it might be a different story.

I had no idea whether or not he ran after me. I didn't bother looking over my shoulder to find out. I just kept running.

Thankfully, I'd grown up in this area, so I knew more than a few places to hide. I ducked into the nearest lane, scooted over several old wooden paling fences, then down several more back lanes before running into the back door of a gaudily painted apartment block, thankful for the siren dislike of locked doors. I caught the door with my fingers to stop it from slamming, then took a deep breath that did little to ease the hammering of my heart or the tension churning my stomach, and walked, with as much calm as I could muster, to the front of the building. I didn't go out. He might be looking for me and he might not, but I wasn't about to discover which was true. Not until it felt safe to do so. I sat on the staircase's bottom step to wait out my nerves.

No one came in or went out of the building, and there was little noise beyond the occasional tread of steps in the rooms above. I glanced at my watch. It was nearing seven, so the men and women who'd answered the call of the sirens the previous night would soon be leaving. I gave it another twenty minutes, then, as the rhythm of life in the rooms around and above me began to increase, I pushed to my feet and cautiously left the building.

The rain was heavier, and the gloom settled around my shoulders, chill and heavy. Or maybe that was just the weight of the ghost from the past. I shivered, shoved my hands into my pockets, and studied the street ahead. I couldn't even see the beach from here, so I had no idea why I was hoping to sense whether Kaij was still there or not. He shouldn't be, but then, he shouldn't even be back in Berren. Not when he'd sworn so vehemently *never* to return.

The door behind me opened and I glanced around. A short, stout man made his way from the building, his gaze avoiding mine as he turned in the opposite direction and hurried away. Obviously not someone who wanted to be spotted leaving a siren's building.

I studied the other end of the street a little longer, then sighed and forced my feet into action. I owed it to Lyle to at least see if I could uncover whether the siren on the beach was Mona. If Kaij was gone, I could hang around and ask some questions.

And if he wasn't?

Well, I'd be running again. *Cowardice, thy name is Harriet.* I half smiled. Cowardice was better than bitterness or anger, I guess. Once upon a time there'd been plenty of both, and the mere fact I didn't feel them now surely meant that I had at least moved on from the pain he'd inflicted.

It was something. And maybe it meant that the next time we saw each other—because there would be a next time, I was sure of that—I could stand there and face him.

I *would* stand there and face him.

Hell, I'd stood up to a trio of trolls. An old flame shouldn't be anywhere near *that* scary now I knew he was back.

The wind caught my hair and tossed it wildly across my face as I turned toward the beach. I caught it with my fingers, holding it out of the way as I scanned the beach.

The cops were still there, but the siren's body had been taken away and the majority of the crowd had lost interest. Kaij had gone.

Relief stirred through me. As I tucked my hair behind my ears, I noticed a lone figure standing on a small, grassy rise of sand further down the foreshore. He was wearing lime green Lycra shorts that seemed to glow in the early morning gloom and a tight-fitting Nike shirt that emphasized his stocky build.

Dwarf, I thought. And given dwarves were passionate avoiders of all things ocean, the mere fact this one was here, staring down at the place where the siren had washed ashore very much suggested he might have known her. I walked over. He didn't look up or acknowledge my presence in any way. He simply stared at the sand.

After a few minutes, I said, "Did you know her?"

He glanced up then. Droplets of rain silvered his bushy eyebrows and lined his handle bar mustache. "What's it to you?"

"I'm a private investigator. I was hired to find Mona Delmare."

His gaze swept me but gave little away. "Oh yeah? Why?"

He'd known Mona. It was evident in the briefly visible pain that mingled with the shock in his brown eyes. "Because she went missing a couple of days ago, and my client was worried about her safety." I hesitated, and then added, "He called the police."

"Who did fucking nothing until it was far too late, as usual."

So the siren *was* Mona. *Fuck.* I pushed the wayward strands of hair out of my eyes again. "Were you the one who found the body?"

It was a guess, but he was dressed for running and there was still sand all over his shoes.

His gaze slid from mine. Hiding emotion. "Yes."

I hesitated, and then said, "Do you often run on the beach?"

He looked up, expression sharp. "I'm not liking what you're implying with that question."

"I'm not implying *anything*. I'm just curious as to why you might be running here when it's generally out of character for dwarves to be near the ocean."

He snorted. "It's out of character for elves to be so damn nosy, but that doesn't seem to be stopping you."

"I'm not an elf."

"You damn well look it." He hesitated, and then added gruffly, "I got a call from a prospective client. She wanted to meet near the beach, and it was easier to jog down here than go to the bother of getting the car out and then trying to find parking."

He met prospective clients in lime green shorts? What the hell sort of business was he in? "Do you know how she died?"

"What does it matter? She's dead, and that's the end of it."

"It's not. The killer is still out there and he needs to be found."

He glanced at me and snorted. "And a slender little thing like you is going to do that?"

"Probably not, but I suspect my client will at least want to know why she was killed."

He grunted and crossed his arms. "She'd be happy to know someone *did* care enough to find out why this happened."

I raised my eyebrows. "Meaning you have no idea why someone might have wanted her dead?"

"No," he said, gaze on the empty sand and sorrow in his voice.

He might not know why she was killed, but he *did* know something. Of that, I was suddenly sure. I hesitated, wanting to push but suspecting he might walk away if I did. "How well did you know Mona?"

He glanced up again, gaze narrowed. "Ten months." His admission was almost grudging. "I used to drive her about, for shopping and the like, when business was slow."

I nodded. A lot of sirens employed drivers, simply because few ever bothered getting a driver's license. Mom had once explained that it was simply easier to pay someone else to worry about traffic and rules. And, of course, cash rarely ever exchanged hands in such deals. "What sort of business do you run?"

"I own Mighty Mouse Bodyguard Services."

I smiled. "Cool name."

"Yeah, it gets remembered." He half shrugged, his gaze going back to where Mona had lain.

"Would she have said something to you if she'd suspected she was in trouble?"

He seemed to hunker down into himself. "She should have. She didn't."

That wasn't really unusual. Sirens usually treated their drivers as little more than another business transaction, but this dwarf's reaction to her death seemed to suggest there was more to their dealings than that.

"When was the last time you saw her?"

"Haven't seen her for a few days." He hesitated and shook his bald head. Droplets of water fell from it like tears. "She was so excited."

"About what?"

"About leaving the business," he said softly. "About giving it all away and becoming a married woman."

"You're kidding, right?" I couldn't help the incredulous note in my voice. As my brother had noted not so long ago, a siren giving up her song was as unheard of as a dragon giving up its wings. It was a part of them, a part of who they were. Oh, some of them certainly tried—Mom had, on numerous occasions, as she'd gotten older. But every time she'd come back, and every time she'd stated it would have been easier to give up breathing. I had no doubt that she was still using her song, even though age had all but crippled her.

"I never kid," the dwarf said, voice sour. He glanced at his watch. "I have to get going. Good luck with your search."

I dug my wallet out of my pocket, pulled out a business

card, and handed it to him. "Call me if you remember anything useful."

The dwarf glanced at it and raised an eyebrow. "So you *are* a bloody PI. Here I was thinking you were just another nosy reporter spinning a tale."

"I don't spin tales." At least, not all that often.

"I'll remember that," he said, and walked away.

I went back to my car and drove home to Abbotsford, but finding a parking space once I'd arrived was an entirely different matter. Some bastard had parked a big black van in my usual spot and, in the process, had managed to block a good half of the narrow street. I edged my old Toyota past it, then continued on, working my way back up Park Street before finding a spot half a block from home.

My house was a single-fronted, double-storey Victorian on the corner of Park and Stafford Streets, and it pretty much faded into the background when it came to looks. The government had declared this section of Abbotsford a heritage area a year ago, and most of the other Victorians in the street had received the required face-lift. I'd been in the process of doing the same when I'd been working at the newspaper, but had concentrated on getting the inside livable rather than the outside pretty.

Of course, I could have done what many other residents had and gone down the quick-fix route, but I refused to shell out a weekly retainer for a wizard to keep a restoration spell on my house. It might be old fashioned, but I'd rather be sure that the place *was* solid rather than simply look it.

The gate scraped harshly along the concrete as I opened it,

meaning it was just another thing to fix on a list that was getting longer by the day. I forced it shut, then headed up the steps two at a time to my front door—which stood wide open.

Laughter drifted out to greet me—raucous, deep laughter I was more than a little familiar with. A mix of amusement and frustration slithered through me as I walked down the long hallway to the kitchen-diner at the rear of the property. Four man-mountains turned and gave me a wide smile of greeting. I knew one of them—Guy, the biggest of the lot. He and I had basically grown up together, having gone to the same all-races primary and high school.

"Welcome back, Harri my friend." He held out a can of beer. "Have a drink."

It was one of my own beers I was being offered. Guy, like all ogres, believed that what belonged to a friend also belonged to him. And really, who in their right mind would argue the point with an ogre? Especially when they had hands and teeth the size of Guy's?

Not that *that* had ever stopped me trying. Being sensible wasn't always one of my stronger points. Besides, I knew well enough Guy was a sheep in wolf's clothing. He really *wouldn't* hurt a fly—not unless his family or friends were threatened. And in that sort of situation, you wouldn't want anyone else by your side.

"Guy, how many times do I have to tell you to stay out of my house when I'm not home?"

"But Harri, you didn't lock the door. And how was I to know you weren't home unless I came in?"

To an ogre, a deadlock was like a fly on the back of a horse—an irritation, nothing more. "You *could* knock. And I want the lock replaced." Again.

"But I did knock. That was when the door opened."

"Then use a little less force next time."

He grinned, revealing more tannin-stained teeth. "I'll try to remember. And I'll get Kristo to fix the lock. He's really good at that sort of stuff."

I rolled my eyes. Kristo was all I needed. The gnome was good at fixing all manner of items, but he tended to be heavily into the planning side of things and not so big on action. It'd take him all week just to decide a new lock was needed.

"Besides," Guy continued. "The only thing worth stealing is the stuff we're drinking and the TV."

"Well, at least with you lot here, no one would dare take the TV."

Guy raised his beer and grinned in agreement. One of his compatriots let off a fart that sounded like the rumble of a jet taking off, and the other two practically fell about the floor laughing. The whole house shook.

I grabbed a yogurt from the fridge and hightailed it to the safety of the loft. At least the air would be less polluted up there.

"You really have to do something about those ogres," Ceri commented, her voice filled with exasperation. Her desk was the larger of the two we'd squeezed into the loft space, simply because, at six three, she actually needed the extra legroom. Especially given she'd not only inherited her gargoyle grandfather's sensitivity to the sun, but also his build. She was, to use an old phrase, built like a Mac truck—but that still made her little compared to the ogres downstairs. "They're really making this place unlivable. Or, at the very least, unworkable. Lord knows how many clients their foul presences have scared away."

I placed the yogurt onto the desk, then shucked off my coat off and tossed it over a nearby chair. "I've tried. They don't listen."

"If we starve to death, it'll be their fault," she muttered, but there was amusement in her tone.

"I'm getting enough photography work to keep us from actually starving." I picked up the coffee pot and raised it in question.

She nodded and then thrust a hand through slate gray hair —another remnant of her heritage. "I rang Numar's mom—she hasn't heard from him, although she did expect him home last night."

"Did she mention where he was staying down here?" I walked across to her desk, the floorboards creaking with each step.

Ceri accepted her coffee with a nod of thanks, and then said, "Apparently he usually stays with a female friend, but Roda couldn't remember her name."

Which didn't make it easier to track him down. I made a mental note to ask Keale and then said, "Luckily, I had a little more luck with Lyle's task. Or maybe that should be a little less luck."

"How so?"

I wrinkled my nose and settled down at my own desk. "A siren washed up on the beach this morning. I suspect it might be the woman Lyle hired us to find."

"Well, there goes our nice fat paycheck," she muttered, expression gloomy. "I was hoping you could string the old bastard out for a few days."

"We might yet. There's no confirmation that it *was* Mona."

"True." She sighed and glanced at her watch. "I better get going. I rang our client and arrange to meet her at a café in town at nine."

"Do you want me to do it? You'll be pushing your sun limitations at that hour."

"She's expecting me so I'd better go. Besides, it's clouded over and I'll be sunblocked to high heaven *and* covered up."

Which didn't mean she wouldn't burn. "Why not just ask her here?"

"Aside from the ogre factor?" Amusement touched the corners of her slate-colored eyes. "I thought she might be less inclined to cry in a public place."

I snorted softly. "You're all heart."

"Totally. Comes from years of walking the streets in the dead of the night." She pushed up from her desk. "Let me know how the siren thing goes."

"Ditto with the crier." I grinned. "And hold your breath as you head downstairs. Gutter humor was alive and well when I left."

"Another damn reason to move the buggers on." She drew in a deep breath and quickly retreated down the stairs.

I fired up my computer, and then transferred all the images I'd taken of Keale. The shot of the dragon, his body aflame with sunlight and mirrored in the Rialto's windows, was a stunner. It almost looked as if two dragons were flying through the sky. But it was the picture of him colliding with the helicopter that caught my attention. I'd managed to take the shot from behind him just as the sun broke above the horizon, and the silver helicopter was practically lost in the sudden glare. If I could hardly see it, then a dragon, with their poorer eyesight, certainly wouldn't have. If ever there was a shot that might provide Keale with an excuse for hitting that helicopter, it was this one.

I stared at it for several more seconds and then emailed the proof across to Greg Harris, my former boss. Technically, I I should have sent it to the police—and that's certainly what Ceri would have advised—but I wasn't above trying to sway the public's opinion in Keale's favor. He needed all the help he could get on this one.

Surprisingly, Greg's response was almost immediate and, for once, he didn't quibble at the cost. Obviously, no staff photographers had managed to get anything, and photos like this on the front page of any newspaper usually guaranteed at least an extra ten thousand newspapers sold.

I waited until I had confirmation that the fee had been transferred to my bank account, and then sent him the full picture. With that all settled, I pulled Lyle's memory card from my pocket and opened a separate file to upload them into.

He was no photographer, that was for sure. There were only five shots on the card—four of them of the car from different angles, and one of the driver in government gray. All were blurred, as if taken on the run.

I blew out a frustrated breath, then opened Photoshop and began working on the images. It took me a good twenty minutes to get anything resembling clarity. I ran off a couple of prints, and then homed in on the driver's face and the muddy number plate, and got a couple of prints of those, too. Lyle could probably use his connections to grab the driver's name, and maybe even the name of the man he'd been chauffeuring.

I studied the five images tiled on the screen for a few minutes longer, then frowned and enlarged the middle one. There seemed to be a vague outline of something in the back window of the car. A passenger, or simply a shadow from the nearby building?

I zoomed in. It definitely resembled the profile of a person rather than a shadow. I reselected the area, then played around with pixels, and shifted some colors and tones, trying to sharpen the image. I didn't have much luck—the image merged too well with the tint-darkened windows.

I sat back, contemplating options as I ate my yogurt. Maybe if I assigned the glass a different color, the darker head shape might stand out more. I did that, changing the glass color to light gray, then hit re-assign all. And, as simple as that, the side-on image jumped into focus.

My stomach twisted. I knew that profile, even if I didn't know the man himself all that well. In many respects, the profile on the screen so very similar to the one I saw in the mirror day in and day out—if you discounted the sharper angle of his aristocratic nose and a chin that was definitely more prominent than my own.

This wasn't any old elf. This was the newly elected head of the Elven Council; a man who not only sat on the High Court bench, but a statesman whose word was practically revered in the halls of state government.

My father, Charles Bramwell Harrison Phillecky.

CHAPTER FOUR

T*his* was unfucking believable. First Lyle's case draws Val back into my life, and then it beats a path straight to the feet of my goddamn father. Who was next? My other half brother? The way things were going, I wouldn't be at all surprised.

I scrubbed a hand across my eyes, then picked up my coffee and leaned back in my chair. What was I going to tell Lyle? For that matter, why the hell hadn't Lyle recognized his own damn brother? I knew his sight was getting worse, but surely it couldn't be *that* bad.

Frowning, I studied my father's profile for several seconds, then sighed and hit print. In reality, it was probably fortunate that Lyle *hadn't* recognized him, because I suspected he was a little unstable—at least emotionally—when it came to Mona. He would have confronted Bramwell—both verbally and physically—and that could only have gone badly for Lyle. This also explained the trolls being set onto him. He'd obviously been spotted taking the photos.

Which meant I had to proceed with caution. But it also meant my next step was talking to my father, and that really wasn't something I wanted to do. I might not have much respect for my Elven kin—Lyle aside, and despite what Ceri might think, I had no illusions that he held any deep affection for me—but I knew full well what my father thought of my existence. If he'd been willing to set trolls onto his own *brother*, I could imagine the lengths he'd go to if he knew I now had the photographs.

Seeing him wouldn't be easy, though. While he'd never denied my existence, he'd never publicly acknowledged it beyond allowing my mother to place his name on my birth certificate. Why he'd allowed this I have no idea, although I suspected it might have been something of an insurance policy. After all, there'd been no guarantee he'd actually reproduce with his wife, and a half-breed was better than nothing. But then my brother had been born, and I'd become valueless. In twenty-nine years I'd met him precisely three times—and never for more than five minutes at a time.

I drained the rest of my coffee, then rose and walked across to the window. Rain slithered down the pane in silvery streaks and the day outside looked even gloomier than it had before. It was a somewhat fitting reflection of how I felt.

Movement below caught my eye. In the yard behind mine, my neighbor—who went by the somewhat ill-fitting name Delilah—was currently attempting to hang out her washing. Why she'd want to do this when it was raining was anyone's guess, but then, in the entire time we'd been neighbors, she'd never once done the expected.

She was perched tippy-toes on the top step of a ladder that was about two rungs too short, thanks to the fact she was a shorter than normal dwarf—a fact she refused to acknowledge. I shook my head and wondered when she'd actually get around to buying a decent ladder—especially when the one she was currently using was the one she'd borrowed from me several years ago. Delilah, as well as being a dwarf, was also something of a magpie.

She must have caught the slight movement, because she suddenly glanced up. "Harri?" she said, her voice deep but holding an edge that grated. "That you hiding up there again, girl?"

I grimaced, but opened the window and leaned out. "Morning Delilah."

"When are you going to do something about that house of yours? The smell coming from it this morning is atrocious."

I somehow managed to restrain my smile. "Guy's bought a couple of his mates over again."

"Guy?" Her stout little body suddenly quivered with indignation. "That ugly ogre bastard owes me fifty bucks."

I suddenly felt sorry for Guy. He didn't have a *hope* against the cyclone that was Delilah on a mission to retrieve.

She clomped down the ladder then marched toward the gate she'd cut into the fence between our two properties. When it came to privacy, none of my neighbors seemed to think I needed or wanted it. I sat on the sill and crossed my arms. There was no way in hell I was actually going down there.

The back door crashed open. "Guy, where the hell are you?"

I could practically feel the ogres cringing from where I sat. Delilah might be a good sixth of their size, but she could be meaner than a pack of dogs fighting over a scrap of food.

"You got my money?" she demanded. She was obviously tapping her foot—the sound was as sharp as a gunshot on the polished boards below.

"Er...no. Mom had to go to the doc and...um...the van needed some work and—"

"In other words, you've pissed it against the wall again."

Guy mumbled something I couldn't quite catch, but I very much suspected from the general tone that it wasn't exactly polite.

"Don't you go cussing me, boy. I want my money, not more of your excuses."

"Look, our strike should be over in a couple of days, and once the additional money comes in—"

"I could starve in a couple of days—"

Somewhat unwisely, Guy snorted. The sharp sound of flesh being smacked echoed.

"Fuck, Delilah, that was uncalled for—"

"Then show a little respect, ogre. That new black van out there blocking half the street yours?"

"Yeah. What of it?"

"Give me the keys." Delilah's voice was imperious. The wise did not ignore that tone. "When I get my money, you'll get back your keys."

"Get real. Shemp and I will need it when we go back to work."

"Then borrow the money from him. I don't really care where it comes from."

"He ain't got no money either," Guy mumbled.

"Then give me the keys."

"Harri!" Guy's voice was plaintive. "Can you lend me fifty bucks?"

I rolled my eyes. Who'd have guess that was coming? I grabbed twenty dollars from my purse—which was precisely half of what remained in there—then slowly headed down the stairs. The four ogres were huddled in the far corner of the kitchen. Delilah stood in front of them, foot a-tapping and hands planted firmly on her hips. A sheepdog working her flock, I thought with amusement.

"I haven't got fifty," I said, and offered her the twenty instead.

Delilah snatched it from my hand and then waved the note fiercely at Guy. The ogre threw up his hands, as if warding off evil.

"I want the rest of my money by payday, and you'd better make sure you give Harri back her twenty, too."

"I'll pay, I'll pay," he said hastily.

"Good." Deliliah glanced up. "You want me to get this scum out of your house, Harri?"

"Thanks, but no." If the ogres went, Delilah might stay, and as much as I knew she meant well, I really couldn't take much of her homespun advice on everything from my love life—or lack thereof—to how to repair my house. Besides, given what I'd just discovered, it might be handy to have a little muscle hanging about. Bramwell might be my father, but that wouldn't stop him pulling any punches once he realized what I had.

"Then I'll get going." She hesitated and glanced around. "There really is a shocking smell in this place. What the hell have you been doing?"

"The plumbing is playing up again." If I mentioned the true source, none of us would hear the end of it.

She harrumphed and stalked out of the house, bleached blonde hair standing on end and waving a goodbye. Once the coast was clear, the ogres erupted into gales of laughter. I rolled my eyes and once again retreated.

Back at my desk, I placed Mona's little black book in front of me and began the long process of retrieving all the images. There were twenty-two cards all up, and each one contained images of at least half a dozen men. Mona had been a very busy little siren.

It wasn't until I was retrieving the images from the last of the cards that I noticed something odd about the book itself. There was a slight discoloration in the page that followed the final card, as if something had been stuck there but was now gone. I ran a finger across the paper. It was sticky, so if something *had* been there, it shouldn't have fallen off. It could only mean it had been taken. Obviously, I *wasn't* the only one who knew a siren's hiding habits.

The question that now had to be answered was, was that person also her murderer?

I leaned back in the chair again. Technically speaking, I should hand the book and all the disks over to the PIT boys, and that's certainly what Ceri would be demanding if she knew of their existence. Given what Val had said, it was obvious that some of her clients *had* known about each other. Maybe one of them would know who had been jealous enough to kill.

But handing it over meant risking a run in with Kaij, and my nerves hadn't yet settled from our first almost-encounter. I needed more time to get used to the fact that he was back in town.

I glanced across to the printer and studied the photo of my father outside Mona's apartment. He knew all about a siren's hiding habits. He'd answered my mother's song for more than ten years, until the call of duty and prosperity had finally become more alluring.

Had my father succumbed to the song yet again?

I couldn't imagine it happening, not given his recent appointment as the head of the high council. When he'd spent all that time with my mother, he had—according to her—been little more than an adolescent looking for excitement, despite the fact he was over forty years old. He hadn't at the time been destined for greatness and a seat on the high council. He *had* been married, of course, but like most Elven marriages, it was an arrangement made to strengthen political and business ties. I doubted the wife had known of his liaison with my mother though—not if the fuss my existence had eventually caused was any indication.

So why the hell had he been outside Mona's apartment?

Only the man himself could answer that question. Somewhat reluctantly, I reached for the phone and dialed the number I knew by heart but had only ever used twice in my life.

After several rings, a polished voice said, "Phillecky residence."

Jose, the butler. I knew a whole lot about where and how my father lived, even if I'd never been there. It was amazing what you could discover when you were a bored teenager armed with a computer and friends who could hack into just any system they wanted to.

"I'd like to speak to Bramwell Phillecky, please."

"And who may I say is calling?"

"Just tell him Harri."

There was a click. Symphony music came online. There was something to be said for elevator music, even if it assaulted the ears. Jose came back. "Transferring you now."

I had no doubt I was being transferred to both a more secure line *and* room. Wouldn't want the dirty washing aired within hearing range of staff, after all.

"What do you want?" My father's voice, deep and impersonal.

"I've seen a photo you might want to explain," I said, doing my best to imitate his tone.

"I haven't got time for games, Harriet."

Impatience edged his voice, and annoyance surged. "Nor have I. This is a photo of you outside the residence of a recently murdered siren. I want a meeting, and I want an explanation, otherwise I will take my knowledge to the police."

Silence fairly crackled down the line. I could almost hear my father's mind ticking over, no doubt figuring ways and means to get out of the situation.

"When?" he said eventually.

"The sooner the better." I glanced at my watch. I still had to contact Lyle, and then go see Keale. I had no idea how long either of those would take, so it was probably a good idea to leave plenty of time. "Coffee at Noah's Ark, in Lygon Street, at five PM."

"Fine," Bramwell said, and slammed the receiver down.

No surprise there. I dialed the café and booked a table, as the place was usually busy on the weekends, then leaned back and studied the photos still tiled on the screen. Given the fact my father had more than likely set the trolls onto Lyle, if I wanted to keep these images secure then they had to be kept elsewhere. While I could keep the card in the safe and the computer key-coded locked, neither were one hundred percent thief proof. Which meant the only place I could store all the images—not just Lyle's, but the ones I'd retrieved from Mona's little black book—and be reasonably assured of their safety was by transferring them across to Cindy's. She was another old school friend, a human who these days ran a large ISP. She'd given me five hundred gigs of storage on their system some time back in return for doing her wedding photos, and while I did pay a nominal fee these days, it was still the safest place I had to store anything vital. No one was hacking into Cindy's system—not when she was a reformed hacker herself, and kept up to date with all the tricks.

I spent the next couple of hours doing precisely that, and then erased all evidence of having done so. Once I'd secured the disks and the book in the hidden floor safe, I finally picked up the phone and dialed Lyle.

"Harriet," he said, voice gravely and tired sounding. "That punch-drunk friend of yours is in a whole heap of trouble."

"Did you get them to test for Prevoron?"

"Yeah. They weren't too pleased, especially since initial breath tests suggest he's been drinking for days. In fact, they're currently keeping a close eye on him because they suspect alcohol poisoning." Lyle's tone was almost scathing, although why when he'd certainly had enough alcoholic binges in his time I couldn't say. Although elves weren't affected by alcohol in the same way as many other races, so maybe it was just an elf's general lack of sympathy for the frailty of others. "The Prevoron results will probably take four or five days to come through. But the biggest problem is the fact they're intending to charge him with murder, not manslaughter."

"What?" I said, voice incredulous. "They're saying he *deliberately* downed the helicopter?"

"Basically, yes. Apparently, air traffic were tracking him at the time, and he made no attempt to get out of the helicopter's way."

"He's a dragon, for fuck's sake. He doesn't come equipped with radar, the sun was in his eyes, and his eyesight is shot to hell." I hesitated. "Besides, the helicopter wasn't exactly in legal airspace either."

"Air traffic say they were."

"Then how do you explain the fact they crashed over Princess Bridge?"

"Sudden wind shift."

I snorted. "It would have taken a gale to blow a dragon and a helicopter that far out of legal airspace." So why would air-traffic lie? Especially over something that could be so easily checked?

"I'm heading over to the airport now to have a nice little chat with the controller in question."

"Good." I hesitated. "Is Keale going to make bail?"

"They won't even consider it until he sobers up, but I suspect he will. They'll just tag him to ensure he can't do a runner."

Something he *wouldn't* be pleased about, although it was infinitely better than remaining cooped up in a prison. "Is he coherent yet?"

"Near enough. He still swears he hasn't had a drink in over a week."

I wanted to believe him, if only because of the Rebecca factor. But if he *hadn't* been drinking, why was his reading so high in the breath test? "Can I get in to talk to him?"

"I've made arrangements for you to, yes." He paused. "How'd things go at Mona's apartment?"

Telling Lyle over the phone that she was more than likely dead was not something I wanted to do. Yet I couldn't lie, either. Lyle knew me well enough to detect it. So I simply said, "Did you know Mona was collecting photos of her clients?"

Lyle was silent for a moment. "No, I didn't."

"Well, someone did. One of the memory cards is missing from the book."

"Book?" Confusion edged his voice. "What book?"

"The little black book I found in the laundry basket. She was keeping the memory cards inside it."

"Why would anyone want to hide something like that in a laundry basket?"

"As my mom used to say, would you go through a pile of dirty socks on the off chance there was something worth stealing within them?"

Lyle snorted. "Good point. You developed the cards yet?"

I resisted the impulse to yet again remind him that photos were digital and were no longer processed—not in the sense he meant, anyway. "I've done both lots, actually."

"Really? Did you get anything worthwhile from mine?"

"Yes. And remind me to give you photography lessons some time." I hesitated. "I've printed several shots of the driver. I thought you might know someone who could run a check on him."

"Great. I'll drop by just after seven tonight and pick it up. Did you uncover anything else?"

Yeah, someone strangled Mona and dumped her in the sea. "Did you know Val owned the apartment building Mona's living in?"

"Really?" Surprise ran through his voice. "He must be keeping a low profile, because I haven't spotted him."

Val and low profile were two words that didn't often associate with each other. "He stopped an argument between two men in Mona's apartment a couple of days before she disappeared. He's working on a sketch for me."

And what would I do if one of them was Bramwell? Maybe I'd better hassle my brother to get the sketches done this afternoon. Forewarned was forearmed.

"Then why didn't he mention it to the cops? It certainly wasn't in any of the reports I read."

"It wouldn't be." And not only because it might have landed him in trouble with the guild. Val had a long history of his brain going to mush when confronted by a uniform. All his boyfriends, past and probably present, had been military, firemen, or cops.

"Push him for those sketches, Harriet," he said, voice edged with exasperation. "The sooner we get them, the sooner we can track the men down and see if they had anything to do with her disappearance."

I frowned. "Why are you so certain that she was in trouble?"

Silence met my question. I swiveled the chair around and

81

stared out the rain-covered window. The response that eventually came wasn't the one I wanted.

"What do you mean, was?" Lyle's voice was flat, devoid of any emotion.

I silently swore. One little slip and the game was up. I sighed. "The body of a siren washed up on Sandridge beach this morning."

"And just when were you planning to tell me?" His voice still held a monotone note, yet somehow managed to hint at fury.

"Certainly not over the damn phone, and certainly not before I knew for certain it was her. Which I don't."

The silence stretched on again. I let it, knowing Lyle needed time to pull himself together.

"I'll see if my contacts can verify ID."

Good. It'd save me from risking an encounter with Kaij. "I *did* talk to a dwarf who was at the scene—apparently he was Mona's driver."

"Darryl," Lyle muttered. "Was he able to confirm whether or not it was her?"

"No." Which wasn't exactly a lie, because he *hadn't* actually come straight out and said it was Mona. "He did mention that Mona had intended to give it all up and save her song for just one man. You know anything about that?"

"It was me." The admission was grudging. "But it was complicated."

"No doubt." For one, Lyle was already married. And two,

he'd lose whatever standing he had left with not only the council, but with Elven society in general. "Did Adelia suspect something serious was going on? Is that why she was having you followed?"

He snorted. It was a fierce, disparaging sound. "The bitch wants to get her greedy little paws on my money. If she can prove I've been having a serious, long-standing affair with a siren, she gets more."

If social standing was the first most important thing to an elf, the second was money, and the third was offspring. Lyle had none of the first, plenty of the second thanks to both his previous job and the fact that the Philleckys were old money, and none of the third. "So even though you've been with Mona long-term, you had no idea she was photographing clients? Or why she might have been doing that?"

"How the hell would I know that, when I didn't even fucking know until-" He cut the sentence off abruptly, making me wonder just what he'd been about to reveal. "Sorry, Harriet. I shouldn't be getting angry at you when you're just doing the job I asked you to do."

"It's okay, Lyle. Really."

He sighed. "I see you tonight. By then, I'll know one way or the other."

"Hopefully."

He hung up. The phone rang almost instantly.

"Finished those sketches for you, darls," Val said, without preamble. "When are we having that dinner party?"

"As soon as I can get the ogres out of the kitchen."

Val's sigh was overly dramatic. "Don't tell me you're still collecting oddbods?"

"I seem to have an affinity for them. Can you scan the pics and email them across?"

"Not a hope, seeing I haven't a computer. But I could magic a copy over, if they're that urgent."

"They are. Thanks, Val." The copies might only last a few hours, but all I really needed was enough time to photocopy them.

"Hang on a minute." The phone clunked down, then Val began muttering an incantation. A few seconds later, two rolled-up pieces of paper plopped into existence, the edges glowing a weird pink color as they hovered at eye level.

"Got them?" Val asked.

Energy tingled across my fingers as I grabbed them. "Yep."

"So, our dinner date?"

I sighed. He was going to harp on this until it happened. "How about Tuesday night?"

"I'm all a-tingle."

"Oh, so am I." My voice was dry. "How many friends are you bringing? Remember, my place isn't that large."

"I'll restrict myself to Bryan, then. He's a fireman."

I smiled. "Fine. I'll get back with details later, Val. And thanks again."

I hung up and unrolled the drawings. The first one was of a man who looked to be in his mid to late thirties, with a heavily receding hairline, a prominent nose, and somewhat narrow dark brown eyes. Whether Val had intended it or not, the impression this sketch gave me was of a personality that was calculating—shifty.

The second man had black hair, striking blue eyes, an arrogant, somewhat aristocratic nose, and wing-tip ears.

I closed my eyes and shook my head in disbelief.

It was Gilroy, my *other* half-brother. Which made me wonder why Val hadn't recognized him, until I remembered he took even less interest in politics and keeping up with the news than I did. And it wasn't like I'd had pictures of Gilroy growing up. I'd had no idea what he'd looked like until he'd gone into politics and I started seeing stories about him at work.

Obviously, though, he'd taken after Bramwell in more ways than one. But how he'd managed to keep his tastes for sirens a secret for so damn long was anyone's guess. Gilroy was a politician—a high-ranking member of the Liberal Party and the shadow minister for Education, which basically meant he and the rest of his cronies in the opposition party did their best to heckle and hamper their opposite number in the government. He had both the desire and the backing to go right to the top—and, in fact, was predicted to become the first ever non-human prime minister. He was a favorite with the media, who followed him like puppies, charmed by his re-tooled smile and effusive personality.

If Gilroy had been hooked by a siren's song, then surely the press would have found out by now. Or maybe they *had*.

Maybe Bramwell was shelling out big bucks to keep someone quiet. It certainly wouldn't be the first time. As Maggie had so aptly noted, there were a lot of skeletons in the Phillecky cupboards, and not all of them were dead.

But it was a development Lyle was *not* going to be happy about. I mean, his *nephew* was sleeping with the siren *he* wanted to marry, and might well have been involved in her disappearance.

At least it *did* explain my father's presence outside Mona's. Maybe he'd been trying to talk some sense into Gilroy. Or, perhaps, Mona.

But no matter what, this was going to get ugly. And I'd put money on the fact that some of that ugly was headed my way. It had been that sort of week, and it certainly didn't show any signs of improvement.

I pushed to my feet and realized everything was quiet downstairs. Maybe the ogres had finally left...then my gaze caught the time. It was two-twenty. Time for the one and only religion ogres truly believed in—football. They were no doubt gathered around the TV right now, on their knees and fervently praying for the center bounce that would start the day's proceedings.

I smiled then gathered everything I needed together and headed downstairs. I hadn't been far off in my estimation— they weren't on their knees, but they were sprawled all over the floor, eyes locked on the screen, expressions filled with expectation and happiness.

"You lot planning to stick around awhile?" I picked my way through the sea of legs and opened the side window. If I didn't get some air into the place, I wouldn't be able to sleep later tonight.

"You kidding?" Guy didn't bother looking at me. "North plays West Coast live tonight."

So they'd be here until ten, at least. "Lyle's coming over later. Try to be polite to the man if I'm not back."

"I'm always a gentleman," Guy said, and belched.

His three compatriots didn't respond with gales of laughter. They barely even twitched. The sermon was about to begin —the umpire had the ball in his hand and was about to bounce. I shook my head and left.

It didn't take all that long to drive to the Melbourne Assessment Prison. It was Saturday afternoon, the Berren Cricket Ground had the full-house signs out, and the game was being replayed live across the country. Berren was the home of Australian Rules Football, and a good portion of her population never missed a game.

I parked in Adderley Street, just around the corner from the prison. After feeding the meter, I made my way around to the main entrance. Two scans later, I was being escorted down sterile white corridors and then out through a side door into what had been the old exercise yards. Four dragon-containment cells now dominated the space. Built with titanium, they were fireproof and fully electrified, and had a hundred percent success rate so far. Once in, dragons didn't get out. Of course, the real trick was getting them in.

"Don't touch the walls or you'll fry," the guard said, and opened the first of the two cell doors. "Just buzz when you want out."

I nodded and stepped into the barren space between the two doors. The first one slammed shut, then another buzzer sounded and the second door opened.

Keale had regained human form. He lay—not quite spread-eagled—in the center of the concrete expanse, a gangly, red-haired scarecrow of a man staring up at the miserable sky framed through the overhead titanium bars. Dragons weren't fond of small spaces, even in human form, so though the cell did have a shelter, it only had three walls. Presumably, the bed, TV, and bathroom facilities were all open to the elements, though I'd hazard a guess that the hut had been built in such a way that there was little chance of rain actually getting in. The dragon coalition—which was basically a union protecting dragon rights and working conditions—would have been up in arms about it, otherwise. Football commentary blasted from the shelter, though I couldn't tell if it were the TV or the radio.

I sat cross-legged beside him. A roar came from the direction of the shelter. The Western Bulldogs—the team I half-barracked for—had just scored a goal and were leading Richmond by one point.

"I've backed the dogs," Keale said. "Got three to one on them."

"Good odds, considering they're second on the ladder."

"I thought so." He continued to stare unblinkingly at the sky for several more minutes, then scrubbed his left hand across his eyes. His right arm had been plastered from elbow to wrist. "The shit has really hit the fan this time, hasn't it?"

"Buried it, I'm afraid," I agreed, voice grim.

"They said I hit a helicopter. Killed four people." Disbelief edged his voice. "I can't even remember leaving the pub, let alone flying home."

"So you definitely can't tell me why you were flying through the city?"

Keale glanced at me, his black eyes bright with confusion. "The city? How the hell did I get there? *Why* would I even go there? For fuck's sake, after working all damn day I was totally knackered. It would have been an effort to fly home —why the hell would I take such a weird detour?"

"I don't know." I frowned. "Do you remember being with Numar? You told me at the bridge after the crash that you'd been drinking with him."

"I did?" He hesitated, and scrubbed his jaw. It sounded like sandpaper being scraped along the concrete. "I can't remember it, but from what the docs have said, I'd certainly been drinking with someone."

Yeah, and if not Numar, then who? "What happened to Rebecca? I thought you had a date with her last night?"

"Yeah, but she called to cancel. Something had come up." He grimaced. "Shame really, given that if the cops get their way, the memory of hot sex is all I'll have for quite a long time."

"Lyle's working your case, and he's one of the best." I patted his arm, though I doubted it provided much in the way of comfort. "But you were with her the night before, weren't you?"

"I did the early shift, and left before eleven."

"Why so early?"

Keale shrugged. "She didn't want me there any longer. Probably had another dragon lined up for the late night shift."

I nodded. Dragons were not monogamous creatures, and females only had a short window of fertility. To give themselves the maximum chance of falling pregnant, it wasn't unusual for them to take on three or four males over the course of the mating cycle. And they could afford to be choosy, because males outnumbered them four to one. Of course, both sexes *did* have sex at other times, in human form. They were just infertile with each other and other races when in that form, which is why you never saw half-breed dragons gadding about. And *that* was probably just as well.

"So why would the police say you've been drinking for days?" I asked. "And why the hell would you be drinking when her mating cycle hasn't finished?"

"Harri, I don't know. Everything is a blur. I have no idea what the hell went on last night, let alone what I thinking."

"So what *are* your first clear memories?"

"Waking up in this fucking cell with a broken bloody arm, a sliced-up back, and a freight train screaming through my head. Bit of a shock, I can tell you."

"Your back is obviously okay." He was, after all, laying on it.

"They shot me full of painkillers and told me to keep off it." Keale snorted. "As if. I would rather soak in the sky than barren concrete walls, even if it does fucking cause more damage."

I glanced down at the concrete. There didn't seem to be any blood staining it, nor could I smell its stink, so he hadn't opened any wounds just yet. "Where's Numar staying?"

"When he's in town he normally bunks down with Olisa, an old girlfriend of his, but I think he mentioned work putting him up at the meeting venue this time."

"You wouldn't happen to know which venue or hotel, would you?"

He frowned. "Ibis, I think. On Springvale road."

I nodded and glanced at my watch. It was just after four, which meant I needed to get moving if I was to meet my father on time.

"Lyle said you were likely to make bail, but they'll electronically track and restrict your movements." I hesitated, and then added, "You got somewhere to stay?"

"I'll head home. My sister lives in another state and I refuse to go to Mother's." He glanced at me. "I'll be all right, Harri. I *can* look after myself, you know."

I smiled, then leaned forward and kissed his cheek. "I know. But if you feel like some company, or just a bed for a couple of nights, then my spare room is always available."

"You're a sweetheart, but I'll see how I go first."

"Good." I rose. "Be careful of your back."

He waved my concern away and kept staring at the sky. Drinking it in while he could, perhaps.

I left. The streets were still relatively free of traffic, so I made it to Brunswick in plenty of time—which was just as well, given the serious lack of parking in the area. I eventually found a spot in a side street half a dozen blocks from the café, and walked back, grateful the rain had at least stopped. The wind, however, still held a chill. I zipped up my jacket and shoved my hands in my pockets to keep them warm. Most sirens loved winter—loved the cold, the wet, and the storms—simply because it was the sort of conditions they might find at sea. But even in that, I'd taken more after my Elven side. I hated winter.

Noah's Ark was a small, single fronted café situated in the heart of Lygon Street's famed restaurant district. It served brilliant coffee as well as a mix of Italian and Greek food at reasonable prices, and, as usual, it was packed. Which is actually why I'd arranged to meet my father here—with all the noise, there was less likelihood of our conversation being overheard.

I ordered a coffee and a large helping of carrot cake, then headed for our table, which was, as I'd requested, tucked into a rear corner well away from the windows. Bramwell wasn't likely to appreciate the chance of roving reporters seeing us together.

Five o'clock came and went. I ordered another coffee. My watch soon tripped past five-thirty and still he hadn't turned up. Either Bramwell had decided he didn't need to explain the photo to me, or he'd resorted to more nefarious methods of checking it out.

I was voting for the latter option.

My phone chose that moment to ring. I half-expected it to be my father, calmly proclaiming he'd either procured the photo, or that he'd rather see it circulated than meet with unwanted offspring.

I was wrong.

It was Guy.

And the ogre sounded madder than hell.

CHAPTER FIVE

"Harri," he growled. "You weren't expecting a couple of trolls to come busting through your door, were you?"

"No." The fact that they obviously *had* meant my father had taken option number one. I wasn't surprised, but I *was* annoyed. "Is everyone there all right?"

"We are. The trolls are a little worse for the wear."

No surprise there. Ogres don't take too kindly to people interrupting their football viewing. "What happened?"

"Nothing much. A little undue force was used, but no damage caused—at least to the house. Missed the bloody end of the footy, though."

And no doubt the trolls had been given an extra punch or two for *that* thoughtlessness. "Where are they now?"

"Here in the kitchen. Moe and Curly are sitting on them."

Two of the ogres were called Moe and Curly? He *had* to be kidding. "Then what the hell is Larry doing?"

"Larry?" Confusion edged Guy's voice. "Who the hell is Larry?"

Amusement rippled through me, though it *did* surprise me that an ogre who absolutely loved slapstick comedy didn't know who the three stooges were. "Nobody. Forget it."

"If you mean Shemp, he's in the lounge relaying the scores."

I barely restrained a laugh. Someone in the ogre community certainly knew about the stooges, even if Guy didn't. "Can you keep them there until I get home?"

"Sure, no probs. It's only a couple of trolls, after all. You're almost out of beer, by the way."

Now, *that* would be a true disaster. "I'll pick some up on the way home."

"Thanks. We'd appreciate that."

I hung up, then scrolled through my contacts list and called Ceri. "Hey," I said, when she answered. "What time you intending to get to the office?"

"Just about to leave home." She hesitated. "Why?"

"Trolls just broke into my place. Guy and his boys are currently sitting on them. Literally."

"I almost feel sorry for the trolls." Amusement filled her voice. "But why are you ringing me rather than the cops?"

"Because I suspect these particular trolls were after something I have, and we need to question them—and then release them."

She was silent for a moment. "Has this got something to do with the case Lyle gave you? He's the only reason I can think of for you not wanting to hand the trolls over."

"It has, and it's not just Lyle involved now. It's my whole damn family." I gave her a quick update, and then added, "You're scarier than me, so you need to be the one questioning them."

She snorted. "Trolls don't scare easily. Trust me on that."

"Well, you have more hope of scaring them than I do. Besides, as a former cop, you know all the techniques to get people to talk."

"And yet *everyone* fucking talks to you," she retorted. "Hell, half the neighborhood practically lives at your house."

"Which is just as well, because if the ogres hadn't been there, the trolls might have gotten more than the memory cards." Not that there was much more worth taking, given our agency was still finding its legs in the paranormal community.

"Okay, we'll do it your way. I'll be there in half an hour," she said, and then hung up.

I headed home, taking a small detour into the drive-through bottle shop of the local hotel to grab the beer I'd promised the ogres. Guy was still parked in my usual spot, so I stole Delilah's—something I'd no doubt regret later.

Ceri was approaching the house from the other end of the street and gave the beer a somewhat amused look. "That's definitely *not* the way to get the ogres out of the house—not unless you plan to bribe them out with it."

"Wouldn't work, because Guy hasn't got a big screen TV."

She forced open the gate and waved me through. "Meaning they're basically parked here for the rest of the football season?"

I grinned. "I'm afraid so."

"Then we really *do* need to sort better office space out. Especially if Guy keeps inviting the fart machines he calls friends around."

I laughed and stepped through the once again open front door. The heat hit me, warming the chill from my bones as I made my way down the hall. Ceri kicked the door shut then followed.

Guy greeted my appearance with a wide smile. "You arrived just in time. The boys were getting a little restless—the next game starts in half an hour."

"And heaven forbid they miss the pre-match roundup," Ceri muttered.

"True, friend Ceri. Very true." Guy's voice was serious. "There's money riding on the game, after all."

And how missing the pre-match roundup could affect *that* was anyone's guess. But I didn't bother asking, just squeezed past him and continued on into the kitchen. Moe and Curly, who were pretty much ogre-versions of their namesakes, had the two trolls hog-tied on the kitchen floor and were currently perched in the middle of their backs. While trolls tended to be bigger height wise, ogres had it all over them when it came to punch per ounce. And while trolls were contract assassins, it wasn't in their nature to fight for the hell of it. Ogres considered fighting one of life's little necessities—much like beer, football, and pizza.

One of the trolls spotted us, and almost immediately said, "Hey, get these bastards off us. They're heavy."

I ignored him and headed to the fridge. Ceri dragged a chair next to the trolls and rather stiffly sat down. She didn't say anything, just contemplated them both steadily. They shared uneasy looks. I restrained my grin, tossed three beer cans to Guy—who was hovering in the doorway—then put the rest away and leaned back against the fridge door.

Both trolls looked rather the worse for wear. One had a puffy eye and several nasty looking scrapes across one cheek, and the other had a split lip and—if the bloody flap of skin swinging to and fro was anything to go by—some gold missing from his ear. Both had been in the threesome that had attacked Lyle, but neither was the one I'd spoken to.

Ceri crossed her legs and leaned back in the chair. She was, I thought, a rather intimidating presence. No wonder she'd risen through the police ranks so swiftly—at least until the shoot-out with a crime boss that had ended with her needing spinal surgery and being pensioned off.

"Would you like to tell me why you were breaking into our house?" Her voice was polite, but there was nothing polite about the look she was giving them. The wise would have 'fessed up instantly, but these particular trolls obviously weren't that intelligent.

"Hey," the troll with the gold in his ear said, "We didn't technically break in. The door was wide open. We just entered."

"Since you want to get technical, you might like to know that I'm a former police officer. As such, I have many friends still in the force. Believe me when I say it would be very easy to call in some favors, and get your asses thrown in jail so long that you might just start wishing for a sunlight bath."

The troll looked her up and down with a slight sneer. "No cop can do that. Not for a crime as minor as breaking and entering."

Ceri raised her eyebrows. "You said you didn't break in. Besides, you'd be surprised what can happen when paper-work gets lost."

"She could do it, too," Guy offered helpfully. "Happened to a mate of mine last year. Totally lost him in the system for months they did."

He was leaning against the doorframe, arms crossed and expression serious. And he was, I thought with amusement, lying through his teeth.

"But it's not the cop you should be scared of, though," he continued conversationally. "It's that slip of a thing leaning against the refrigerator."

The trolls gaze shot to me. Recognition stirred in their eyes. "Why?" the one with the damaged ear asked.

"Because she's an elf-siren hybrid." Guy gave me a slight wink. He was on a roll and enjoying it immensely. "And has the nasty tendencies of both."

"Sirens have a nasty side?" the troll said, not looking convinced.

"Oh, hell yeah." Guy waved a hand. "Not all siren calls end up with a little humpy. Sometimes, their tastes run to flesh and blood. The things I've seen Harri here eat would curl my mother's hide, I tell ya."

It was all I could do not to laugh. Ceri looked to be having the same sort of problem. The two trolls, however, looked nervous. They really *weren't* all that bright, because anyone who knew anything about sirens knew that the only flesh they ate was fish. Red meat—which is generally what most humanoid beings would be considered—made them sick. Unfortunately, this was one siren tendency I *did* get.

"So," Ceri said quickly, before Guy could roll on. "Tell me why you were sent here."

"Well, shit," the troll with the piece of ear missing muttered. He glanced at his companion, who simply shrugged. "We were sent here to collect whatever memory cards, cameras, and photos we could find downstairs."

Bramwell wasn't taking any chances, it seemed. Anger surged, but I held it in check—if only because it wouldn't have done any good to vent anyway.

"Who by?" Ceri asked.

"Oh man, come on. You know I can't tell you that. Contractual obligations, and all."

"Fair enough," Ceri said easily, and dug a hand into her pocket.

When the troll saw her phone, he said, "For fuck's sake, okay. It was an elf. He didn't leave no name."

"What about a contact number? You have to know that given you were sent here to retrieve items for him."

"I can't tell you that," the troll said, voice sullen. "It's against policy."

"You can always call in Delilah," Guy said thoughtfully. "I'm sure she'll find a way to change their minds."

"Who's Deliliah?" the troll asked, his gaze darting between the three of us.

"Man, you're better off not knowing, believe me." Guy, shuddered and took a long drink.

The troll started to sweat. Whether it was fear or simply Moe's weight pressing down on him was anyone's guess. I bit back another grin.

"You have plenty of options, troll," Ceri said quietly. "You can tell me, you can tell the police, or you can tell Delilah. Trust me when I say we're the easiest of those three options."

"Okay, okay," the troll muttered. "He was supposed to ring back tonight to arrange collection. I won't ask his name—he'll know something is up if I do—but I will run a trace and get his number."

From what I knew of troll business practices, running a trace was second nature, even though there were few people around foolish enough to renege on a deal with them.

"We'll expect a call by midnight then," Ceri said.

"Yeah, sure. Can I get up now? My back is really killing me."

Guy raised an eyebrow at me. When I nodded, he motioned Moe and Curly. The two ogres undid the ropes then climbed to their feet, but kept close to the trolls as they did the same. The troll with the torn ear did several back-stretches. Bones cracked into the silence.

Ceri pushed to her feet. She was tall enough that she didn't actually have to tilt her head too far up to meet the troll's gaze. "You got a business card, troll?"

He muttered something unpleasant, but dug into the pocket of his overalls and handed us both a card. *Ramjets Investigations*, it said. *Problems solved. Professionalism guaranteed.* I glanced down at the name on the bottom of the card.

"Xavier?" I couldn't help saying. "Really?"

"Ma was working her way through the alphabet," the troll said. "And it's better than Winifred." He cast a sympathetic glance at his companion.

I wasn't so sure about that. I shifted away from the fridge and picked up a card from the stack sitting on the nearby dresser. "Here's our card. Make sure you phone us after you talk to the man who employed you for this job."

"But what do I tell him?" He eyed me with uncertainty. "It's not like we actually succeeded, and telling him we did wouldn't be right."

Ceri snorted. "And yet it was right to accept a job to break in here?"

"That's different. That's money." He glanced back at me. "Taking money for a job not completed is bad for business."

"Trust me, the elf you're talking about won't raise any waves for you over not getting the job done. He can't afford to."

He didn't look convinced. "So I just say we got what he wanted and arrange a meet?"

"Yes. And then you ring me and let me know where that meeting is. I'll turn up in your stead."

"And the money?"

"Consider it an incentive not to come back here," Ceri said.

The troll still looked dubious. I waved a hand toward the front door, and Moe and Curly escorted them out.

Guy glanced at his watch. "Whoops, the footy is on."

He quickly disappeared. Ceri shook her head then glanced at me. "Your father might not make waves for the trolls, but I'm betting he'll raise hell for you. Especially if you're intending to confront him—which you are, aren't you?"

"Yes." I grimaced. "I really have no choice. Like it or not, he *is* my dad, and my mum would haul me over the coals if I didn't give him the opportunity to explain."

"Your mum doesn't have to know."

I snorted. "Mum knows *everything* when it comes to my father, even if it's been nearly years since they've been together."

Ceri's expression remained concerned. "You want me to come along?"

"No. He won't talk if you're there." Hell, he mightn't talk when it was just me there. I opened the fridge and pulled out the makings of a sandwich. "You want one?"

Ceri shook her head. "I've got to get ready for another night of tailing."

"Really? Why? I thought we had enough proof."

"I think she wants indefensible proof. As in, something mid-coitus." She grimaced. "It's money, as you said, but it somehow feels dirty to get pics of him in action."

I wondered what she'd think of all the shots Mona had collected of—the thought stilled as something else occurred to me. The trolls had come here to collect memory cards, cameras, and photos, from downstairs, but not the computers or anything else that was upstairs? *That* didn't make any sense. And besides, my father wasn't likely to rely on just the trolls—he couldn't afford to.

Meaning maybe, just maybe, the trolls had been a diversion. The ogres certainly wouldn't have noticed someone else slipping into the house when they had the trolls to contend with. Fuck, I thought, and raced upstairs.

The computers were all present, the safe appeared untouched, and the photocopies of the images Val had drawn were still on my desk. I didn't immediately relax, just walked over to my computer and hit the start button.

Ceri came up the stairs carrying my sandwich and a coffee for herself. "What did you remember?"

"That my father is a sneaky bastard." And the computer wasn't firing up.

I checked all the cords were connected, and then rose, walked across to Ceri's desk, and hit the power button on her computer. It also didn't fire up.

"What the hell?" She placed the plate and cup on the desk and checked the cords. "It's connected, so it should start."

"Unless it's been tampered with." I lifted the box. It was light. *Too* light. "He's ripped out the fucking hard drives."

Ceri snorted. "Why would he bother doing that? Why not take the whole bloody box?"

I glanced at the window. It was open. "Maybe he just wanted the give the illusion that everything was untouched. Maybe he intends to erase and return them."

Ceri frowned. "He could have erased them here."

"It takes a while to erase drives that large. He might not have wanted to risk it." As I looked around some more, I realized there were two damn cameras missing, too. Not my good ones, thankfully, as I tended to keep them locked away.

"Well, if they *are* going to return them—and I seriously doubt they'd bother—it might be better if I stayed."

"Trolls won't fit through that window, so it'll probably be someone human. Them I can cope with."

I hope. After all, I'd never really used my fighting skills, and it had been a long time since I'd practiced against anyone.

She looked doubtful. "You sure? As you just noted, you father is a sneaky bastard-"

"You need to get that mid-coitus photo." I grabbed my sandwich and headed back to my desk. "Paying customers have to come first."

"I guess." She sighed, and then cocked her head sideways. "I think that was the doorbell."

I glanced at my watch and saw it was close to seven. "That'll be Lyle."

"You should make the old bastard pay for our computers if we don't get them back," she said. "It's his fault they were swiped in the first place."

"If we don't get them back, I will." Sandwich in hand, I made my way back down the stairs and opened the door for Lyle.

He didn't look good. He leaned against the wall, arms crossed and face more haggard than usual. He'd torn off the Band-Aids Maggie had applied earlier, but her colorful salves still covered his skin, and mixed garishly with the purple bruising beginning to appear.

"You obviously need coffee," I said, and stood to one side.

"You can take your coffee and shove it somewhere unpleasant. I want a proper drink, and it had better be a triple." He walked toward the living room, made a face when he spotted the ogres, then continued on to the kitchen. "It's been that sort of day."

Something of an understatement given his day had started with him being bashed by trolls and had ended with the discovery his missing girlfriend was more than likely dead. Still, I didn't really want to offer booze to someone who was the closest thing to an alcoholic as elves could ever get.

"I think a coffee-"

"Don't start telling me what I should and shouldn't be fucking drinking, Harriet. You're not my fucking wife."

No, just someone who stupid enough to care about the old sod. "Lyle-"

"Do I have to walk down the road to the pub and buy my own?"

"Fine," I muttered, and raided the stash of top-shelf alcohol I'd hidden from the ogres in the laundry room.

"What's with the ogres? Haven't they got a home of their own?" He accepted the glass with a tight smile, downed it in one gulp, and then reached for the bottle.

I clenched my hand against the urge to whip the whiskey out of his reach. "I've got a big screen. They haven't."

"In that case, remind me never to get a big screen." He poured himself another generous glass. "I've just come back from the Sandridge police station. Had to ID Mona."

"So it was her?" I didn't have much doubt that it was after talking to Darryl, but there was always the slight chance he'd been wrong.

"Yeah." There was a haunted, desperate look in Lyle's eyes. He downed the second glass just as fast as the first, then added, "She'd been strangled, Harriet. Strangled and raped."

Horror crawled through me. Rape was a crime of power, not passion. Whoever had murdered Mona had made damn sure before she'd died that she knew who was in charge.

Goosebumps crawled across my arms, despite the heat in the house. I'd like to think that neither Bramwell nor Gilroy were capable of such a despicable act, but the truth was, I just didn't know them well enough to be sure.

"I'm sorry, Lyle."

The old elf nodded, and said, voice fierce, "I'm going to find him, Harriet. You know that, don't you?"

"We'll find him together." There was no point in warning him not to do anything stupid. Not while he was in this sort of mood. "What else did they say?"

"Nothing much. If they have any DNA evidence, they're not saying."

If Kaij was in charge of the investigation, that wasn't surprising. "Do you think you can get an ID check on the driver of the car you spotted?"

Lyle nodded again, but didn't elaborate. He just poured himself more alcohol. "I talked to the air traffic controller. It's a dead end."

I blinked at the sudden change of subject. "Why?"

Lyle shrugged. "I listened to the recordings. It does sound like Keale kept heading directly for the helicopter. The pilot did take evasive action."

I frowned. "No, he didn't. I was there, and saw it. Besides, we're not disputing he hit the helicopter, we're just saying there might be extenuating circumstances."

Lyle snorted. "It doesn't really matter if there was Prevoron in his system or the sun in his eyes. The fact is, he hit a helicopter and killed four people. His butt is busted for good this time."

"Which is why we need to find out if Prevoron was in his system or not," I said, more than a little fiercely. "It's very possible someone *wanted* him to down that helicopter."

Lyle stared at me for several seconds. "You really don't believe that, do you?"

"Yeah, I do." Mostly. I crossed my arms and returned his stare evenly.

"But that's insane."

And maybe *I* was for believing Keale. I mean, he *had* been caught drink-flying more times than I could remember, and had come close to hitting aircraft more than once. But this time, it just didn't feel right. And I couldn't ignore it.

Of course, it was a theory that could fall apart very easily if Numar confirmed they'd not only been drinking last night, but also indulging in a little Prevoran high.

"You'll never be able to prove it in a court of law. Not in a million years." He shook his head. "It's too far-fetched for anyone to believe."

"Unless we can get some solid proof." I hesitated. "Did you know Frank Logan was supposed to be on that helicopter?"

"Why the hell would I? It's not like I associate with the man."

"Well, he was. Only he had a last minute change of plans and his brother went instead."

"I cannot see your point, Harriet." He downed his third glass. Elves might not be as affected by alcohol as humans, but at this rate, he was going to be drunk in no time.

"The point is, why the last minute change of plan? Was he, perhaps, warned not to go?"

"For fuck's sake, you're really reaching for straws now. Besides, if he was warned, why wouldn't he also warn his brother?"

"Maybe the warning came too late. Or maybe he simply didn't care if his brother died. They weren't exactly bosom buddies, after all."

"Family is still family, Harriet."

Said the man whose family had more than likely set trolls onto him.

"Besides," he continued. "There sure as hell are easier ways to get rid of someone than feeding Prevoron to a dragon and pointing him in the direction of the city in the vague hope that he'd hit a helicopter."

As daft as it sounded, that's exactly what I suspected someone might have done. After all, Prevoron wasn't only deadly to dragons in high doses, it also made them highly susceptible to the power of suggestion.

According to the article the paper had printed, Prevoron might be available on the street, but it wasn't actually cheap —though it only took the smallest amount for a human to get high. Dragons, with their different biology, had to take far more, which is why it was so much of a risk for them. Too little, and they didn't get high; too much, and they could die. The amount needed to affect a dragon Keale's size as badly as it *had* meant someone with money and means had to be behind it. The question was, why? Hell, most trolls would kill for half the cost of buying that much of the drug.

"Is there any way you can hurry the blood tests up? I mean, if he's been given too much of the stuff, he needs to be treated." Because if too much Prevoron was introduced into a dragon's system, it began to act like a virus, first overriding the body's natural defenses, then infiltrating cells and reproducing its toxic presence to the point where it began shutting down the central nervous system and eventually killed its host.

"I can try." He sighed and wearily rubbed his eyes. "I'd better go home and get some sleep."

"I'll call a taxi."

He glanced at the now half-empty bottle of whiskey and smiled. "Yeah, I guess you'd better. The way my luck has been running, I'd be picked up by a Breathalyzer."

I called a cab. Lyle downed another two glasses by the time it arrived.

"Time to go." He rose a little unsteadily. "You got the photos of the driver?"

Oh, god, the photos. I hadn't even *thought* to check they were still there. "I'll go get them now."

He waited in the hall as I raced upstairs. Thankfully, the thief had missed them, probably because they were underneath some other paperwork. Lyle contemplated them silently when I handed them to him.

"I'm going to kill him," he said eventually. "I'm going to find him, and kill him."

He meant whoever had killed Mona, not the driver of the car.

"No, you're not," I said calmly. "We're going to find enough evidence against whoever it is, and then we're going to let the cops pin his ass to the wall."

Lyle's gaze met mine. The fury so evident in the sapphire depths shook me. "I meant exactly what I said."

"Do that, and Adelia will have grounds for divorce and get *all* your money."

He didn't say anything. I helped him into the taxi, gave the driver his address, then slammed the door shut and watched it disappear down the street.

And wondered just what it was about sirens that captured my Elven kin so completely.

———

Xavier rang back at midnight, as promised. By that time, the ogres had gone home and I finally had the TV—and the house—to myself.

"Got the phone number," he said, without preamble. "But it's a public telephone. No way to trace who was using it."

"Where was it located?"

"Near as I can figure, it's one of the ones inside the Jam Factory, near the cinemas there. Doesn't help you much, I guess."

No, it didn't. But then, it didn't help the trolls much, either, and Xavier didn't seem all that fazed about it. "How do you get paid?"

"Oh, come on, you know we can't tell you that."

"You can't? Then perhaps I better tell you that we've done some checking since you left. You can't afford another breaking and entering charge, because this time, it *will* mean jail time." It was, of course, nothing more than a wild guess, but I figured—given what his compatriot had said this morning—they were all likely to be in the same boat.

I guessed right.

"But I *can't* break a contract. We'll be out of business if word gets around."

"Your employer doesn't have to know. Just tell me how you get paid and where the exchange is so I can then follow them home."

"But we didn't come away with the intended goods. We won't get paid."

They obviously hadn't been told they were only a diversion. I lightly bit my bottom lip for a moment, and then said, "Okay, I'll give you an old camera and a couple of memory cards. Will that do?"

"Yes," he said, resignation in his tone. "But you didn't get *anything* from me, okay?"

"Okay."

He hesitated, then said, "We've worked for this particular fellow a few times-"

"I'm guessing he's the one who employed you to beat up the elf this morning."

"Yeah." He paused again. "Sorry about that, but it was just a job, you know?"

I knew—though I would never understand the weird ethical code that allowed trolls to beat up and even murder people, and still feel able to call themselves pacifists. "Go on."

"He always pays by cash, which is placed in unmarked envelopes and dropped by a person or persons unknown at a pre-arranged time and place."

"And the payment drop tonight?"

"McDonald's on the corner of Smith Street and Victoria Parade."

Which was, very conveniently, not very far away from me.

"So you park and go in?"

"Yep, order a burger, head outside, a car pulls up and we exchange bags."

"Thanks, Xavier. And a word of advice—stop taking work from this particular client. He doesn't play nicely with other people."

"We can take care of ourselves," he said. "What about the camera and stuff?"

"Drive by my place on the way through."

"Will do." He hesitated. "We square after this?"

"Unless you attempt another break-in here, yes we are."

"Oh, you've hit the top of our avoid list, trust me."

I grinned as he hung up. At least that was one lot of trolls we no longer had to worry about. Trouble was, there were plenty of others around who'd no doubt be pleased to step into Xavier's shoes, and *they* might be harder to bluff.

I picked up the remote and channel surfed for the next half an hour, and then went upstairs. After collecting a couple of old cameras, I scooped up some memory cards that were either faulty or had capacities too small to be very useful, and headed outside to wait for Xavier.

Five minutes later, a blue pickup cruised to a halt beside me. Winifred wound down the window, plucked the bag of goodies from my hand, gave me a nod of thanks, and then left.

I jumped into my car and followed, parking in the shadows several cars up from Xavier's and sliding down in the seat so I wouldn't be as noticeable.

The trolls climbed out of their truck and ambled toward the store, my canvas bag of goodies slung over Winifred's shoulder. I leaned across the seat, grabbed my spare camera out of the glovebox, and flicked it to infrared.

Five minutes later, right on the dot of one, a black Mercedes pulled slowly into the car park. Xavier and Winifred re-appeared, bags of burgers and fries in hand.

I raised the camera and started taking shots. The passenger side window of the Mercedes slid down, and a hand holding an envelope appeared. The trolls smoothly exchanged the bags for the envelope and the Mercedes kept going with barely a pause. I would have missed it if I'd blinked.

I waited until the car turned left out of the car park, then quickly started my car and followed. For several horrible seconds I thought I'd lost them, but I finally spotted the Merc heading towards Hoddle Street. They turned right, changing lanes several times, as if they suspected they were being followed. I kept to the left, keeping them in sight but not obviously so. Ceri, I thought with a smile, would have been proud of me.

They crossed the Yarra River and headed into the very prestigious section of South Yarra. I continued to follow them and—surprise, surprise—they eventually turned into Rocklea Road. Which just happened to be where my father lived.

I parked in Toorak Road then grabbed my camera and jogged down. The big Mercedes had stopped up ahead, its rear brake lights glowing like demon eyes in the darkness of the night. Waiting for the gates to open, I thought.

I stepped off the footpath and kept to the deeper shadows of the treed nature strip that lined either side of the road. The Mercedes drove forward, and the gates began to close again. I snuck up, aimed the camera, and started taking shots as the car came to a halt and two men climbed out. They were little more than blobs of white through the lens, but with a little bit of processing, I might just be able to sort out some facial details.

They disappeared inside. I stepped back and studied the house I'd seen online but never in person. It was a big, two-story gothic-like structure, all turrets, gables, and soaring windows. Concrete gargoyles poked their tongues out from the corners of the roofline, as if to frighten bad spirits away.

They obviously didn't work—Gilroy managed to come and go without trouble.

Light shone from a window on the top floor—my father's study, if I remembered the layout of the place correctly. I toyed briefly with the idea of pressing the intercom and demanding a meeting here and now, but I'd promised Ceri I'd be careful. Meeting my father in the dead of night when nobody knew where I was certainly wasn't that.

Besides, once he'd figured out neither of his forays had been a success, he'd more than likely ring for a meeting himself.

Sighing, I spun on my heel and headed back to home and bed.

I woke with a start some hours later. For several minutes I did nothing more than lay there listening, my heart thundering and throat dry.

There was nothing to be heard other than the usual noises made by an old weatherboard house, and there was little sound coming from the office upstairs. Ceri had gone home rather than come back here.

So what the hell had woken me?

I glanced at the clock and saw it was nearly five. Which wasn't anywhere near time to get up, let alone eat, but my stomach rumbled its opposition to that particular thought. I untangled the blankets from my legs, grabbed the glass of water from the bedside table, and gulped it down. It helped with the dry throat, but not the belly rumbling. Given I hadn't actually eaten all that much over the last twenty-four hours, I guess it wasn't really surprising.

I tossed off the bed sheets, pulled my sleeping-shirt over my hips and butt, and headed downstairs. The moon filtered in through the side windows, casting its silvery brilliance across the shadows and revealing cupboards in a serious state of disarray. Delilah, I thought grimly, really needed to keep out of my place when I wasn't home. I picked my way through the mess across and opened the fridge up, inspecting the contents for something edible and eventually deciding on the leftover vegetarian lasagna from the other night.

As I closed the door, a gentle breeze stirred around my ankles. I looked up and realized the back door was open. Which was odd, because Delilah had a key, and it was unlike her to leave a door open like that; she tended to be a bit of a stickler when it came to security.

Frowning, I put the lasagna on the counter and walked down to close it. As I did, more air stirred and the back of my neck crawled with the sensation of danger.

I wasn't alone in the house.

Heart suddenly racing, I ducked and swung around. The length of two-be-four that had been aimed at my head sliced through the air several inches above it and thudded into the wall with enough force to send plaster and dust flying.

If it had hit me, it would have killed me.

At the other end of the bit of wood was the biggest damn troll I've ever seen. He made Xavier and Winifred look like gnats by comparison. Hell, even Guy would have seemed puny beside him.

He pulled the wood from the wall and prepared to swing again. I surged upright, took two steps, and launched myself feet first at him, hitting him hard enough to knock him several strides backward. Waves of flesh rolled away from the impact point, but he certainly wasn't winded, as I'd intended. I hit the ground, flipped back to my feet, then turned and ran. There was bravery, and then there was foolishness. Fighting this troll would definitely fall into the latter category.

I didn't get far. Fingers grabbed my hair and yanked me backward. I flew back through the kitchen and crashed into the pantry door with enough force to shatter it. Wood and cans of food rained down around me as I landed in a heap on the floor.

The troll laughed. It was a guttural, raw sound that sent shivers down my spine. This was one troll, I sensed, who didn't have any boundaries.

"Tell me where the cards are." He thumped the slab of wood into his palm so hard the sound reverberated like a gunshot. "And you might just get out of this with little more than a few bruises."

My fingers closed around a sharpened remnant of a door. "I have no idea what you're talking about."

"Come, come now." He shook his fat, ugly head, his expression sorrowful. "We both know that is not true."

I climbed slowly—unsteadily—to my feet, keeping my body side-on to the troll so he couldn't see the stake I held. "I'm a photographer. I've got tons of memory cards."

"Then I shall take them all."

"Like fuck you will."

I ran at him, the stake held fiercely in one hand. He laughed again and raised the four-be-two. But I had no intention of getting close enough to stab him—*that* would be nothing short of insanity. Instead, I flung the bit of wood, as hard as I could, at his face, and then ducked under the swinging two-be-four and raced for the back door. Only to all but fall down the steps and land in a heap at the bottom, winded and seeing stars.

The trolled roared, and I swear the earth shook as he thundered toward me.

Get up, get up, something inside me screamed, and somehow, I did. I staggered several feet then tripped over something, almost landing face first in the grass. I regained my balance and looked down. A shovel. It was better than nothing, I guess.

I swept it up and swung around. The troll was in the air, the wood held high over his head. I flung myself out of the way, then twisted around and fended off a second blow with the shovel. The sound of metal connecting with wood ricochet across the night. If we weren't very careful, we'd wake...I blinked, and then screamed, "Delilah!"

The troll came at me again. I turned and ran. He followed. Despite his size, the bastard was fast

"Delilah!" I screamed again. "Fucking wake up!"

The air whistled in warning. I threw myself out of the way and swung the shovel again. The metal end thudded into the troll's right elbow and he released that hand from the slab of wood with a bellow. I spun and sprinted away, but not fast enough. The edge of the plank caught my hip and again sent me flying. I crashed into some roses, tearing shirt and skin, but ignored it and scrambled out of the way as the troll came at me again.

As I sprinted around the yard, I couldn't help but feel like I'd fallen through the rabbit hole into some third-rate movie. Where else would you find an elf running for her life around a postage stamp size plot of land chased by a troll built like a fucking mountain?

Again, the air screamed its warning. I swore and pivoted around, swinging the shovel as hard as I could. This time it smacked into the side of his head, and with enough force to send him staggering sideways. He bellowed—a sound that was both pain and anger.

"That you making all the noise down there, Harri?" Delilah yelled, her voice high-pitched and grumpy sounding.

Never in my life had I heard a sound so sweet. "Yeah. Call the cops—I have trolls."

"Fuck girl, what are you doing with—"

"Delilah," I cut in, "just call the fucking cops--*now!*"

The troll was shaking his head and looked somewhat unsteady on his feet. I raised the shovel and ran full bore him. He saw me at the last moment and tried to dodge, but his reaction time had slowed. This time the shovel cracked his head open, and he fell like a sack of bricks. The ground shuddered as he hit.

I stepped back, shovel raised, ready to hit him again if he so much as twitched. He didn't. He was out cold. Not that I got close enough to check. I wasn't that stupid.

I lowered the shovel and leaned against it heavily. Now that the immediate danger was over, every part of me decided to ache. My nightshirt was ripped across my right shoulder and back, and there were numerous cuts and scratches, thanks to both the pantry door and rose bushes. The bruises I'd have tomorrow I didn't want to think about.

The sudden sound of footsteps filled the silence, and I jumped back, shovel held at the ready, before I realized it was Delilah rather than another troll. It was a realization that left me shaking.

Delilah bustled through the gateway, wrapped in a hot pink robe that matched the rollers in her hair. "What in the hell is going on, Harri?" Her gaze fell on the troll and she stopped abruptly. "You beat *that?*"

"With some help from my trusty shovel." Not to mention a whole lot of speed and a lot more luck.

"Shit girl, you've got some grit." She approached the troll and toed him none too lightly. "Know who he is?"

"No." My legs suddenly felt like jelly, so I plopped down on the porch steps. At least I couldn't fall much further from there. "Did you call the cops?"

"Yep. Five minutes, they said."

I ran a hand through my hair, and it came away bloody. I couldn't even remember hitting my head. "Could you find his wallet and see if he has a name?"

"Happy to." She dug chubby little fingers into the troll's pants pocket then went through his wallet. "He goes by the moniker of Gunner Brown."

"Address?"

"All it says is Labertouche Caves."

Labertouche was one of the main Troll enclaves, and though it was about ninety minutes out of Berren, it was the closest of the three. Because of the distance between home and here, most trolls had secondary—and generally communal—living quarters to bunk down in when they were in Berren on a job. But if we wanted to uncover that, we'd have to wait for him to wake—and that wasn't something I was willing to do.

"You want to grab some rope from the shed and tie him up?"

She dropped the wallet onto his belly and bustled away. I rested my head in my hands and contemplated getting some painkillers. But that would mean moving and I really wasn't up to that just yet.

Delilah trussed the troll tighter than a turkey on Christmas day, and then stepped back to contemplate her handy work. "Should hold him a little while." She cocked her head sideways. "The cops are coming."

"Good." I sighed and sat up straighter. "Are you hanging around to be questioned?"

"I'd prefer not to." She hesitated, nose wrinkling. "Unless you want me to?"

I shook my head. "I don't think there's much need. Thanks for your help, Delilah."

She waved it away. "Anytime, love, anytime."

I smiled as she bustled away. She might be bloody annoying at times, but god, she always came through when I needed her.

The wail of police sirens began to bite through the air. I stayed where I was and kept an eye on the troll. His fingers were beginning to twitch, so he wasn't that far off regaining consciousness.

The police siren came to a halt outside my place and, two seconds later, someone knocked on the front door and a gruff voice said, "Police."

"Come through," I yelled, then pushed carefully to my feet. The night did a three-sixty around me, and it was only my grip on the shovel that kept me upright.

Footsteps echoed on the wooden floorboards. One pair, not the two I'd expected. Tension slithered around me. Maybe it hadn't been so smart to offer the invite without actually knowing if it *was* the police...

I gripped the shovel a little tighter, tension knotting my belly. The footsteps came through the kitchen, and then a tall, slender figure was silhouetted in the doorway.

It wasn't one of the boys in blue.

It was Kaij.

CHAPTER SIX

For several heartbeats, neither of us moved, our gazes locked, blue eyes clashing with green. And yet something stirred deep within, something I'd thought long dead. Anger, bitterness, hurt—all that was there. So too was sorrow for all that we'd lost, for all that we could have been. What surprised me was the ache—an ache of a heart not quite as dead to this man's presence as I'd thought.

The sharp planes of his face had always given him a remote sort of beauty, but age had filled out his features, and the creases around his eyes and full mouth softened the remoteness and hinted at a nature that was light and easy going. It wasn't a lie, although it was hard to remember the sunnier days after the bitter way in which we'd parted.

"What are you doing here, Kaij?" My voice was even, surprising given I'd expected it to be anything but.

His expression was closed. "You called the police, did you not?"

His voice flowed across my senses like the whisper of the

wind on a clear summer day—warm, rich, and inviting. *Don't go there*, I told myself fiercely. *Just don't.*

"Last I knew, you were with the preternatural boys, not the police."

"I still am." His gaze moved past me. "That the intruder?"

"Hell, no." There was an edge in my voice that hinted at anger more than sarcasm. Obviously, I wasn't quite as in control as I'd thought. "It's just a rather large garden ornament."

"Given your taste in ornaments, I wouldn't actually be surprised." He paused, his cool gaze meeting mine again. "Is he the only one?"

"Yes. And he was more than enough, thank you very much."

He crossed his arms and leaned against the wall of the house. A casual looking pose that wasn't. "What did he want?"

"You know, I really didn't take the time to ask him. Especially given he seemed intent on making as big a mess of me as he did my house."

"An aim he partially succeeded in, from the look of it." His gaze skimmed my body, and I had to resist the urge to pull down the hem of my nightshirt. "You really don't look so good. I think you need-"

"What I need," I cut in, "is to know why you're here."

Both in my house, and in Berren itself.

He knew what I was asking—I saw the flash of it in his eyes.

But all he said was, "I heard the call over the radio, and recognized the address."

"And decided to race to my rescue?" I snorted softly. "A little late for that sort of thing, isn't it?"

The surge of his emotion was so sharp and cold it felt like an ice shard being thrust into my flesh. "The past is dead—buried," he snapped. "Leave it there, Harri."

The past was definitely buried, but how could I possibly leave it when I visited her as often as I could?

"I'm here because I was nearby," he continued. "I needed to talk to you about the siren on the beach, anyway."

"I can't tell you much about her." I grabbed the banister and climbed the steps. Every movement hurt.

He stepped back, but didn't offer me any help. Didn't even comment. Tears stung my eyes and I blinked them away angrily. Damn it, it shouldn't be this hard. Not after nearly ten years.

I made it into the kitchen as two more cops entered the house. "The intruder is contained out in the yard," Kaij said. He was so close behind me that his breath washed warmth across the back of my neck and sent shivers down my spine. "Call an ambulance."

I half-turned. "I don't need-"

"Yeah, yeah, you don't need help," Kaij said, expression almost as contemptuous his voice. "Heard that song many times before, and still not believing it."

"And yet when I needed help the most, you walked away." It was out before I could stop it and I almost instantly regretted it. Not because I'd said it, but because we weren't alone. I shouldn't be hanging out our dirty washing for others to see.

Kaij went still, but it was the stillness of a snake about to strike. Tension crawled through me. He'd never been a violent man, but I had the sudden suspicion he was fighting the urge to lash out, either physically or verbally.

Well, fuck him, an inner voice snarled. *He deserves it for leaving you as he did.*

I flexed my fingers, but somehow managed not to say what I was thinking. It wouldn't have helped the situation, and it certainly wouldn't have made me feel any better. Not for long, anyway.

The two police officers walked out into the yard. I pulled out a kitchen chair and dropped more than sat.

Kaij walked across to the cupboard that held my medical kit, pulled it out, then opened it on the table. In silence, he washed down the wound on the top of my head, his touch gentle and body too close. It took all my strength to be still, to not run.

Eventually, he said, "this is going to need stitches."

"If it does, I'll go to the hospital and get them. Until then, let's get on with the questioning." I leaned back in the chair, which was as far away from him as I could get without physically getting up. "What did you want to know?"

"Why you were at the beach, for a start." He tossed the bloody cloth in the nearby bin, then leaned against the counter and again crossed his arms. "You once said you'd never go back to that area."

"And I haven't. I was there on a job."

"So you and Ceri got the agency up and running?"

"Yes." I didn't bother telling him it was a recent thing—and that it had only happened because of Ceri's accident.

"Did you know Mona? Was she one of your mother's friends?"

"No, and no." I rubbed my forehead a little gingerly. It was beginning to feel like there were a dozen tiny men armed with pickaxes inside. The last thing I needed was a question and answer session—especially when the man doing the questioning was my ex.

"And yet you obviously know it was Mona who washed up."

"I do now, but at the time I didn't." I reached for the kit and got out a couple of painkillers. Kaij filled a glass with water and handed it across without comment. "How did she die?"

He raised an eyebrow. "I dare say you could probably tell me, given Ceri's contacts."

"Probably, but we prefer not to use them unless absolutely necessary." I shrugged. "If you came here looking for answers about Mona, I'm afraid I can't help you much."

"Considering one of the men who answered her song was Lyle Phillecky, I seriously doubt that."

I guess I should have seen *that* coming. I swallowed the painkillers, and then said, "My uncle doesn't actually regale me with tales of his time with Mona, you know."

"But you were attempting to find her for him, weren't you?"

For a heartbeat, I considered lying, but one glance at his set features and that thought went out the window. He'd be well within his rights to drag me to Preternatural's headquarters to question me more formally, and I wasn't really up for that.

"Yeah, he did. Unfortunately, the killer found her before I could."

"And he has no idea who'd want to kill her?"

I cocked an eyebrow. "Why don't you ask him that yourself?"

"I would, but your uncle has been decidedly slippery to track down. Tell him to ring me, or we'll get a warrant out and arrest him."

"You can't do that. He's not a suspect—" I hesitated, "is he?"

He just smiled. It wasn't an altogether pleasant smile. "I cannot answer the latter and, as for the former, you'd be surprised."

"No, I wouldn't." Not when it came to what he'd do to inconvenience one of my relatives, anyway. "Is that it, then?"

His being here seemed pretty pointless if it was, but maybe all he'd actually wanted was for me to pass the message on to Lyle.

"For now, it seems it is." He pushed away from the counter. "But I suspect there's plenty you're not telling me, Harri."

"I can't tell you how Mona died or who killed her. I have no idea. As for anything else that might be going on—" I gave him a smile that was as hard as the one he'd given only moments before. "You lost the right to question me about *that* a long time ago."

Again anger surged, but this time it heated the flakes of gold and made his eyes burn like fire. "Do not be so sure of that."

And with that threat lingering in the air, he turned and stalked out.

I stared after him, my stomach churning. What in the hell had he meant by *that*? He couldn't want to resume our relationship—and his actions here certainly hadn't given any indication that this was his intention—so why make such a statement?

But maybe he hadn't intended *anything*. Maybe it was just my aching head and overall weariness reading intent into comments where none existed.

It was something I'd have to stop doing, especially if he was back in town for good. Berren might be a big city, but the supernatural community was relatively close-knit and our paths would no doubt cross more than either of us might want. At least I'd gotten through the first face-to-face with emotions relatively intact. Surely it would only get easier from now on.

The ambulance turned up a few minutes later and medics treated the troll before the cops hauled him away. Other than a nasty egg on his head, he hadn't been seriously harmed. Which was probably a good thing given there would have been a more serious investigation into the circumstances surrounding the break-in if a critical injury had occurred. And *that* might have just resulted in information that was better kept confidential—at least for the moment—getting out.

As Kaij had predicted, my head did need stitches. I changed and locked up the house as best I could, given the battered front door, then was hauled away and given a proper check-up before being patched up.

It was close to eight by the time I got home. I was damnably hungry, so I grabbed the lasagna still sitting on the counter and munched on that as I headed back to my bed and a few hours sleep.

The phone woke me. I groped for it without opening my eyes and said, "You'd better have a good reason for calling at this ungodly hour."

"It's past one, for god's sake. What are you still doing in bed?"

Lyle's voice was surprisingly upbeat, and I blinked, wondering if I'd stepped into some weird time warp. This did *not* sound like the same morose man I'd dumped into a taxi last night. "I didn't get much sleep last night. Why are you so cheerful?"

"I tracked down government car. It was assigned to James Logan."

"Why? He wasn't the politician, Frank is." And government cars were only supposed to be used by government officials. But regardless of that, what the hell was Bramwell doing in it? Frank Logan and my father were not what anyone would call political allies, and James himself had made more than a few disparaging public remarks about Gilroy's political aspirations.

"Frank had apparently called and organized for James to use it."

"That still doesn't explain the rush of happiness." I pushed into a sitting position, and almost instantly regretted it as a myriad of aches sprang up all over my body.

"Well, the bastard got what he deserved, didn't he?"

It took me a moment to remember that James had been one of the four killed in the helicopter crash with Keale. And maybe the battle with the troll last night had rattled more than a few brain cells loose, but for the life of me, I still couldn't understand why Logan's death made Lyle so happy.

"And just how do you figure that?" I tossed the bed sheets off and gingerly climbed out, biting my lip against the various aches that started screaming even more loudly for attention.

Lyle cleared his throat. "Well, he was one of her clients, wasn't he?"

He was? Christ, what sort of allure did Mona have to catch so many high-profile men? It was certainly an unusual feat for a mid-level siren. Then I blinked. James Logan and my brother had been seeing the *same* siren. Talk about an explosion waiting to happen.

In fact, maybe Logan was man Gilroy had been arguing with the night Val had stepped in and given them both temporary wings. The second picture Val had drawn could easily have fitted either Logan brother without the hair pieces they habitually wore—a fact that had been commented on often enough in the press that it made me wonder why they actually bothered to cover-up their baldness. Maybe it was just vanity.

"How do you know that, Lyle? And what has this got to do with Mona's murder?"

Lyle was silent for a long moment. I stopped in front of the mirror and contemplated the bruises. There were a lot of them, though many jostled for prominence with the scratches I'd received from the rose bushes. No dresses for me for the next couple of days, I thought—not that I tended to wear many, anyway. And it wasn't like I actually went anywhere fancy enough to warrant getting all dressed up.

"I went up and talked to Mona the day after I saw the car," Lyle said, almost reluctantly, "She was very upset—said she'd been threatened."

I wondered what else he wasn't telling me. Because there was more, I was sure. "By whoever was in the car, or someone else?"

I wouldn't have been surprised if it *had* been Bramwell who'd threatened her, although he generally believed such actions were somewhat unbecoming when it came to dealing with those he considered beneath him—and sirens were certainly that. Maybe that was why he'd been sitting in the car that day—maybe he was leaving the dirty work to James.

Although James *was* human, and I couldn't imagine Bramwell allowing any human—even one with a brother as powerful as Frank—an insight into Phillecky family dealings.

Lyle said, "I'm presuming it was James."

Never presume anything, Lyle had once told me. Besides, both Bramwell and James had been in that car, so either of them could have been the culprit. Just because my father had been photographed inside the car didn't mean he'd stayed there the entire time. "She wouldn't tell you who?"

"No. She was scared, though. I could tell that."

I hesitated, then asked, "Why didn't you talk to her the day before? You were curious enough about the car to take the photos—why didn't you go up and ask her about it once they'd left?"

"I couldn't, because she might have been working." He paused. "I know she was a siren and all, but that didn't mean I like seeing who she did."

And he didn't like the fact he had to share her with others, if the catch of anger evident in his voice was anything to go by. It had to have torn him apart, knowing that the one thing he hated was the one thing she couldn't give up.

Yet the dwarf had mentioned her retiring. Maybe Mona really *had* loved Lyle enough to at least try.

"Did you ask who was threatening her?"

"Yeah, but she refused to tell me. The only thing I could get out of her was that he was a fairly high-ranking politician."

"Which James Logan is not." Neither was Bramwell. But Frank Logan *was*. Had he been protecting his brother, as Bramwell had been protecting his son? While everything I knew about the Logans suggested that wasn't likely, sometimes the bond of blood made you do strange things. "Did you talk to the driver?"

"No. He's gone on leave for a couple of weeks."

"Might be worth checking when he actually applied for leave, because that seems a little convenient to me."

Lyle was silent for a moment. "What aren't you telling me?"

That there's more to this than meets the eye. I hesitated. "It wasn't James Logan in that car."

"Why do you think that? Logan did hire it."

Because it was my fucking father. His brother. Somehow, I bit the words back and I thrust a hand through my tangled hair. I hit something solid and pulled it out—a rose-twig.

"He might have hired it, but he wasn't the only one using it. I managed to pull an image of the passenger through the back window. It's not James Logan."

"Then who the hell is it? And why didn't you mention it before now?"

"Because it isn't clear enough to provide proper ID, but trust me, the profile *doesn't* belong to James Logan."

I swung away from the mirror and walked over to the window. Yesterday's rain had cleared, but the skies still looked wintery—which pretty much summed up my life at the moment.

"Are you positive it's not Logan?"

"Yes." And I was just as sure that it *was* Bramwell. Hell, his reaction to the news that I'd seen the photo provided certainty if nothing else.

"Then who is it?"

"Lyle—"

"Don't mess with me, Harriet. You know I can tell when you're hiding shit. Just spit it out."

If I spat it out, he'd be over there in a shot, all temper and flying fists. And while I wouldn't have minded my arrogant parent getting knocked down a peg or two, it would be Lyle who'd come out of it worse for wear. My father was too well protected.

I sighed. "Look, I'm going over there later today—"

"I'm coming," he cut in, voice cold. Determined.

"Lyle, I really don't think—"

"Put yourself in my shoes, Harriet. Think about someone you love being killed—how would you react?"

I didn't have to think all that hard, because I *had* lost someone I'd loved—and all my hopes and dreams had gone with them. And while the death I'd suffered through wasn't murder but rather fate and my body dealing a harsh blow, it was still an ending, and everyone coped with those in their own way. Lyle's was with anger and the need for revenge. Mine had been tears, and an almost total withdrawal from everyone who'd cared.

I really *did* understand. I just didn't think it wise. Especially once he realized who I was going to see.

"Lyle, please, you employed me for a reason. Let me do my job—"

"Don't make me get nasty, Harriet. I *am* coming with you."

Just what I needed right now—another goddamn threat. But instead of getting angry about it, all I felt was frustration. I was trying my best to do what was right by both Lyle and

Mona, and all I kept getting was beaten up on—literally and figuratively.

If Lyle really wanted in, then in he would be. And when the shit began to flow, I'd reminded him that *that* was what he'd wanted.

Not that I thought he'd care.

"Fine." I glanced at the clock and noted it was just after one. I knew from past years of snooping that every Sunday, the Phillecky clan—minus the bastard daughter, of course—got together for dinner and a weekly catch-up session. Up until five, though, Bramwell and Tianne—his wife—would more than likely be alone. "I'll pick you up at two."

"Make sure you do," he growled, and slammed the phone down.

"Goodbye to you too," I muttered, then tossed the phone on the bed and headed to the bathroom.

A hot shower didn't really make me feel any better, but at least it washed away the blood and grime. I pulled on a pair of jeans and a loose-fitting sweater, then shoved on some runners and grabbed my coat as I made my way downstairs. To find Delilah ass-up in the cupboard under the sink, putting away a variety of pans that were lined up behind her like terrified soldiers. Guy was re-stacking the pantry, his expression glum. A far from willing participant, I thought with a grin.

"Hey guys," I said, stopping in the doorway. "Thanks for tidying the place up."

"The devil made me do it," Guy muttered, casting a sullen look Delilah's way.

"Don't you go giving me no mouth, ogre. You owe Harri more than an hour of your time, and you know it." She sat upright and gave me a critical once over. "You look like shit."

"Just what every girl likes to hear," I said, voice dry.

"Now you know I don't mean it like that. You should be resting, not gallivanting about."

"I know, but I have mouths to feed."

"The mouths appreciate it," Guy said solemnly. Then he grinned. "Heard about that troll you took down. Their network is going to be filled with warnings about the need *not* to mess with Ms. Harri Phillecky, that's for sure."

"I doubt it, given I came out of it far worse than he did."

"The point is, you came out of it. That, friend Harri, is what is so impressive."

I guess it was, given the troll's size. I half-turned away, and then remembered I owed Val a dinner. "You two up for a meal Tuesday night?"

If Val wanted a party with all my friends, then that's *exactly* what he would get.

"You cooking lasagna?" Guy asked, visibly brightening.

I smiled. Pasta was right up there with beer and pizza on an ogres 'vital for life' food list. "Probably."

"Then count me in."

Delilah sniffed and shoved the rest of the pots in the cupboard. "Can't say I'm overly fond of pasta."

139

From what I'd seen over the years, she wasn't fond of anything that didn't involve copious amounts of sugar, cream, and chocolate. "What about pavlova? Or cheesecake?"

"Both will do nicely. Thank you."

"Then be here at six." I hesitated again. "Are you sticking around, Guy? I have to head off, but I wouldn't mind someone keeping an eye on the place if you've got nothing else to do."

"The second prelim is on, so I was planning to watch it here. Got good odds on Essendon beating the Dockers, too."

"Moe and Curly making an appearance?"

"Yes. Shemp's got something on with the missus."

"Then tell them to bring their own beer. I really can't afford to keep four of you fed and watered." I hesitated, then added, "And keep an eye out for trolls."

He waved my concern away. "I doubt they'd make a third appearance. Even trolls aren't that stupid."

Maybe not, but my father might be. At the very least, he'd be mightily pissed off that his efforts so far had not produced desired results—which could make my planned invasion of his home this afternoon all the more interesting.

Delilah harrumphed. "Well, I guess that cuts me out from staying, what with them three fouling the air and all."

"There is a god after all," Guy muttered.

Delilah grabbed a pot and flung it at his head. It hit with a resounding clang. Guy bellowed and glared at her.

"I did warn you not to give me sass, ogre."

"But that was uncalled for," Guy said. "Damn it, you might have busted something."

Delilah snorted. "With your thick head? Doubt it."

I grinned and left them to it. Twenty minutes later I pulled up in front of the old four-story warehouse Lyle had purchased some years ago and converted into apartments. He was sitting on the front steps, looking darker than the sky and puffing heavily on a cigarette. Odd, given it didn't have the same calming effect on elves that it did on humans.

"When the hell did you start smoking again?" I asked, as he climbed in.

"There are lots of things you don't know about me, Harriet." He took a last drag and then flicked the butt out the window. "We might be related, but we ain't really family."

And there, I thought grimly, was our relationship summed up in one neat sentence. Related by blood but not considered family. I guess I should have been grateful he *did* acknowledge kinship, but I suddenly wasn't.

"Well, I do know one thing about you—you can get dangerously fired up and react without thinking." My voice was harsh, but I doubt it made any sort of impact. "I want you to behave yourself today. There's no proof the man we're about to see was involved in any way with Mona or her murder."

"We've got his photo outside Mona's apartment." Lyle shifted in his seat, sapphire eyes narrowing. "What are you afraid of, Harriet?"

"Your anger, as I said."

"Oh for fuck's sake, I'm not going to do anything stupid—"

"Promise me, Lyle. No action—or reaction—until we get the facts straight."

He snorted. "Don't go quoting my own phrases back at me, Harriet."

"Then don't go off half-cocked." It didn't escape my attention that he hadn't actually acknowledged my request, let alone make any sort of commitment.

"Have I ever?"

"How would I know, Lyle? As you said, I'm not family."

A trace of bitterness had crept into my voice, but if he noticed, he certainly didn't comment on it. He simply watched the road, no doubt trying to work out where we were going and who we were about to see.

When I turned into Toorak Road, his anger surged, just about setting the air alight.

"You *bitch*," he said. "You could have warned me we were going to see my own damn *brother*."

"We both want answers, Lyle," I snapped back. "You confronting him in a drunken rage is not the way to get them."

"I would not—"

"Bullshit, and we both know it."

I pulled into my father's driveway, then wound down the car's window and pressed the intercom buzzer.

"May I help you?" a bored voice said through the speaker.

"Lyle Phillecky to see Bramwell." It was infinitely better to use my uncle's name rather than mine, as I had no doubt my father would have turned me away. Especially as he'd made no effort to contact me, even after his more recent failed attempt at photo stealing.

"He has an appointment, ma'am?"

"No, I'm afraid he hasn't."

Lyle chose that moment to lean across the car. This close, I could smell the traces of alcohol on him. He might not be drunk, but he *had* been drinking. "Just tell the bastard his brother is here."

"Oh yeah, that's going to help," I muttered.

Lyle gave me a somewhat malevolent glare. Great, I'd pissed off the one Elven relative who actually bothered to talk to me—and right now I couldn't help thinking that might be a *good* thing.

"Just a moment," the voice said, tone still polite.

I tapped the steering wheel and wondered if Bramwell would be any more willing to see Lyle. He was, after all, on the outer with his family, even if not quite as far as me.

"Mr. Phillecky is able to spare his brother a few minutes," the voice said. "Please proceed through the gates."

Said gates slowly opened. I drove up to the house and parked in the area marked family only. We were that, even if we belonged to the section no one wanted to know about. Lyle all but scrambled out of the car and stalked across to the door. I followed several paces behind, more to avoid any fists that started to go flying than anything else.

The butler met us. His gaze swept my length, but if he knew who I was, he gave no sign of it. "This way, if you please."

"I know my way around my brother's fucking house, Jose," Lyle growled. "Just tell me where he is."

"In his private office."

"Good. Now get out of my way."

He did, and with all the grace my uncle lacked. I murmured an apology and followed Lyle through the white and gold opulence of the entrance hall and up a sweeping mahogany staircase that would not have gone astray on the set of *Gone with the Wind*.

The first floor was even more luxurious than the entrance hall. The walls were white, but color abounded in everything from the toe-sinking richness of the wine-colored carpet to the ancient tapestries and paintings that lined the hall. Lyle thrust through a set of double oak doors at the far end of the hall and stalked inside.

Bramwell turned, one black eyebrow raised in query, his expression disinterested. "What can I do for you, Lyle?" He hesitated, his gaze falling on me. Just for one fleeting moment, anger pierced the bored expression. "What the hell is *she* doing here?"

Lyle didn't answer. He just strode forward, and let loose with the best right hook I'd ever seen.

So much for hoping Lyle would behave himself.

I jumped forward, grabbed the collar of Lyle's jacket, and hauled him back before he could unleash another blow. Lyle turned, fist swinging wildly, one blow barely missing my chin and the other hitting my arm. I swore and kicked him hard in the shin. He bellowed and went down.

"Enough, Lyle," I snapped. "That's not what we're here for."

He blinked and glared up at me. He was still very angry, but at least the unthinking glow of rage was leaving his eyes. "There was no need for that, Harriet."

"You said you'd behave."

"I said no such thing." He winced as he climbed slowly to his feet. Good, I thought uncharitably.

Bramwell picked himself off the floor and moved across to his desk, pressing the intercom. "Jose, call the police."

"Yes, Jose, please do," I said, imitating Bramwell's cool indifference perfectly. "Perhaps Mr. Phillecky would care to explain to *them* why he was so desperate to gain possession of certain photos that he employed not one, but two sets of thieves to get them. Unsuccessfully, as he is no doubt aware."

Bramwell contemplated me for several seconds, then said, "Jose, forget that order."

"Wise move," I commented.

"Do not think I was swayed by your threat." He sat down and regarded me with some amusement. "I merely wish to understand why you would be under such an impression."

"Stuff the goddamn photos—"

I gave Lyle a quick, somewhat fierce look, and he stopped, surprise flitting across his expression.

"It's no impression," I said to Bramwell. "I have photos of the trolls exchanging items stolen from my place with person or persons within a black Mercedes. I also have photos of the same black Mercedes pulling into your drive, the occupants getting out and carrying said items into your house. At the very least, that suggests collusion in a crime."

He leaned back in his chair. "It seems I underestimated your resourcefulness."

It seems he did. "And you might also want to know that the second troll is currently in police custody."

Bramwell waved the comment away. "That is of no concern to me. He won't talk. What do you want, Harriet?"

"What I wanted yesterday—an explanation."

Bramwell sniffed. "The mere fact I was seen outside a missing siren's apartment doesn't mean I had anything to do with either her or her disappearance. In fact, I did some checking, and she disappeared *long* after I left."

"What about Gilroy?"

Lyle gave me a sharp glance. "What do you mean, Gilroy?"

Bramwell didn't even blink. The Elven shutters were well and truly up. "Yes, what do you mean, Gilroy?"

I smiled without amusement and kept my gaze centered solely on my father. "Seems he was following Phillecky tradition and sowing some wild oats down in the siren district before settling down to a career and family. Only for

Gilroy, that could prove disastrous for his prime ministerial aspirations if ever discovered."

Bramwell's answering smile edged towards condescending. "Gilroy has nothing to do with any siren, I can assure you of that."

"Really?" I pulled copies of Val's sketches from my back pocket. "Then you won't mind if I hand these sketches over to the police? They were produced by a witness who can place him and a second man—who just happens to resemble one of the Logan brothers—arguing outside her apartment five nights before she disappeared. The same man will also testify that one of those men was more than likely arguing with her the day after you were spotted in the government car."

Lyle snatched the drawings from me and studied them. "It's James Logan," he said, after a moment. "You can tell by the mole near his mouth. Frank doesn't have one."

Bramwell held out an imperious hand. "May I?"

Lyle threw more than handed the copies to him. I half expected him to follow them with another wild punch, but he spun around to face me instead.

"You knew all this, and you didn't tell me?"

"I needed to be sure before I made accusations—"

"Don't lie to me, Harriet. You were protecting *him*, despite the fact he's done nothing for you."

"No," I said. "I'm merely doing what my mother would wish."

He snorted. He didn't understand, and I didn't expect him

to. Elves didn't rate emotions very highly, even if they were as every bit susceptible to them as the rest of us.

I glanced back to Bramwell. He placed the copies on the desk and leaned forward, his hands clasped. "Where are the originals?"

"Somewhere safe from whatever thieves you might think of employing next. Like the photographs, really."

He contemplated me for several seconds. "What is it you wish to know?"

"I want to know what you and James were doing at Mona's place."

"Do you think that is wise with my brother here? It's is obvious he was emotionally involved with the siren." His distaste came through so clearly it was almost amusing—especially given I was testimony to what he obviously now considered his own unpleasant encounter. "He might not be too pleased with the sordid details."

I glanced at Lyle. There was little emotion to be seen on the old elf's face, but his fists were clenched, knuckles white. He was still a firecracker ready to explode. Yet I knew there was nothing I could do or say to get him out of this room—and really, I could understand that. Could understand the need for answers, even when the answers might hurt.

"We both want the truth," I said.

"Very well." He steepled his fingers and regarded us for several seconds. "Gilroy had apparently been seeing the siren in question for several months."

"She told me she that no new men had answered her song recently," Lyle growled.

"Never trust the word of a siren." Bramwell's gaze met mine. "They tell you only what you want to hear. It is a game they play."

I clenched my fists then forced myself to relax. "Funny, my mother says the same thing about elves."

A cool smile touched Bramwell's lips. "A week ago, she told Gilroy she was giving up the song. She didn't say why or for who, but she wanted Gilroy to provide stake money for a new start."

"And threatened to expose him if he didn't?" I asked.

Bramwell nodded. "That's when I got involved, of course."

Of course. Couldn't have the pride and joy wrecking his political career now, could we? "What did you do?"

"Paid her the money."

"In return for the memory card?"

His dark brows furrowed slightly. "What memory card are you talking about now?"

His confusion *seemed* genuine, and suggested he hadn't known about Mona's collecting habit. But if Bramwell didn't have the card, who did? "Mona apparently had a penchant for taking photographs of all the men who answered her call. She kept them in a book I now have, but there's a memory card missing."

"Neither Gilroy nor Mona mentioned photos or memory cards."

And Gilroy would have, had he known. Maybe Mona had been keeping them as insurance. Maybe someone else had taken them—someone we were yet unaware of.

"What were James and Gilroy arguing about that night?"

"Gilroy walked in on James arguing with the siren."

"Did he happen to mention what they were arguing about?"

Bramwell gave a cool smile. "He didn't, but I was reliably informed after the event that he was reacting to her very recent blackmail threat."

I wondered if the reliable source was Frank. "So, you and James were both there to pay her money?"

"Yes."

Which made me wonder just how many other clients Mona was blackmailing.

"Where did James get the money from? I thought he had a serious cash flow problem thanks to excessive gambling."

"He has. I presume Frank provided the cash."

I studied him for a moment, and then said, "Why did you go with James? I would have thought you'd prefer to keep this sort of activity off the radar, and James is something of a loose cannon, isn't he?"

Bramwell smile was both cool and calculating. "Which is why he was the perfect cover. The car was in his name and I never stepped inside that building."

I considered what he *hadn't* said. "Which doesn't mean you didn't go in."

"No." He paused. "That was a good catch, Harriet."

Be still my heart. A *compliment*. "You used some form of magic to get in?"

"A minor transport spell. Easy enough to acquire if you have the right contacts."

The right contacts *and* cash. Transport spells weren't cheap. "If both you and James paid her, why did Gilroy go back the next day?"

Bramwell frowned. "He didn't. She called him and said it wasn't enough. She wanted more."

Then who'd been arguing with Mona? James? And why was she so desperate to get her hands on all that cash? Lyle had more than enough money to keep them both comfortable for the rest of their lives—even if his wife got her mitts on half of it. "What was Gilroy's response?"

"That she'd had all she was going to get, and he wasn't going to be blackmailed the rest of his life."

"And that's what she intended?"

Bramwell's nod was almost imperceptible.

"She wouldn't," Lyle growled. "She didn't have any reason to do any of this. It doesn't make sense."

"Sirens are capricious creatures even at the best of times." His gaze was once again on mine. Pushing. Judging. "It is never wise to plan anything more than a good time with them, as it is not within their nature to offer anything else."

Which is probably as close to an explanation as I was ever likely to get from him, and not one I needed. Mom had

151

never been anything but truthful when it came to the reasons their long relationship had ended. Nor had she placed the blame on either his shoulders or hers, but rather on the fact that they were simply different people, with different goals.

My father's refusal to formally acknowledge the daughter that had come out of that relationship *had* annoyed her, though. It was only the concern over the effect of a protracted court battle might have had on me that had stopped her from pursuing the maintenance and acknowledgment he owed.

"You didn't know her," Lyle muttered. "She was different."

Yes, she was—if only because she was collecting photographs of all her men. And if Lyle hadn't known about that, what else hadn't he known about?

I glanced at my father again. "Did you or Gilroy make any attempt to see or talk to Mona after Gilroy received that phone call?"

"No, of course not."

"Are you *certain* that Gilroy had no further contact with her?"

"Yes." Disdain crept into the cool tones. "He left on a skiing holiday the same day. He's not due back until later this evening."

"And you're certain that he didn't come back without telling you?"

"Again, yes. He's in New Zealand and has been on the news

there. Call the TV stations and view the tapes if you doubt me."

"I certainly will," I said, "And I'll need to talk to him on his return."

"I don't think that will be necessary."

"Well, it's either me or I'll hand everything over to the cops and let them talk to him."

Bramwell began to tap his desk. The sharp drumming echoed in the brief silence, and tension crawled down my spine. "I don't suppose offering you a large amount of money to forget all this, and to lose those photos and drawings, will do any good?"

"We're trying to find out who killed the woman I love, and you're offering us *money?*" Lyle took one step forward, then stopped. "You are fucking incredible, brother."

"One has to try." Bramwell shrugged. "And don't act all high and mighty, Lyle. We both know you can hardly call the kettle black when it comes to paying hush money."

Which was just another indication of how little I knew my uncle. And I had wonder just who he'd paid off—and why. "Or you could just try doing the right thing for a change."

"I always do the right thing," he said urbanely. "At least when it comes to family."

And you are not. He didn't say it, but it lay there between us nevertheless.

"Am I going to be able to talk to Gilroy?"

He studied me for several seconds, and then made a motion

with his hand. "All right, but only in my presence. When and where?"

"My place, straight from the airport." I might as well have the advantage of home ground. "You obviously know the address."

"I can't see what this will achieve," Bramwell commented. "Gilroy wasn't in the country when she was killed."

"Maybe," Lyle said, "But I can look him in the eye and ask him straight out if he was in any way involved with her murder. And he's blood, so I'll taste it if he lies."

Which is one elven trait I really wished I *had* inherited.

"He has nothing to lie about, brother."

"Then neither of you have anything to worry about," I said, "And I'll see you

"Unfortunately, yes, you will."

I turned but at the doorway, I paused and asked, "Does Gilroy drink beer?"

Bramwell expression was one of distaste. "Of course not."

"Then what about James?"

"Probably. He had more than a few vices." His gaze narrowed slightly. "Why?"

"Just curious." I shrugged and walked out.

After several seconds, Lyle followed. "He really *is* a bastard."

I smiled grimly. In my father's estimation, there was only

one bastard around here, and she was currently making her way out of the house. Jose reappeared at the front door and opened it for us. I exited without comment, and breathed deep the cool crisp air. It felt good after all the bitterness and anger that had filled my father's study.

"He certainly knows the trouble breeding one can cause," I said, voice dry.

Then I froze.

Mona had threatened to blackmail Gilroy, but hadn't used the photos she'd been keeping. And she'd also said the money she'd been paid wasn't enough.

It might be a leap, but I suddenly couldn't help wondering if Gilroy had followed my father's footsteps in more ways than one.

Had Mona been pregnant with Gilroy's child?

CHAPTER SEVEN

I f ever there was a straw that could break Lyle's back, *that* would be it. It was bad enough that his nephew had answered the call of the woman he loved; if he'd also gotten her pregnant...God, what a mess.

I glanced up at the house and saw a shadow in the study window. Bramwell, making sure we left.

Had he told us the entire truth? I very much doubted it, but I couldn't really be sure. People might talk to me rather easily but I couldn't always see the lies behind their words.

If Mona *had* been pregnant, Bramwell would have gone to great lengths to protect his son. Or rather, protect his son's political ambitions, which to my father were more important. And while I had no doubt he could and would employ someone to kill anyone who got in his way, I also had no doubt that he *wouldn't* have condoned rape. His views on that crime were widely known and, during his stint as a judge, he'd thrown the book at any rapist proven guilty in his court.

So where did that leave us, besides knee deep up that well-known creek?

I climbed into the car and started it up. First things first. Get Lyle home, and then somehow find out if Mona *had* been pregnant. Maybe Ceri could use some of the contacts she still had—although Kaij's mob were in charge of the investigation and they were known for keeping information to themselves. Ceri's contacts didn't have that sort of reach.

"Don't take me home," Lyle said, voice sharp. "Because I'm parking myself at your place. I intend to be there when Gilroy turns up,"

"Why? So you can punch him out too?"

"Damn it, Harriet, I thought you of all people would understand."

I pulled into the Toorak Road traffic. "And why would you think that?"

"Because your mother was a siren. Surely it couldn't have been easy seeing all the men coming and going."

"I grew up with it, Lyle. Besides, it *is* part of their nature, whether you like it or not." He didn't say anything, so I added, "And I still don't see how my being raised by a siren would make me more understanding of *this* situation."

"Well, you would have seen how a siren's call can warp a man's mind. I mean, it hooks you, hooks you deep, until you can't think straight and all you want is her call. But you also know others answer her call, and sometimes you even see it. Deep down, the knife twists. The anger burns."

Actually, it was very rare for a man to get hooked *that*

deeply by a siren, simply because sirens generally made sure it didn't happen. Mom and her friends had always been wary of calling any man too often, just to avoid that sort of event.

But it did make me wonder who he'd seen with her—though it wasn't hard to guess, to be honest. "You walked in on James Logan?"

"The bastard got what he deserved," he said, doing everything but meeting my gaze. "It's a shame Frank wasn't in that helicopter, too. If I'd known that bastard was the one who'd threatened her—"

He shook his head. The unspoken threat hung in the air, twisted and poisonous.

"James might have gotten his just desserts," I said sharply, "But there's no evidence whatsoever that Frank was the one who'd threatened her."

"Who else could it have been? James hasn't got the guts, and besides, she said it was a politician."

"Which Gilroy is."

"Which is why I want to ask him myself. I'll know if he's lying."

"There's always Bramwell."

"He said he didn't do it. I believe him."

Because he wanted to? Because blood called to blood and he really didn't want to believe otherwise? As much as I also didn't think my father had killed Mona, I very much suspected my reasons for believing so differed to Lyle's. "Then maybe it was whoever took the damn memory card.

Someone knew about that book, Lyle. Find out that, and we may well find our killer."

"Maybe." He glanced out the window. Not wanting to hear anything resembling sense.

I bit back my frustration and said, "Besides, while you think James deserved his death, the other three people in the helicopter certainly didn't."

He waved a hand. "I didn't say they did."

Maybe, but he never gave them a thought, either. "Did you get around to talking to the cops about Keale?"

Lyle wound down the window then lit a cigarette. "They're releasing him tomorrow, once he's been charged. The case won't be slated for court for a couple of months, and they'll shackle him with a tracker that'll restrict his movements."

"What about the Prevoron tests?"

"I told you before," he said, voice irritated, "they'll take a while to come through."

"If we can prove there's Prevoron in his system—"

"It won't make a goddamn difference." Lyle blew a ring of smoke out the window. "You need to face the fact, Harriet, that your friend is very likely going to jail."

It would kill him if he did. You couldn't confine a dragon in a cell barely bigger than a toilet, and expect him to survive. And hell, the animal rights mob would be up in arms if they did that sort of thing to zoo animals. "What sort of sentence is he looking at?"

"Ten to fifteen, minimum." Lyle shrugged. "As you noted, he killed four people when he hit that helicopter."

"I know. I just don't think it was a deliberate act on his part. Can you please hassle the cops about those tests again?"

He sighed and rubbed the bridge of his nose, coming dangerously close to burning his eyebrows. "Okay, okay."

"Good."

In the meantime, I might find out where on Springvale Road the Ibis Hotel was, and see if I could find Numar there. Maybe *he* could give me some answers.

The rest of the trip was spent in silence. Lyle stared out the side window, every now and again raising the cigarette to his lips and puffing the smoke out the window. It made me think about anger burning so deep it poisoned your thoughts. Made me wonder if perhaps Lyle had slipped beyond love and into the realms of obsession.

The ogres had pinched my parking space yet again, forcing me further up the street. Their roars could be heard clearly over the booming noise of the TV as we approached the house, a combination that was practically deafening. It was a wonder Delilah wasn't complaining. I glanced toward her place and saw her car was missing. Maybe she'd given up and headed off to find new souls to hassle.

"Fuck it, Harriet, when are you going to do something about those ogres?" Lyle's voice held more than a hint of distaste. "They practically live at your place."

Amusement twitched my lips as I led the way into the house. "Only in the football and cricket seasons."

"So, what, you get two or three months to yourself?" He snorted. "You need to put your foot down more."

"I would, but their feet are bigger than mine."

"This is no laughing matter," he said sternly. "Your house is in danger of becoming half-way house for the community's dregs—"

"Hey," I said, giving him a sharp look. "They're my friends. I don't care how pissed off you are at the world at the moment, don't insult them."

Lyle held up his hands. "No insult meant."

Oh yes, he *had*. But I let it slide and made my way down the hall to the living room. Guy greeted us with a grin and raised a can of beer. "It's Curly's," he said. "And I called Kristo about the front door. He's down the street, choosing a new lock."

"Tell him I want it installed before Christmas."

I headed up to the loft. Ceri wouldn't arrive until night fell, so the large room was shadowed and quiet.

"You do all this yourself?" Lyle stopped in the doorway and looked around.

"Well, with some help from the dregs." I grabbed my camera and a few memory cards.

"I said I was sorry." Then he frowned. "You going somewhere?"

"Yeah, I've got an appointment I forgot about. Bloody wedding photos." Why I felt it necessary to lie, I wasn't entirely sure.

For once, he didn't seem to detect it. "Reduced to taking wedding photos." He shook his head, a mix of amusement and disdain in his expression. "That *is* a sad state of affairs."

"Hey, it pays the bills, so don't knock it." I picked up the wedding sampler book and a couple of my photography business cards from the spare desk just to flesh out the lie. "You want to come?"

"I could think of nothing more boring—except, possibly, listening to the ogres give a blow by blow description of a game two hours after it had finished."

"Nothing is *that* boring." I shoved everything into a carryall and hoisted it over my shoulder. "I should be back by six."

It was just before three now, so that gave me just over two and a bit hours to find the Ibis and hopefully get some answers from Numar.

Lyle nodded. "I might go down and cheer on the Dockers. That should piss the ogres right off."

I grinned. "It certainly will. They hate the interstate sides, and Guy's bet on Essendon."

"Should make for an interesting afternoon then. You got any whiskey hidden?"

I hesitated. I really didn't want him any drunker than he already was, but there was little point in refusing given the hotel was within easy walking distance—it was one of the reasons Guy had purchased the house three doors down from mine. Two suppliers of beer within easy reach was the closest thing to ogre heaven imaginable.

"There's half a bottle in the cabinet above the laundry sink."

Lyle nodded. I headed back down the stairs and out to my car.

The Ibis was easy enough to find. It was situated just down from Canterbury Road, and was an L-shaped, glass and concrete affair. It wasn't exactly pretty, but then, I'd always been a fan of old style architecture rather than new.

I stopped in the car park and made my way inside. Two people manned the reception desk, one female, and the other male. I headed towards the male, not only because he wasn't currently helping anyone but also because siren magic was gender specific. It worked with the wielder's sexual orientation. I preferred the opposite sex, so it wouldn't work on females.

He greeted me with a smile warm enough to touch his brown eyes. "Welcome to the Ibis. How may I help you?"

I returned his smile and backed it with a touch of siren magic. "I'm here to see Numar Boyd—could you tell me if he's still staying here or not?"

"Just let me check." He did some typing and, after a moment, met my gaze again, "According to our records, he was supposed to have left yesterday, but extended his stay at the last moment. Would you like me to ring him and inform him you're here?"

I applied a little more magical influence. I knew well enough he wasn't supposed to give me the information I was about to ask for. "Could you actually just tell me his room number?"

He frowned, so I hit him a little harder with siren mojo. He blinked and glanced down at the screen. "It's room four-thirteen."

"Oh, brilliant." I hesitated. "And a key?"

He produced one immediately. "There's nothing else I can do for you?"

"No. Thanks." I gave him another smile and headed for the lifts, but didn't actually release him until the doors were closing behind me.

There was a 'do-not-disturb' sign hanging on the door of room four-thirteen. I ignored it and knocked. There was no response, so I knocked again. Silence remained the only answer. I shoved the key in the lock and opened the door—and was knocked backward by the stench of alcohol and vomit. I swore softly and hurried inside.

Numar was sprawled on the bed, half undressed and on his side, his skin pale, with vomit covering the pillows and floor around him. I ran around the bed, avoiding the stinking puddles as best I could, then leaned over and pressed two fingers against his neck. He had a pulse, but it was as irregular as his breathing.

I swore again, then grabbed the phone and called for an ambulance. I made a second call to the front desk to let them know what was happening and, thankfully, it didn't take too long for either the management or the ambulance to arrive. Numar was quickly whisked off to hospital. I gathered his wallet, some fresh clothes, and then followed. The next few hours were spent anxiously pacing the waiting area, hoping like hell he was going to be okay. Eventually, a nurse appeared and I took a step towards her.

"Harri Phillecky?" Her gaze met mine, one eyebrow raised in query.

I nodded. "Is Numar okay?"

"He will be, but we're keeping him overnight, just to be sure."

Relief slithered through me. I didn't know Numar all that well, but he'd seemed a decent enough bloke the few times we'd met. I knew Keale thought the world of him. "Is he awake? Can I talk to him?"

She hesitated and glanced at her watch. "If you're quick. We're hoping to transfer him to a bed in the next five or ten minutes, and he'll need to rest after that."

"That would be great, thanks."

She nodded and led the way past several curtained off cubicles before stopping at one and pushing the curtain aside. "Remember, you can't stay too long."

"I won't," I said, and went in.

Numar was wearing a blue hospital gown and sitting upright, but he looked even more washed out than he had when I'd found him. Although he—like most dragons—was on the skinny side, his face looked almost emaciated, as if he'd been drained of almost all his bodily fluids.

"Harri," he said, his voice on the raw side, "I'm told you were the one who found me."

"Yeah, and stinking mess you were, too." I propped myself on the end of the bed and dumped his fresh clothes beside me. "What the hell did you and Keale do last night?"

He scraped a hand through still matted hair, confusion touching his pale features. "I don't really know. Drink, obviously, but I can't tell you where or when because it's all a blur."

Which suggested he'd been even drinking *before* they'd met. "I thought you were supposed to fly home yesterday?"

"Yeah, I was." He gave me a grin that was little more than a ghost of its usual self. "But I met a stunning blonde with the most beautiful blue eyes in the bar the night before, and we hooked up."

"Was she also at the conference?"

He shrugged. "Don't think so. She was just at the bar having a drink and I decided to chance my luck. Couldn't believe it when she all but fell into my arms."

I smiled. "Meaning women don't usually fall so readily into your arms?"

"Well, not women who looked *that* classy." He grimaced. "Unfortunately, I only know her first name—Mandy—and forgot to ask for her phone number when she left at ten past eight this morning, so unless she's downstairs again, there won't be a repeat performance."

I snorted softly. "You almost died of alcohol poisoning, and you're worried about a repeat performance with a blonde?"

"I'm a dragon. Trust me, my priorities *are* in the right order." His smile faded. "How come you were looking for me? I mean, I'm grateful and all, but it is a little unusual, really."

"Keale mentioned he'd been drinking with you, and given

the mess he's gotten himself into, I figured it might be worth-while checking to see if you were okay."

He raised his eyebrows. "I'm surprised he could even move if the doctors are right about the amount we must have consumed."

"So am I, actually." So how the hell *was* he flying? He should have been as comatose as Numar by all rights. Unless, of course, his poison had been Prevoron rather than booze. "Did either of you do anything more than drink?"

He frowned. "What do you mean? Like drugs?"

"Prevoron, actually."

"No way. I'm allergic to the fucking stuff and, for as long as I've known Keale, he's barely had enough money to keep up with his weekly booze consumption. How the hell would he be able to afford Prevoran, especially in the quantities he'd have to take to get high?"

Good question. But if it wasn't Prevoron then it had to be booze, and given he *had* been flying, it meant he couldn't have consumed as much as Numar. And that, in turn, meant there were no excuses for his actions—and no way out of a murder charge.

I didn't want to believe he would have been that foolish—that careless. I wanted to believe the inner niggle that said there was more to this than met the eye.

Even if that niggle was getting drowned under the mounting evidence.

The nurse reappeared and said, voice crisp, "I'm afraid you'll have to go now."

I nodded, and then said to Numar, "I've bought in your wallet and a change of clothes, but if you need anything else, just give me a call."

He nodded, looking wearier than he had a few minutes earlier. Talking had obviously washed him out again. "Thanks, Harri. I really do appreciate it."

"No problem."

I slipped off the bed and headed back to my car. By the time I got back home, the ogres were rummaging through the freezer, dragging out pizza and party pies. Lyle was lying on the living room floor, snoring loud enough to rattle the glass doors in the nearby Blu-ray cabinet.

"How long has he been like that?" I dropped the carryall on the table and walked across to turn on the percolator.

Guy shrugged. "Half an hour. He finished the Johnny Walker all by himself, I might add."

I smiled. Such an action was practically a crime in an ogre's view. "He never was very good at sharing."

The microwave pinged. Curly opened it, and the smell of ham and pineapple pizza wafted out.

"Want some?" Guy asked, reaching over Curly's shoulder to grab a slice.

I shuddered. "I can think of nothing worse than microwaved pizza."

"How about a party pie?"

"Except that." I walked across to the fridge and opened the door. The seafood curry I'd made was still there, although it showed signs of a recent spoon attack. Obviously, none of the ogres had liked it enough to eat it. I'd have to start making it more often. I threw it in a pan to heat it up and shoved some bread into the toaster. "You guys hanging around very long?"

"If you want us to shove off, just say so." Guy gave me a wide grin. "I've got a microwave and the pizza is portable."

"My father and brother are coming around. It's not likely to be pleasant."

"The gay brother or the snotty politician?"

I smiled. "The latter, I'm afraid."

"Saw him on the TV the other day," Guy said. "They were asking about his prospects for the upcoming election. I ain't voting for him, I tell ya."

"Neither am I." Not that our votes—or lack thereof—would affect Gilroy's chances in any way, given the polls had him streets ahead of his opposition. "They're due here at seven."

"Then me and the boys will head off." He paused, giving me a somewhat concerned look. "Yell if you need help. We'll come a running."

"I will. Thanks."

He nodded, collected the stack of party pies and sausage rolls they'd pilfered from the freezer, and headed out. Ceri walked in just after they'd left.

"That's what I call perfect timing." She peeled off her coat then headed for the percolator. She poured two cups and handed me one. "What's been happening? And who the hell is that snoring?"

"Lyle. You want some curry?"

She walked over, gave it a sniff, and then wrinkled her nose. "Seafood. No thanks."

I shrugged and spooned it out onto my toast, and alternated between eating and updating her on events.

"So," she said gloomily. "Keale is basically up shit creek without a paddle."

"Unless the blood results come back showing Prevoron, he could be." I scooped up the last bit of curry. "I don't suppose you have anyone in the force who still owes you a favor or two, do you?"

She regarded me steadily. "Why?"

"Because I'm a little curious about the woman Numar met."

"Again, why? She left his room well before he met up with Keale and starting drinking."

"Yeah, but it's been bugging me. He has absolutely no memory of what he did either during the day or with Keale, and yet he can remember the exact time a woman left his bed?"

"We *are* talking about a dragon here." Her voice was dry. "Their lives to tend to revolve around sex at certain times of the year."

"I know, and that fact alone makes me wonder why Keale would risk getting drunk. He was still seeing Rebecca—who is in season, remember—so why would he go on such a bender when she apparently hated the smell of the stuff?"

"Good question." She paused for a moment, then said, "The

only way we're going to get a picture of her is to pull it from the hotel's security tapes—and success depends whether they write over the same disk or not."

"Doesn't hurt to try."

"That it doesn't. I'll see what I can organize before I go meet the weepy wife again."

I raised my eyebrows. "You got the pictures she wanted?"

"In full, glorious color." She grimaced. "I hope we start getting meatier cases. I don't want to spend the rest of my life doing this sort of stuff."

"We've only just opened. They'll come once word gets around."

"Maybe." She hesitated. "I'll be upstairs if things get a little heated with your father, brother, or uncle."

"Lyle's the only one I have to watch, and him I can cope with."

"I'm not here to cause problems, Harriet," he said, voice tart as he appeared in the doorway. He gave Ceri a barely civil nod as she walked past him, and then dropped heavily into a chair. "I told you, I'm just want to hear what Gilroy has to say for himself."

I rose, poured Lyle a coffee, and then refilled my own mug. His fingers shook as he wrapped his hands around the mug. "You really need to cut the drinking, Lyle. It's not doing you any good."

"And who appointed you my fucking keeper?"

I raised an eyebrow and sat back down. He scrubbed a hand

across his eyes. "Sorry. I don't know what's gotten into me lately."

I did—a hell of a lot of booze. "Were you and Mona having any kind of trouble before she disappeared?"

His gaze sharpened. "Why would you ask that?"

I shrugged. "Just curious. I mean, I know it must be hard for you living with a siren, and I wondered if that was why you've been drin-"

"I wasn't living with her," he cut in. "Couldn't, with Adelia sniffing around for excuses."

"Then who was? Because someone was keeping beer in her fridge."

"Yeah, well, it wasn't mine. Can't stand the stuff." He took a large gulp of coffee that must have scalded his tongue, though he gave no evidence of it. Maybe there was enough booze in his system to dull sensation. "Why do you keep asking stupid questions?"

"Because that's what you are paying me to do."

He didn't answer. He just sat there glowering at me. Thankfully, the doorbell rang before the silence got too grating. I walked down the hall and undid the chain that was all that was keeping the door closed. My father and Gilroy stood on the other side. Neither looked particularly happy. No surprise there.

"Come on in, gentleman." I stepped aside and waved them in. "The coffee has just been brewed."

"Let's not make any pretense at civility." Bramwell's voice

was cold as he stepped past me. "We will be here no longer than necessary."

I'd expected nothing less. Gilroy—a younger replica of my father—didn't even acknowledge me as he went past, but the faint look of disdain etched into his features grew as his gaze roamed the shadows of my hallway. No doubt the house was nowhere near the level of comfort *he* was used to.

They walked down to the kitchen, their footsteps sharp against the old wooden floorboards. Bramwell stopped just inside the kitchen doorway. Gilroy did the same, and I was surprised to discover my brother was a good three inches smaller than our father. In fact, he was only a little taller than me, and at five six I would have been considered a runt if I'd been of pure Elven stock. He was slightly broader at the shoulders, and though I was slender, he was even more so. My gaze slipped down to his hands. White and soft. Not the hands of anyone who'd ever worked an honest job. Not the hands of a murderer.

Frowning at the thought, I squeezed past the pair of them then waved toward the free chairs. "Take a seat."

Gilroy looked at the chairs and his expression, if anything, became more disdainful. Something I hadn't thought was possible. "Are they safe?"

"If they can take an ogre's weight, they can take yours." I sat down next to Lyle. The old elf hadn't acknowledged the arrival of his kin in any way. I wasn't sure whether this was a good thing or bad.

"Ogres. God." Gilroy pulled a handkerchief out of his pocket, brushed the seat, and then sat.

My father continued standing. "We're here, as requested. Ask your questions."

Lyle finally raised his head. His eyes were bloodshot and glinted with sapphire fire, but there was little emotion to be read in his expression. "Did you kill Mona?"

Gilroy looked shocked. Ever the actor; ever the politician. "I certainly did *not*."

"But you wanted her dead, didn't you?" Lyle's voice was little more than a growl. "She was trying to blackmail you, and you wanted her dead."

"Please, cut the dramatics, uncle." Just for a moment, there was a hint of Bramwell's steel in Gilroy's voice. "I paid her off, end of story. The bitch wanted more, granted, but she was very much alive the last time I saw her."

I could sense no lie in his words, but then, would I? Bramwell would have schooled him on the proper responses on the journey over here, of that I had no doubt.

"She might have been alive when you last saw her, but what about the men you sent after her?"

Gilroy snorted. "I wouldn't waste the time or money on the bitch. In fact, I told her to go to the press. We'd see who they believe soon enough—and it wouldn't have been a two-bit siren past her prime."

Lyle jumped to his feet, face mottling. "You *bastard!* She was good enough for you to bed, so what right have you—"

I saw his fist clench and lurched upright, grabbing his arm. He turned on me and, just for a moment, the hatred aimed at Gilroy shone on me. I shivered. There was no love there. No friendship. It was almost if kinship didn't exist and we were nothing but strangers. Then he blinked and the moment was gone, but it left me feeling decidedly uneasy.

"Damn it, Harriet, let go of my arm."

"Not until you sit down."

"I am not a child—"

"Then stop acting like one and *sit*."

"No. I'm going out for a cigarette."

I frowned. "But I thought you wanted to hear what—"

"I've heard all I need to hear." He pulled free of my grip and stomped out, leaving me somewhat confused. Why demand to come here, then not hear the entire story? Did that mean he believed Gilroy was telling the truth?

"Is that all, Harriet?"

I sat back down. "Certainly not, brother of mine."

Irritation flashed through Gilroy's thin cheeks. "Do not call me that—"

"Why not? It's the truth, even if you and daddy dearest have no wish to acknowledge it." I crossed my arms and leaned against the table. "Was Mona pregnant with your child?"

Just for a moment, he looked totally thunderstruck. It was the first honest expression I'd seen so far, and it told me everything I needed to know. If she was pregnant, he hadn't known about it.

Then the mask of disdain slipped back into place. "I am not so careless as to allow a whore to conceive my child."

"Accidents happen. Hey, I'm here blighting your existence thanks to one such occurrence."

"Mona was *not* carrying my child."

"Then what did she threaten you with?"

"I told you—she threatened to go to the press with our relationship."

"So there was never a mention of photos?"

Gilroy hesitated. Bramwell said, "Tell her."

He grimaced. "She said she had proof. She didn't say what type and I didn't ask. She demanded money in exchange, I gave it to her, but she reneged and wanted more. I walked out. End of story, as I said."

"How much did she demand?"

"Initially? Two hundred and fifty thousand."

He said it without even blinking. But then, that sort of money was pocket change to people like Bramwell and Gilroy. "And the second time?"

"One hundred and fifty. I told her I had no intention of being blackmailed for the rest of my life, and to go ahead and do her worst."

"It would have killed your political aspirations." My gaze was on Bramwell more than my brother. He was giving away little, but I knew Gilroy's aspirations were just as much his.

"Short term, yes," Gilroy agreed. "But long term? People forget. In this day and age, a single politician having a little fun is not quite the scandal it was back when you were born."

"Gilroy learned from my mistakes," Bramwell said, voice quiet and yet holding the sharpness of a knife. "If the siren was pregnant, it was not his."

I believed him. He might not be telling me everything he knew, but I don't think he was lying when it came to the pregnancy. Although these two *were* well versed in telling the world what they wanted to hear, and it might be that I didn't know them well enough to sense fact from fiction.

"Why were you and James Logan arguing?"

"There was no real reason. I stopped the stupid bastard from punching the siren and he started in on me."

So much for thinking James was as spineless as Gilroy. "Did he say why he was about to punch her?"

He snorted. "Yeah, he said the stupid bitch was attempting to blackmail him."

I glanced up at Bramwell. "Is this when Frank Logan got involved?"

"I have no idea whether James confided in his brother or not. I merely presume he did, as I cannot imagine James would have been able to produce that sort of cash on his own."

Meaning I might just have to talk to Frank. "I don't suppose James gave any indication about what she was blackmailing him with? I mean, he wasn't a politician, so she could hardly threaten his reputation."

Gilroy sniffed. It was a disparaging sound. "Trust me; I did not talk to the man any more than I had to. But he *did* have a habit of reproducing unwisely, so there's a good chance it was his if she was pregnant."

"Who was pregnant?" Lyle said from the doorway. "Mona?"

I groaned inwardly. This was all I needed. I turned around. Lyle stood in the doorway, his face as dark as thunder. The Elven discipline of being in complete emotional control had well and truly slipped.

"It's just supposition, given she could hardly use the same sort of blackmail threat on James as she did Gilroy."

"A siren becoming pregnant would be a far greater threat to Gilroy than it would James," Lyle snapped. "So if she didn't use the pregnancy possibility to threaten Gilroy, why the hell would she bother with James?"

Good question—and one I didn't really have an answer for.

"Because," Bramwell said, voice hard, "If she'd had a long-standing relationship with James, she'd more than likely have established a connection, and would probably have discovered that James was in danger of being disinherited if he produced one more by-blow."

"Connection?" Lyle looked at me, confusion evident. "What sort of connection?"

"It's similar to telepathy," I said, meeting my father's gaze evenly. "It's rare, simply because sirens rarely form such long-term attachments."

But Bramwell and my mother had, and I very much suspected that was part of the reason mother had never felt truly bitter about the way he'd treated us at the end. Somewhere deep in the darkest reaches of his mind, she must have sensed some caring.

Lyle grunted. "It's still a stupid supposition to make, Harriet."

"Perhaps it is," I agreed. "But we still have to consider it as a possibility when nothing else seems to make sense."

"*We* do not have to consider anything," Bramwell cut in. "There has been enough of this foolishness already. Will that be all?"

"If I remember any other questions, I'll be in contact."

"Then ring at the office," Bramwell said. "Come along, Gilroy."

My brother dutifully rose then dusted imaginary specks of dust from his suit. "I can't say it's been a pleasure, Harriet, because it hasn't. You have a nasty little mind."

"Maybe, but you're the one with the nasty little habits, brother."

He looked down his nose at me for several seconds, then turned and left.

Bramwell made to follow, then paused and met my gaze again. In those sapphire depths, fury mingled with death.

"Threaten my son's future," he said, voice soft, vehement. "And you will not see the sun rise on another day."

For several seconds I couldn't respond, pinned not so much by the threat, but the sheer depth of the anger and hate that briefly resonated in his eyes.

Anger I could understand, given the circumstances, but where did the hate come from?

"The only one threatening your son's future is himself," I somehow managed to retort. "Perhaps you should sit him down and explain the political facts of life to him. Sooner or later, his affair with Mona would have come to light, and you of all people know what that can do to political aspirations."

"The Mona situation I can control. You I cannot."

He couldn't control his brother, either, and of the two of us, Lyle was the more dangerous.

Still, I couldn't exactly be unhappy about the fact he'd realized I *wasn't* someone he could manage on a day-to-day basis—unlike my brother.

"See you around," I said, a little more cheerfully than I otherwise would have.

"Not if I can help it." And with that, he followed Gilroy out the door. It slammed shut behind them.

"Well, that was fucking useless," Lyle said in disgust.

"No, it wasn't. It was quite the opposite, actually."

Lyle rested his arms against the back of the chair to my right, and gave me a somewhat sullen look. "In what way?"

"Well, for one, I believe Gilroy when he said he didn't kill Mona."

Lyle didn't say anything to that. I guess that meant he believed it, too.

"Which means either Bramwell, Frank, or James could have killed her. And James is dead, so if he *is* the killer, we've reached an impasse." Unless, of course, she *was* black-mailing other clients. She did have an entire book filled with memory cards, after all, and I couldn't help but wonder why if not for nefarious purpose. Of course, they might just have been her version of notches on a bed head.

"Bramwell didn't do it."

I met his gaze sharply. "You still believe him?"

He grimaced. "My brother is as smooth as they come, but yes, I believe he didn't personally kill her."

"Meaning you think it's possible he hired someone?"

Lyle hesitated. "He's capable of such an act. We all are, when it comes to protecting our own."

Which still didn't mean he *had*. I picked up my coffee and sipped it thoughtfully. "We did glean another bit of useful information out of that little interview."

"Other than you coming up with wild pregnancy theories, you mean?"

I gave him a flat look. He returned it evenly. Not willing to even consider the possibility she'd been pregnant—which was interesting given there was as much chance of it being his as anyone else's.

"Bramwell and Gilroy both state they paid Mona the money, so the next question is, what the hell happened to it?"

"She would have banked it."

"Sirens don't bank. It's like driving—an inconvenience they'd rather pay someone else to handle."

He frowned. "I don't think she'd trust anyone enough to bank that amount of money."

Which made Mona different to just about every other siren I'd known. If they didn't lock their doors against thieves, why would they worry about someone stealing their cash? After all, their song had more uses than calling in prospective clients. It could also be used to lure thieves back to the scene of the crime.

"What about Darryl? He was her driver, so if he didn't do her banking, he might know who did."

"Good luck finding the little creep." Lyle pushed away from the chair. "He's made himself rather scarce of late."

I raised my eyebrows. "Why have you been trying to find him?"

"Wanted to talk to him about Mona, that's all." He waved a hand, as if the question wasn't important. Which made me suspect the opposite. "I'd better go."

"You want me to call you a taxi?"

"No."

"You sure? Because you're not going to find one easily around these parts—"

"I meant what I fucking said." Something flared in his eyes, something dark and unpleasant. "Just leave me be, Harri."

And with that, he stomped out, leaving me wondering if the somewhat eccentric, sometimes aloof, but generally easy-going uncle I'd known for all these years actually existed.

I sighed, finished the last of my coffee, and then headed up to the loft to do some long overdue paperwork. Ceri came back from her appointment with the weepy wife just before midnight and took over watching the stubbornly silent phones while I headed to bed.

The next morning I decided to try and catch Darryl. Lyle had said he couldn't be found, but given the outfit the dwarf had been wearing the day I'd met him, it was a fair bet that jogging around the streets of Sandridge was a regular part of his training routine. It was worth a shot, anyway.

After a shower in which I discovered a rainbow of bruises and more sore spots, I pulled on a fresh set jeans and a baggy sweater, and then headed downstairs.

Kristo was standing in the middle of my hallway, contemplating my front door.

"How did you get in?" I asked. The chair I'd jammed against the door last night to keep it closed was still in place.

"Back door," he said absently, and scratched a pointed ear. "Fixed the squeak in the bathroom door, by the way."

I hadn't noticed any squeak, but I guess that was beside the point. "What about the front door lock? The one you're being employed to replace?"

The gnome shrugged. "I'm considering it now. You've got to

have the right tools for these operations, you know, or things could go horribly wrong."

"Just consider fixing it before Christmas, would you?"

"Well, yes, I think that should be an achievable goal."

I rolled my eyes and walked away. Knowing Kristo, he'd probably be standing in the same position three hours from now. I walked into the kitchen to discover the back door was wide open and Delilah nose deep in the pantry.

"Hey, Harri," she said, "Where do you hide the sugar?"

"Second shelf, left-hand side. Listen, could you do me a favor? Kristo's here to fix the front door—could you provoke him into action? I need the lock fixed today."

Delilah grinned. "A bit of gnome rousting is always a nice way to start the day. Just watch and learn, my love." She deposited the bag of sugar on the nearest chair and pushed up the sleeve of her hot pink dressing gown as she marched to the hallway door.

"Hey, Kristo!" she yelled.

I winced. The gnome jumped a good six inches and pirouetted in the air to face us.

"Start moving that bony ass, or I'll have to stay here and nag you."

What little hair Kristo had on his head stood on end at the prospect. He nodded, then motored past us and out the back door. I half-wondered if he was making a run for it, but he reappeared seconds later, lock in hand.

Delilah smiled and patted my arm lightly. "See, you just need to use a firm tone. Get's results, every time."

"Totally," I agreed solemnly. "Can you lock up after he leaves?"

She nodded, opened the sugar, and then poured it into a bowl. At least she wasn't taking the whole packet. I left her to it, grabbed my keys and purse, and headed out.

The wind that was little more than a whisper in the confines of the suburbs was sharper and colder down near the beach. I parked near the pier then pulled out my phone and Googled Mighty Mouse Body Guard Services. As I suspected, his office was only a couple of blocks away. I grabbed a jacket off the rear seat and shoved it on as I made my way there. Joggers went past at regular intervals, most red-faced despite the chill in the air. It made me wonder when Sandridge had become so fitness orientated.

His office was a single story, glass-fronted building squeezed in between a coffee shop and a hairdresser, and it looked a whole lot shabbier than either of them. It was also closed, so I crossed my arms and leaned against the window to wait.

Twenty minutes later—just as I was considering grabbing a warming cup of coffee from the shop next door—he came running into view. He spotted me a second later and slowed.

"What the hell do you want now?"

"I need to ask some more questions about Mona."

Darryl dragged keys out of the small pack on his back and opened the shop's door. "Five minutes. And I hope you don't mind me getting on the treadmill. I don't want to cool down too suddenly."

The front room of his office contained little more than a desk, several filing cabinets, a couple of worn leather chairs and the aforementioned treadmill. Unlike like the rest of the equipment in the room, it was shiny new. As he started the machine up, I said, "Did Mona ever talk about her clients?"

He snorted softly. "Never names, if that's what you're after."

"But surely she mentioned a name when she was talking about getting married?"

"Nope. She was always very careful." He shook his head, his expression sad. "But not careful enough, obviously."

No. Especially not if she was blackmailing the likes of James Logan. "Did she say anything that might pin down who she meant to marry?"

"Well, she said that he had to go through divorce proceedings, so they had to be discrete until it was over."

If she'd been talking about Lyle, she would have been waiting a very long time. He would never proceed with a divorce, simply because it would have cost him too much. "What about pregnancy?"

He glanced up sharply, blue eyes narrowing. "What about it?"

"Well, for starters, was she pregnant?"

His gaze slid from mine. "What gives you the idea that she was?"

I shrugged. "It's a theory, nothing more."

He upped the speed on the treadmill. "Why are you still chasing this? Why not let the police handle it?"

"I can't."

He studied me quizzically. "Why not?"

I hesitated. "The man Mona intended to marry is my uncle. He asked me to try to find out what happened."

"Why you?"

"Because I'm half siren, and he thought people around here might be more willing to talk to me than the police."

"Ah," he said, half smiling. "That explains it. You sing?"

I shook my head. "Not a note. I'm afraid I take after the Elven part of my heritage."

"Probably just as well for the world, given your ability to get people to yak. You'd be bloody dangerous as a full siren." He sniffed slightly and shook his arms. "This uncle wouldn't happen to be a former high flying lawyer who could still bust a murderer to hell and back if he wanted to, would he?"

So Mona never talked about her clients, huh? "He might be."

Darryl's expression went hard. "I want this bastard caught." The words were flatly said, but the emotion lacking in his voice was there for the world to see in his eyes. "I want him hung out to dry."

"Then you and the lawyer have similar ambitions."

"Good." He hesitated. "I've been checking up on you."

"Why?"

"Wanted to be sure you could be trusted."

"And what was the general consensus?"

"I think it came down to three things—pretty, remote, and fiercely loyal. And you're nothing like the rest of your family."

"That's four." I frowned. "People think I'm remote?"

He raised an eyebrow, amusement briefly lifting the sadness from his face. "Oh, trust me love, you may get mouths to move quicker than butter can melt on hot pavement, but there's something very untouchable about you."

No, there wasn't, I thought automatically. But there again, I *would* think that. It was altogether possible I *had* been giving off that sort of vibe—especially after the whole Kaij mess. It would certainly explain my lack of progress on the whole boyfriend front.

But I wasn't here to talk about me. "Look, all I'm trying to do is solve Mona's murder. And if you know anything that could help, I'd appreciate knowing it."

"But what would you do if a clue led to your own backyard?"

A chill ran through me. Was Darryl saying Gilroy was the murderer? My brother might be a pompous asshole, but after our talk last night I would have sworn on a stack of bibles he was *not* also a murderer. "I know who the three high-profile men seeing her were. I'm investigating regardless."

He nodded. "One of them was the father. One of them was the murderer."

So she *had* been pregnant. Holy crap, that really did put the cat among the pigeons as far as Lyle was concerned—and it certainly wasn't something I was about to mention. He had enough police contacts—he could discover that particular bit of news himself. "Why are you so certain if Mona never talked about any of it?"

He smiled, but his expression was wistful. "It wasn't hard to work out who her song had caught, even if she never mentioned names. Mona was a lovely lady, but she wasn't particularly bright."

As evidenced by the fact she'd tried blackmailing both my brother and Logan. "And your guess as to who or what might be behind her murder?"

"The what is obvious—none of them could afford the press finding out they might be the father of a siren's kid, now, could they? I tried to tell her—" He bit the rest of the sentence off and shrugged.

So Mona had trusted him enough that he not only knew about her pregnancy, but also her blackmail attempts. "And the who?"

"Anyone in their right mind would be scared of the Logan brothers." His gaze came to mine. "She never did fear your half-brother in the same way."

Which didn't put Gilroy in the clear. Not by a long shot. "Was he the father?"

"From what I could gather, probably."

189

So much for Gilroy's assurance he would never sire a child on a siren. "Then why was she also threatening James Logan?"

"Money, pure and simple." He raised an eyebrow at me. "How well do you know your uncle?"

I remembered the darkness I'd glimpse briefly in his eyes last night, and shivered. "I'm beginning to think not half as well as I'd thought."

He nodded. "Mona said he was extremely possessive. She liked that in him, liked the fact he didn't want to share. Most men come to a siren entranced by their song and the sex, but they rarely see the woman behind it."

I nodded. Mom had once said that her relationship with Bramwell had lasted so long simply because he saw *her*— saw who she was, not just what she was. Maybe it was a peculiarity of the Elven race that those who *could* overcome their aversion to sirens were able to see past the power of the song to the soul underneath.

"Then why doesn't he know she was pregnant?"

"Because she wasn't absolutely sure who the father was, and she feared his reaction if it turned out that the kid wasn't his."

He certainly *would* have asked for a paternity test. He wouldn't have risked supporting a child that wasn't his—not given the reception Bramwell had gotten after producing me. "So why was she thinking about settling down with him?"

"As I said, Mona wasn't the brightest soul on the patch." He shrugged again.

"Have you any idea what happened to the money she was paid? Did you bank it for her?"

"No." He paused. "Last time I talked to her, she said she'd gotten the money but was considering asking for more."

"You didn't try to talk her out of it?"

He sighed. "She could be stubborn when she had her mind set on something."

I guess we all could, but surely even Mona could have seen she was playing with fire.

"She didn't ask me to bank anything for her," he continued. "And I didn't see or hear from her again until I found her on the beach."

I frowned suddenly. "Did that client who wanted the meeting at the beach ever get back in contact with you?"

"No. Why?"

"Because the timing seems a little more than just a coincidence. I mean, a woman rings you out of the blue wanting a meeting at the beach at almost the very same hour a siren is washed up? Then she doesn't turn up for said meeting?"

"Hadn't thought about it, but yeah, it *is* odd."

"I don't suppose you have her contact number or name, do you?"

"She told me her name was Mandy, and she was ringing from a public phone." He must have seen my surprised expression, because he added with a grin, "I have a program that runs an automatic trace if caller ID is concealed. One can never be too careful these days."

No, one couldn't. But was it just another coincidence that his caller's name was the same as the woman Numar had met in the bar? There was certainly more than one Mandy in the world, but it still struck me as odd.

I let it slip for a moment, and got back to my questions. "I take it you normally did do her banking?"

He nodded. "I have her cards, if you want me to check whether the money made it into her accounts."

"I dare say the cops have frozen her accounts. Checking them might just make you a person of interest."

"Which I probably am, given I'm her driver and I found her, but I see your point." He paused and squinted up at me. "I want in, you know."

I raised an eyebrow. "In?"

"On any action you take to catch this bastard." His sudden smile held a bitter edge. "You know what these high-flying types are like—slippery as eels. But if you're setting a trap, call me."

"If and when I find enough evidence to pin her murder on anyone, I'm going to the police." But Bramwell's threat swam through my mind, and I had to wonder if that was actually true. It might be easier to hand it all over to Lyle and let him deal with the fallout.

"The offer is there, if you need it." He glanced at his watch again. "I have to go shower. That all the questions for now?"

"Just one more—were you staying with Mona?"

He considered me for a moment, and then nodded. It was a

short, sharp movement. "Temporarily. She was a little afraid after Frank beat her up."

I blinked. "*Frank* beat her up?"

"Yeah. Made a right mess of her."

"When was this?"

He hesitated. "I'm not entirely sure, but it was before she got the money from James."

If Frank had beaten her up, why would he then give James the blackmail money? It didn't make any sense. I rubbed my forehead wearily. *None* of this was making any sense.

"Mona had alcohol in the fridge—was that yours?"

He nodded. "She bought it for me. Her way of saying thanks for staying to protect her."

Which is why he'd been so grief-stricken at the beach—he might have been mourning her, but there'd been guilt, as well.

"Thanks for your help, Darryl."

"No probs. Just remember what I said."

I nodded then headed out of his office and made my way back to my car. If Frank Logan had beaten her up once, then maybe he'd tried it again. Maybe he was the one Val had heard arguing with her the day after Bramwell and James had paid her the money. If I wanted to go further with this case, I really needed to talk to him.

But before I did, I had better find out if the money had been found in Mona's apartment. If it hadn't, and Frank *was* the one who'd been arguing with her just before she'd disappeared, it made him a damn good suspect for theft, if not murder.

Of course, it would also be handy to know for sure if she *had* been pregnant. While Darryl had no doubt that she had been, a siren who apparently thought blackmail was a damn good idea surely wouldn't be above a lie or two. And no matter how bad a liar Darryl thought she was, maybe he was a little closer to her than he should have been, and mightn't have detected it.

But there was only one way I was going to get that sort of information—I had to talk to someone who'd know.

And that meant facing Kaij again.

CHAPTER EIGHT

I headed home first. The front door was wide open, but the new lock was in place and Kristo was perched on a ladder, doing god-knows-what to the hinges. I shook my head and squeezed past him; I'd learned long ago that it was better not to ask. The one time I had, I'd gotten a twenty-minute lecture on the intricacies of fitting a washer.

I glanced into the living room then stopped in surprise. Keale was sitting there, a beer in hand as he watched the morning news. "What the hell are you doing here?"

"They released me this morning. I went home, but it was too damn silent after the pen. At least there's always someone here." He squinted at me, expression suddenly concerned. "You haven't changed your mind, have you?"

"About you staying here? No." What was one more body in the house, after all? "I was just surprised the tracker device would allow you. I thought it was meant to track and restrict your movements?"

"Only flight movements—they don't want me taking off."

I snorted. "You have got feet in human form. You can run if that was your intention."

He grinned. "Yeah, but it's border alarmed. Go out of the state, whether by car, plane, or train, they'll jump me."

"What about work? You need to fly to do your job."

"I can do that. The fire authority just has to report my hours and flight areas." He grimaced. "Not that I'll be doing much of that until my arm heals."

Which wouldn't take all that long—another week at the most and he'd be out of plaster and into flight rehabilitation. I continued on to the kitchen. "Was Lyle at the court?"

"Yeah." Keale trailed after me. "He didn't look happy, I'm telling you that."

Not entirely surprising given he'd consumed a fair amount of alcohol last night. "Did he say anything after the case?"

"Nah. He pretty much pissed off as soon as they bailed me."

Going where? I wondered, a little uneasily. He had a day job, but given his recent obsession with all things Mona, I doubted that he'd actually been sighted at work recently. Hell, if I was perfectly honest, I was surprised he'd turned up to represent Keale.

"You had breakfast?"

"Yeah, at the assessment prison. I could go for something decent though, if you're making it." He sat somewhat stiffly at the table. "Numar told me he probably owes his life to you."

"I'm not sure about that, but he *was* pretty well out of it when I found him." I grabbed some eggs and smoked salmon out of the fridge, then lit the stove. "Oddly, he couldn't remember anything about that night, either."

Keale snorted. "Not surprising if we drank as much as the cops are suggesting."

"If you *had* consumed that much, you would have been as comatose as he was. You certainly wouldn't have been flying anywhere."

"Maybe I've just built up more of a tolerance to the stuff than he has."

I shot him a severe look. "What, you're trying to end up in jail now?"

"No, but facts are facts, Harri."

"They are, and when we get all of them, we'll know if the cops are right or not." I paused to break a dozen eggs into a bowl. "Tell me about Rebecca."

He frowned. "Why?"

"Because, at the very least, she can confirm that you hadn't touched a drop the week before your apparent binge. Remember, the cops suggested you'd been drinking for days."

"Well, a dragon *can* in one night consume enough to make it seem that way." He half-shrugged, and pain flickered across his features. Obviously, the painkillers weren't deadening all sensation. "She began working in the hotel near home about a few weeks ago. I started chatting her up, just for the hell of it." He smiled. "Couldn't hurt, I figured, even if she seemed way out of my league."

"I can't imagine why you'd think a woman working at a hotel bar would be out of your reach." I seasoned the eggs then poured them into the pan. "And hey, you *do* work for the Country Fire Authority."

Which these days was a pretty important job, especially in the more rural communities. Dragons generally handled the back-burning and clearing undergrowth duties—important tasks given the volatile nature of the Australian bush—as well being a major resource with it came to putting out fires.

He grimaced. "She just seemed classier than that—she gave off the vibe that she really didn't really belong there, if you know what I mean. She was way above my usual type, anyway."

And *that* was almost the exact same words that Numar had used to describe Mandy. Coincidence? Maybe, but there seemed to be an awful lot of them happening recently. "But you applied the Finch charm and she succumbed?"

"Totally. Putty in my hands, she was." He gave me a side-ways glance. "You're too fucking easy to talk to. I normally don't say things like that to women."

"We've known each other since high school." My voice was dry. "I don't think there's anything you could say or do that would actually shock me."

Except, perhaps, crash into a helicopter.

I peeled the smoked salmon apart and added that to the omelet. "Did you ever bother asking her much about herself?"

"Nope. Too busy enjoying myself."

And no wonder, given the narrow window of mating fertility. Then I frowned. "You said you met Rebecca at the hotel?"

"Yeah, and it was the stuff dreams are made of. I mean, not only classy and fertile, but able to get me free drinks. I was in heaven."

And why wouldn't he be when male dragons usually had all of the fun, and none of the responsibility when it came to their offspring? "Didn't you tell me last week that Rebecca hated the smell of alcohol?"

"She did." Keale hesitated. "That really doesn't make much sense, does it?"

No, it didn't. There was something rotten in Keale's Garden of Eden, that was for sure. "Where about in Research does she live?"

He wrinkled his nose. "She had a little place on Joslyn Road, just off the Research-Warrandyte Road. Pretty, but filled with antiques. I was always wary of breaking something."

"Number?"

"I never took much notice. It was a little wooden place on the right-hand side of the road. Had all these white and yellow daisies crawling through the fence."

"I'll find it."

He frowned at me. "Why? I mean, even if she does confirm that I hadn't been drinking the days before, it still doesn't alter the fact I was before I crashed into the helicopter."

I cut the omelet, then pulled out two plates and handed him

the bigger half. "It still can't hurt to question her, Keale. There's always a chance you mentioned where you and Numar were going that night. We need to piece together exactly what happened—even if it does no good."

"Maybe." He accepted the omelet with a nod of thanks. I retrieved some cutlery from the dishwasher and then sat down opposite him. He added, "Just be careful. A female in heat can be very fucking touchy. I wouldn't like to see you crisped or anything."

It wasn't exactly on the top of my list of things to experience, either. "Did you ever remember to ask her last name?"

"*That* I managed." He grinned. "It's Price."

"Which hotel does she work at?"

"She works at the Grand. Does day shift Monday to Friday."

I nodded and waved a fork at our food. "Dig in."

We both did. The phone rang just as I was scooping up the last bit of egg. The number wasn't one I knew. "Hello?"

"Harriet Phillecky?" a male voice said.

"That's me. What can I do for you?"

"My name is Bryan." He cleared his throat. "I'm a friend of Val's."

Something deep in my gut clenched. "What's happened?"

"I was asked to call you. It's about Val," Bryan said. "He's been beaten up pretty badly."

Oh fuck, I thought. *I'm going to kill my father.*

"How bad is bad? Is he in the hospital?"

"No, the little fool refuses to go. I called an ambulance, and they've patched him up."

I breathed a little easier. If Val had been truly bad, he would have insisted on being taken to the hospital. He used to go to emergency if he had anything more serious than an infected toenail. "Where is he? Home?"

"Yes. I'm here for a little while, but I'm rostered on later."

I glanced at my watch. "It'll take me twenty minutes to get there. You able to stay that long?"

"Sure. As I said, I'm not rostered on until later."

"See you soon."

"Problem?" Keale asked, as I hung up.

"Yeah, someone's beaten Val up."

I grabbed my coat and purse, and then hesitated. My house had been raided twice, and now Val had been beaten up. It might have no connection to Mona, but dare I take the chance? Keale could take care of himself, but he had a still healing arm, a battered back, an electronic restriction device on his ankle, and the possibility of Prevoran in his system. In human form, he wouldn't have much hope if another Goliath turned up. I might have beaten the bastard, but I suspected *that* had only happened because he hadn't been expecting a slender, elven female to put up so much of a fight.

The next time—if there were a next time—he'd be ready.

"Look, you might want to call Guy and invite him over.

This case I'm investigating for Lyle has turned nasty, and I'd rather you not be caught alone."

"I can take care of myself," he said mildly. "I don't need—"

"The last time we had an uninvited guest, it took three ogres to bring him down, and even they had trouble." I didn't bother mentioning my battle with Goliath. Keale would figure anything I could handle, he could.

"Oh. I'll invite Guy over, then."

"Good move." I handed him the house phone. "Tell him there's beer wasting away in the fridge. That'll get him here faster than you can hang up."

"He's not working today?"

"No. The union called a strike on the demolition site he's working on—apparently, they're still arguing working conditions. They've been out for weeks."

Keale nodded and dialed Guy's number. I squeezed back past Kristo and headed for Sandridge. I found parking just down the street from Val's and jogged back to his hot pink building. Mona's apartment still had the blue and yellow police tape strapped across it, and I wondered if Kaij thought she'd been murdered within. I rapped loudly on Val's door, and it was almost immediately answered by a tall, red-haired man whose muscular frame practically filled the doorway. Val obviously had far better luck with men than I did—but then, he *could* sing.

"You must be Harriet," he said, and stepped to one side.

"I prefer Harri. Val in the bedroom?"

"Yes." He closed the door then fell into step beside me. "See if you can talk some sense into him, will you? He won't report this to the police. Bedroom is to the right."

"Directions are somewhat superfluous given all anyone has to do is follow the sound of the dramatic sighs."

Bryan chuckled. "Yeah, he does rather like them. Would you like a coffee?"

"That would be great, thanks. White with one."

Walking into my brother's bedroom was like walking into the past. And it wasn't only the scents of orange and sage that swirled through the air, but also the color. He'd painted the room pastel pink, and offset it with lime green furnishings—the very same colors he'd had in his bedroom when we were both kids.

Val was propped in the middle of his king-sized bed, wearing a yellow nightshirt that clashed something shocking with the lime green sheets and comforter.

"Be still my heart," he said, clutching at his chest. "A voluntary visit from my sister! I don't know if I can take the shock."

Despite the bravado, someone had very definitely worked him over. Bruises were beginning to appear down the left side of his face, and his left eye had already closed over. There were cuts across his knuckles and raw looking scrapes visible through the open neck of his shirt. More serious was the cut across his neck. It was a good two inches long, though shallow. Someone had held a knife to my brother's throat.

Anger swirled, but I held it in check and sat on the edge of the bed. "What happened?"

"Walked into a rather large troll, didn't I?" He sighed heavily. "Now, if he'd been large and gay, I wouldn't have minded as much, but he wasn't."

"Just tell me what happened. Bare bones. No dramatics."

"You do take all the fun out of it, darls." He sniffed. "Bare bones, then. I was walking home with an arm full of groceries, and the fucking troll jumped out at me from the shadows two doors down and thrust a knife against my throat. Said if I so much as *thought* about trying anything funny, he'd slit it."

My gaze went to the wound again. *Bastards.* "So he knew you're a magician."

"Yes. So I did what any sane and normal person would do in that sort of situation—I fainted." He raised a hand, studying it intently. "I chipped three nails, too."

I snorted softly. Only my brother would worry about nails when his throat was in danger of being sliced. "What happened then?"

"I woke up in here, tied to a chair. Again, I wouldn't normally mind, but with trolls—"

"Val, I do not need or want to hear details of your love life," I said patiently. "Bare bones, no embellishments, remember?"

He grinned. He may have been beaten up, but he certainly wasn't beaten. "You're so straight, sister dearest, it's sometimes scary."

I gave him the 'look'. His grin widened. "As it turns out, the troll wasn't alone. There was a man—human, I think—with him. He started smacking me around to wake me, but the troll was to one side, knife at the ready should I try an incantation. I didn't bother."

"Wise move."

"I thought so. Anyway, when the human saw I was awake, he asked me if I remembered seeing anyone arguing in Mona's apartment. When I said I did, he smacked me. Needless to say, I caught on pretty quick."

"And once you told them what they wanted?"

"They asked about the sketches I did for you. I'm afraid I handed them over."

"If you hadn't, I'd be smacking you."

"Be careful, Harri, or I might think you actually care."

"Well, you *are* the only brother I can stand for more than a few minutes."

"Which is not exactly a compliment."

I grinned. "What happened after they got the drawings?"

"They patted me on the head and said that as long as I *didn't* remember, I'd be fine."

"You able to draw their images?"

"Way ahead of you, darls." He reached across to the bedside table and grabbed the two rolled-up pieces of paper sitting there. "Here you go."

I unrolled the sheets. The human was bald, with thin, almost gaunt features, pockmarked skin, and beady blue eyes. The troll was the Goliath who'd attacked me. Obviously, the police hadn't held him for very long.

I folded them up and tucked them into my purse. "You can't stay here."

"Which is what I've been telling him for the last few hours." Bryan walked into the room. He handed me a coffee, placed one on the table beside my brother, and sat down. "Those men are still out there, and I wouldn't like to trust the fact that they won't come back."

"But they got what they wanted—"

"For now," I cut in. "But you're still a witness, and they might just decide it would be easier all round to get rid of you."

His gaze slid down my body, and his expression got serious. "They did that?"

"Yes. And I've been threatened with death if I do anything that could destroy career aspirations. So, if he's willing to go that far with me, his daughter, then he's not likely to be concerned about doing the same to you."

"Who is this 'he' we're talking about?" Bryan asked.

"It's better you don't know," Val said, before I could. "Let's just say he's rich, well thought of, and extremely unpleasant."

"Then you definitely need to get out of here," Bryan said.

I glanced at him. "Could he stay at your place?"

"That has already been suggested," Val said. "But tell me, why can't I stay at yours?"

"Because they've already hit my place twice, Val."

His gaze scooted down my length again, and just for a moment, I saw fear in his eyes. Not just for himself, but for me. He knew as well as I did just what Bramwell was capable of.

"Okay," he said eventually. "Bryan's it is. But it is the most boring shade of beige I have ever seen. My light will definitely fade if I stay there for too long."

I snorted softly. "I doubt there's ever a chance of *that* happening. You, brother, are garish to the core."

"I know. And you love it."

I rolled my eyes and glanced back at Bryan. "Have you got time to take him there now?"

He glanced at his watch, then nodded and rose. "I'll start locking up. How long do you want him staying?"

"Hopefully, no more than a couple of days."

"I think we can both survive that."

"Not in a beige environment I won't," Val muttered, but there was a twinkle in his eyes. "Any other orders while you're bossing me about, sister?"

"Yeah, make like a wallflower and stay away from the clubs. If you have to go out, make sure you have someone with you."

He eyed me for a moment, amusement fading. "You be careful too, Harri. You're the one in the firing line, more so than me."

"I know, and I will." I squeezed his hand, and then rose. "You want me to pack some clothes for you?"

"No, it's faster if I do it." He waved his hands, muttered a few words, and pointed at his drawers. His clothes became mini missiles that flew across the room and jumped into an overnight bag.

"Next time I decide to go on holiday, remind me to get you over to pack for me."

He grinned as he climbed out of bed. "We both know that will never happen—a, because you don't take holidays, and b, because you'd be too scared I'd pack all the garish things."

"I don't own garish things." Which wasn't totally true—I did own a few rather bright dresses. I just didn't get to wear them anywhere these days.

I hovered close as he began to dress. Despite his bravado, he was obviously weak—a fact borne out by his choice of clothes. A red sweater and ochre pants were rather dull plumage when compared to what he normally wore.

"What about dinner tomorrow night?" he said, grabbing his bag from the nearby chair. "Is it still on?"

"If you're feeling up to it. If not, we can wait a week or so."

"Darls, even if I was half dead and in the hospital, I'd still drag myself there. We both know if it's delayed it may never eventuate."

Which wasn't exactly a fair statement—I had given my word, after all. But I didn't say anything, just stepped back and waved him past.

"Everything is locked up," Bryan said, coming to the bedroom door and taking Val's bag from him.

I followed them out. As Bryan locked the front door, I said, "Is it worth putting a transport spell on the door?"

Val's sudden grin was decidedly wicked. "I like your thinking. Suppose we send them to the local police station, huh? Let them explain *that* one."

"Brilliant idea."

"I do get them occasionally."

"Emphasis on occasionally," Bryan said, voice dry.

Val gave him a whack on the arm and Bryan grinned. Just for a moment, regret stirred through me. I'd once had a relationship like that—a relationship filled with warm teasing—and I so wanted to find that with someone again.

Once Val had set his spell, we walked down the stairs and across the road to Bryan's car. Like everything else about him, it was a conservative dark blue Toyota sedan. It had to be love, I thought with a smile. Normally Val wouldn't be caught dead in something so...normal.

"What time tomorrow?" Bryan said, over the top of the car.

I shrugged. "From six onwards. There's no rush."

Bryan nodded then climbed into the car. I watched the pair of them drive away, then resolutely dug my phone out of my purse and rang the bastard otherwise known as my father.

"Phillecky residence," came Jose bored tones. "How may I help you?"

"I'd like to speak to my father please."

Jose paused. I suspected he was surprised. "Whom may I say is calling?"

"His daughter."

Again the pause. "One moment."

Take that, father dearest, I thought, though I knew it would do little to endear me to him. Like that was *ever* going to happen, anyway.

There was a click then, after several seconds, Bramwell came onto the line. "Don't ever do that again-"

"Or what?" I cut in. "You'll beat me up? Just like you did my brother?"

"I did no such-"

"Bullshit. The only persons who have any knowledge of—or interest in—getting the drawings and ensuring Val stayed quiet are you and Gilroy, and we both know your son doesn't like to get his hands dirty."

Silence met my reply. I continued on.

"You made a major mistake in doing that, father. For one, it was only when *you* were told of their existence that Val was threatened."

Bramwell sniffed. "Frank Logan's temper is well renowned. He has as many reasons as Gilroy for wanting this event hushed—"

"I haven't talked to Logan, so unless you've suddenly decided to confide all to him, he certainly doesn't know about the drawings. Not even the cops do. Besides, Frank would have confronted Val himself, not hired a troll and a thug to do his dirty work."

"You have no evidence to prove any of this—"

"I haven't finished yet," I cut in again, more brusquely this time. "So shut the fuck up and listen."

I could practically feel the fury leeching down the phone lines. I continued on regardless. In for a penny, in for a pound, as the old saying went.

"If he's touched again, if he has so much as a hair mussed out of place, every scrap of evidence I currently have will not only find its way to the cops, but will be splashed across the front page of every newspaper in this country. And that threat is not an idle one—I still have enough contacts in the industry to ensure it happens."

"I will do what I must to protect my son." Bramwell's voice vibrated with anger. The legendary Elven coolness had well and truly left the building.

"Yeah, well, I'll do what I must to protect *my* brother."

"Gilroy is your brother, too."

I snorted. "Oh, that's very convenient, isn't it? You inviting me to the next family get together, then?"

The silence that met my question was almost contemptuous. "Didn't think so."

"Gilroy did *not* murder the siren."

"I've never said he did. But he was involved with her, and she was definitely blackmailing him. That alone is enough mud to destroy his immediate political plans. Oh, and don't bother sending someone around to my place to beat me into submission or force me to hand over the cards. I've made several copies of them and deposited them in safe places. If anything happens to me, they *will* be sent straight to the cops."

And that, I thought, was something I had better fucking do. Never poke a bear if you couldn't protect yourself from the bear's response.

"You will live to regret this course of action."

As long as I lived, I didn't really care. "Just remember, you value your reputation more than I do mine. You might be better reconsidering your position, and offering me and Lyle the help we need to find the killer."

"I have told you the truth, and you will get nothing more than that from either of us."

"If you *have* told the truth, fine. If you haven't, expect to hear from me again."

And with that, I hung up and blew out a long, somewhat shaky breath. Deed done, warning given. Now I just had to hope that Bramwell reacted with common sense, not emotion, not fury. If he did the latter, then the shit would *really* hit the fan.

I shoved my phone back into my purse, then resolutely turned and headed for my car. One problem faced, several more to go. I needed to go talk to Rebecca, and I also needed to talk to Kaij. He might not be inclined to confirm whether Mona had been pregnant or not, but I still had to try.

But it wasn't something I could ask over the phone. He

could wave the question away far too easily that way. But *that* actually meant enduring another physical meeting.

I bit my bottom lip, dithering between the need to get it over with and the desire to delay it as long as feasibly possible, and eventually fell on the side of avoidance.

Forty-five minutes later I was in Warrandyte, and parking at the Grand Hotel. It was a majestic, two-story wooden building complete with wrought-iron lacework and gleaming stained glass windows. It had always looked like something pulled out of the fifties to me—an ancient remnant of an era that enjoyed detailed exteriors as much as they did interiors.

I made my way inside. The fire had been set within the old hearth, and smoky warmth filled the air. I walked around the casual burgundy and dark wood furniture and gave the bartender a friendly smile interlaced with just a hint of siren magic.

"Hey," he said, an answering smile tugging at his lips. "What can I get for you?"

"A lemon-lime and soda would be great, thanks." I waited until he'd started, then added, "Is Rebecca around?"

"No, she's not, I'm afraid."

"Damn." I got out some notes to pay for my drink. "Don't suppose you know where I can find her?"

He handed me the drink and scooped up the notes. "Not sure. She rang in sick a day or so ago, and we haven't heard from her since."

Interesting timing. "Do you know if she lives around here?"

"She might." He studied me, brown eyes curious. "Why?"

"She asked me here to talk about some photos she wanted done." I dug out my card and handed it to him. "I was supposed to meet her after she finished her shift today."

"Oh." He glanced at the card then tucked it under the till. "Well, as I said, she hasn't been in for the last couple of days —bloody inconsiderate when we're short staffed, I tell you."

"Damn," I muttered, forcing an edge of disappointment into my voice. "I guess it means she doesn't want those photos."

"Hey, she might turn up. She certainly has the balls to walk into the bar after not bothering to call us." He gave me a somewhat cheeky grin. "I'm Jack, by the way. And I certainly don't mind standing here talking to a pretty lady."

I smiled. He was human, but he exuded a warm, country boy charm even if he wasn't exactly handsome. We chatted comfortably until I finished my drink and was able to leave without blowing my cover story.

Back in the car, I pulled out the street directory and looked up the street Keale had mentioned. Joslyn Road was only a couple of streets away, and it was easy enough to find. I cruised along until I found a picket fence covered in white and yellow daisies, then stopped and climbed out.

Number eight, like most of the houses in the street, had been built into a slope steep enough to ski down. The driveway was as close to vertical as you were ever likely to get, and not something I'd want to chance, even if my car's brakes were top notch. The house itself was nondescript—a small, double fronted brick house surrounded by huge gum trees that kept it in shadow and covered the red tin roof with leaves.

After grabbing my bag, I locked the car and made my way down the steep, mossy steps to the front door. I pressed the doorbell and heard it chime inside, but there were no answering footsteps. The place seemed empty—not that I was surprised given what Jack had said.

I stepped back and studied the windows to either side. The curtains were fully drawn, making it impossible to peer inside. I made my way around to the side gate, unlatched it, and then whistled softly, just to ensure there was no dog. Nothing came bounding around the corner at me, so I opened it fully and entered. The back door presented a similar story to the front—fully locked and no response to my knocking.

"The owner's not here," a voice said to my right.

I jumped and turned around. A gray-haired woman was giving me the evil eye over the top of the run-down paling fence. I restrained my grin. Nosy neighbors were one of the best resources of information around—certainly there was nothing going on in my neighborhood that Delilah didn't know about.

"That's odd, because I got a call from Rebecca asking me to come here and take some photos of the house."

The woman snorted. "Don't know what for. She was only renting the place, wasn't she?"

"Really? How long was she living here, then?"

"Came here a couple of weeks ago. There should be a law

against her type, you know. They shouldn't be allowed in the suburbs."

I raised an eyebrow. "Her *type?*"

"You know, dragons. Bloody bitch was in heat, wasn't she? Making a goddamn racket all night and whoring it up in the skies. I had to keep the grandkiddies in all week. Can't have them seeing that sort of stuff, can I?"

"I guess not." I hesitated. "Any idea where Rebecca might be at the moment? She gave me her work address, but she's not there, either."

"Well, she wouldn't be, would she?"

"Why not?"

"Because she left again, didn't she? Packed up everything and took off yesterday. Maybe someone *did* complain." She sniffed. It was a self-righteous sound. "I was out there, I can tell you, making sure she put nothing in that van that wasn't hers."

If it had been Delilah, she would have been out there telling the removal guys how to do their job properly. "Don't suppose you know where she was going?"

"Didn't care, did I?"

"What about the removal van—do you remember anything about it?"

She eyed me for several seconds, her expression dourer. "You ask a lot of bloody questions for a photographer."

"Well, she paid me a deposit." I shrugged. "I have to make an effort to return it if I can't take the photos she wanted."

"Honest, huh?" She sniffed. "That's a rarity these days. Most folks seem related to sharks, especially those in the damn supermarkets-"

"The van," I interrupted, sensing a tirade coming on.

"It was white."

And there were only a few thousand of them tootling around Berren. "Any distinguishing marks? Logos?"

"It had the word *express* painted in green. And a picture of a little truck doing wheelies—I remember that. My grandson thought it was cute."

It was something, at least. "Did she use the same truck when she arrived?"

She frowned. "Couldn't be certain, but I think so."

"Did she have any friends helping her? Someone I might be able to contact her through?"

"Well, she had plenty of men friends over the last week, I can tell you that."

"But did any of them help her move in or out?"

"No, there was only the elf."

The hairs on the back of my neck prickled. "Elf? Could you describe him?"

"They all look the bloody same, don't they?" Her gaze suddenly narrowed. "You're one of them, aren't you?"

"My father was an elf," I said, beginning to run out of patience. "What about—"

217

"It shouldn't be allowed," she said, voice somewhat belligerent. "Like should keep to like."

And what a boring world *that* would be. "Was the elf young or old?"

"Hard to say with bloody elves, isn't it? You're all blessed with long life and good preservation. Bloody unfair it is—"

"Well, thanks for your help," I cut in, before she could go off again. I dug the business card out of my pocket and handed it to her. "If she does happen to return, can you ask her to ring me?"

I spun on my heels and walked back toward the gate, but she wasn't quite finished with me yet.

"I did get a number plate, if that's any use to you."

I paused, closed my eyes briefly, and then forced a smile as I turned around. "Rebecca had a car?"

"No, not the dragon. That wouldn't make much sense, now, would it?"

Well, actually, it did. Dragons might be able to fly, but they did have the twelve-hour restriction when shifting into either shape, and that made casual flight a tad more problematic.

"Then who?" Despite my best effort, irritation edged my tone. This woman was even more annoying than Delilah, and I hadn't thought that possible.

"The elf, of course. He was here Friday night. Thought he was a burglar at first, because the dragon wasn't home and he didn't park in the drive but down the street some. The dragon came home later, just before one of her skinny male friends arrived." She stopped and frowned. "Odd that. It was the only night we didn't hear them making out."

Friday night was the night Keale had gone on his drinking binge, so it couldn't have been him she'd spotted. "Did the elf leave before or after they arrived?"

"Didn't see him leave." Her tone implied she would have.

"Would I be able to grab a copy of the number plate? I might be able to get a friend to track down the owner for me."

"Sure. Hang on a sec."

She disappeared from the fence line, but reappeared a few minutes later, cheeks flushed, as if she'd been running. "Here it is."

I accepted the grubby piece of paper with a smile of thanks. It wasn't a number plate I knew, but that didn't mean anything given it was easy enough to hire a car. "Do you remember what type of car it was?"

"Red Toyota. Rented through Avis."

I raised my eyebrows. "You sure?"

She looked down her nose at me. "Of course."

I had a sudden image of her scurrying up the street, nose twitching inquisitively as she jotted down all the details, and had to restrain a grin. "Thank you very much for your help. If you happen to see the elf come here again, could you give me a call?"

Not that I expected either of them to turn up again. Whatever had been going on here, they'd obviously moved on.

"There money in it if I do?"

If it helped make sense of this mess, then why not? "Sure."

She nodded, looking pleased. "I'll keep a look out then."

"Thanks," I said, and made my escape.

But back in my car, I was confronted by two more choices. See Kaij, ask my questions, or go home.

If I wanted answers, I had to choose the former, even if every part of me was desperate to choose the latter.

If I was going to do this, I had to do it now, before I totally chickened out.

I took a deep breath that did nothing to calm the butterflies in my stomach, then started the car and headed back to Berren.

CHAPTER NINE

M y gut had twisted itself into serious knots by the time I walked into the preternatural squad's Matthews Street headquarters. My footsteps echoed softly on the marble tiles, and the pleasant-looking woman sitting at the security desk looked up.

Her smile was warm, but her gaze assessing. "Can I help you?"

"I'd like to see Kaij Raintree, please."

"Do you have an appointment?"

"No, I'm afraid not."

"I'll see if he's available." She picked up the phone, then raised an eyebrow and added, "And you are?"

"Harri Phillecky."

"One moment, then."

She pressed a button then waited. I turned away and studied the austere foyer. It was all glass and grayness, with the floor tiles practically merging into the walls. There were no chairs, nothing in the way of color, and little that would, in any way, invite someone to wait around. If not for the small silver sign announcing this was the divisional headquarters of the preternatural squad on the wall behind the security desk, it would have been hard to guess this was even a police station. Although the banks of scanners that divided the foyer from the lift area certainly left the impression that this was no ordinary office building.

"Detective Raintree will be down shortly," the security guard said.

"Thanks."

I walked over to the front windows, but the sunshine pouring through didn't do much to lift the chill from my skin. I rubbed my arms, my stomach still doing flip-flops as I fought the urge to run.

So much for the thought that subsequent meetings would be easier than the first.

After what seemed like ages, one of the lifts behind the scanners swished open, and footsteps echoed softly. I took a deep breath that didn't calm the tension, then slowly turned to face him.

His gaze swept me briefly then rose to meet mine. Once again, there was little in the way of expression and absolutely no way to tell what he might be thinking.

He came to a halt several feet away and crossed his arms. "What do you want, Harri?"

I hesitated. "That depends on how willing you are to share some information."

"You know I can't—"

"What I know," I interrupted, "is that the preternatural squad can play hard and lose when it comes to the rules. I might have some information you'll find useful, but I need a favor in return."

For several seconds he did nothing more than stare, his expression remote, yet somehow so judgmental. I didn't flinch or react, returning his gaze evenly even though his warm, foresty scent filled every breath and stirred to life the long dead ashes of love and desire, pain and anger.

Eventually, he said, "There's a coffee shop down the road. Let's go."

He didn't wait for me to respond, just strode past me, all energy and brooding darkness. I released a breath, prayed for strength, then spun on my heels and followed him out.

The coffee shop was large and crowded. He wove his way through the tables with a deftness that spoke of easy familiarity—a thought that was confirmed when a pretty blonde waitress came over to us.

"Same as usual, Kaij?"

A smile briefly broke the austerity of his expression. "Make it a double. I think I'm going to need the caffeine hit."

"Been one of those days, has it?" she said, voice sympathetic.

"Let's just say it's taken a dramatic nosedive."

He said it lightly, but it didn't take a genius to know where that particular barb had been aimed. I forced a smile as the waitress glanced at me inquiringly. "A regular coffee, and a slice of cake, thanks."

"Chocolate, carrot, or white mud?"

"Carrot would be nice."

She wrote it down then tucked her notepad away. "Won't be long."

Kaij waited until she left, then leaned back in his chair and crossed his arms again. "What do you want?"

"Two things." My tone was as blunt as his. "But first, I'd like to pick your brains about Prevoron."

Surprise flitted briefly through his green eyes. "Why?"

I hesitated. "I suppose you heard about the dragon crashing into the helicopter?"

"You'd have to have your head stuck in the sand *not* to hear about it. It's all over the news."

"Well, that dragon was Keale."

He snorted softly. "Which is not entirely surprising. The stupid bastard should have had his wings permanently clipped years ago."

Which was probably true, given the amount he tended to drink. "Despite all the evidence to the contrary, I think he might have been drugged rather than drunk."

"That's no excuse." Kaij's voice was grim. "Drunk, drugged, he still killed four people and he has to pay."

"What if he wasn't responsible for either the drug or his subsequent actions?"

He studied me for several seconds, his expression still neutral and giving little away. "If Prevoron is in his system, it would have been detected during blood tests."

"Not if they weren't looking for it. Prevoron is virtually undetectable when first administered unless you're specifically looking for it, isn't it?"

His nod was a short, sharp movement that spoke of annoyance. Whether its source was my presence or the subject matter was anyone's guess.

"So, if a Prevoron test was requested, how long would it take to come through?"

"It would depend on how busy the lab is, but generally only twenty-four hours, especially on a high-profile case like that."

"Then my first request is, can you check Keale's blood results, and if he hasn't been tested for Prevoron, could you arrange it?" And soon, I wanted to add, but didn't push my luck. Although if he wasn't tested soon, it wouldn't matter, because the drug would have started leeching from his system.

He gave no indication he would, just said, "And the second request?"

"I wanted to know if Mona was pregnant. And, if she was, was a DNA test performed on the fetus?"

"What gives you the idea she might have been pregnant?"

I hesitated. "I've been talking to her driver."

"Who we have been unable to track down. It appears he's been absent from his office, has shifted out of his house, and left no forwarding address." He studied me for a moment. "How did you find him?"

So Darryl had gone into hiding. I couldn't say I blamed him after what had happened to Val, especially given his knowledge of events were a whole lot more damaging than Val's ever could be.

"I was lucky enough to run into him."

"I just bet." His voice was skeptical. "And, of course, you have no idea where he is now."

"No, but he does appear sporadically at his office. I caught him there this morning."

The waitress appeared with our drinks and my cake, and a smile briefly lifted Kaij's expression again. It made me remember all the times he'd looked at me with such warmth, and found myself fighting the sudden sting of tears.

Which was stupid, because there was no hope of us going back to the way we were. Not now, not ever. Too much had happened between us.

I kept my gaze down, concentrating on stirring sugar into my coffee until I had the memories and tears under control. Not that it would do much good—he was a dark fae, and sensitive to the currents of strong emotion. It was part of the reason he was such a good cop.

Of course, that sharing was a two-way street—or rather, it had been—simply because I was siren enough to have formed a connection with him. Whether that connection still held after so many years apart I had no idea, and I certainly had no desire to test it. But if the flashes I kept catching were any indication, it was there to be explored if I *did* want to.

"Why do you want to know whether Mona was pregnant?" he asked, almost brusquely.

I raised my gaze again. There was no sympathy in his eyes. No echoes of the past. No pain. What had happened between us had obviously been dealt with, and he'd moved on.

I thought I had, too.

I pulled the cake toward me and picked up the spoon. "Because it might just provide a clue as to who killed her."

He leaned forward abruptly. "If you know something, it is in your best interest to tell me."

I met him glare for glare. "*Was* she pregnant?"

I wasn't about to give him any information if he wasn't at least willing to give me that crumb.

"No." His voice was flat, but an odd sort of tension surrounded him. "She apparently had a miscarriage five days before she was murdered."

A *miscarriage*. Just for a second, all the old pain rose and I had to close my eyes against the grief that never went entirely away. No wonder she'd been acting a little crazy. Grief made you do strange things. It certainly had for me.

God, if Lyle ever found that out, Frank was a dead man. I met Kaij's gaze again. There was nothing to be seen in those green depths. Not even ashes.

It hurt, but it also made me angry, even if I'd expected little else from him.

"Look," he said, before I could react in any way. "I'll see what I can do about Keale, but you really need to tell me what you know. Otherwise, I'll have to make this interview official."

I ate my cake as I contemplated my options, but the truth was, I really didn't have that many. If the information I passed on was kept off the books, then I had a chance of going under the radar as far as my father was concerned. But if it became official, there was no damn chance of that happening. My father had many contacts in the force, and far too many of them owed him favors.

"Okay," I said. "But you heard none of this from me."

"Meaning," he said, voice holding the slightest hint of distaste. "Your damn family is involved."

"Yeah." Dark fae and elves generally co-existed pretty nicely, but the Phillecky clan had never been afraid to step on toes, and over the years had become *persona non grata* in the dark fae community. Which hadn't made it easy for me, either before or after Kaij and I had split. "Lyle wasn't the only Phillecky seeing her. Gilroy had been, too."

"Fuck." He scraped a hand across his chin.

"Yeah. And it gets worse." I told him about James Logan, Mona's blackmailing efforts, and Frank beating her up. "Both Gilroy and James paid her, but according to Gilroy, she wasn't happy and demanded more."

"Which makes him a prime suspect."

"Except for the fact he was in New Zealand when she was murdered."

He raised an eyebrow. "You really think that clears him?"

"I know what my family is capable of, so no." I paused. "I do, however, believe him when he says he did not kill her."

"And why would he have to, when he has a father who would do it all for him?"

I grimaced. "Yes, but I don't think he killed her, either. Mona was raped, and my father's views on *that* are well enough known."

"How did you know—" He stopped, then shook his head. "Lyle had to identify the body. He obviously got the information from someone in the coroner's office."

"He has plenty of contacts—"

"Your whole damn family has plenty of contacts. And *far* too many powerful ones." He eyed me grimly. "You know I'll have to talk to them all."

"If you go to them with the information I've given you, they'll know I'm the source."

And they'd make me pay. I didn't say the words out loud but it hung between us all the same.

He was silent for several minutes. Weighing up the pros and cons of tackling my father and brother against the backwash I'd cop. His gaze flicked briefly to bruises and scratches on my arms, and something ran through his eyes. Not concern, but maybe frustration.

It was something. Not much, but something.

"Then what the hell do you expect me to do?"

"Talk to Frank Logan. He beat her up once—maybe he did it again. Someone was arguing with her the day after she was paid the money—maybe it was him." I hesitated. "Did you find any money in her apartment?"

"No. And it didn't make her bank account, either." He eyed me for a minute. "I suppose you asked her driver about it?"

"Yes. He generally did her banking, but not recently."

"And you think he was telling the truth?"

"Yes."

He grunted. "We still need to talk to him."

"And then go talk to Lyle. It won't take very much pressure to get the information you need out of him, and my father won't kill him. He's family."

"Is that what he's threatened? To *kill* you?"

I smiled, but it was a bitter thing. "Why do you sound surprised? My family hates me almost as much as your family does."

"My family doesn't—"

I snorted. "Your mother practically did a song and dance when we broke—"

"*Don't*," he cut in, his expression suddenly fierce. "Because it is neither true nor warranted. She was as broken as you and me by events."

Events. Even now, all these years later, he couldn't bring himself to acknowledge the miscarriage. It was both sad and infuriating. Damn it, we'd lost our *daughter*. And just when I'd needed him the most, he'd retreated. Physically, mentally. Unable to cope, and blaming me for the loss.

I grabbed a pen and a piece of paper from my bag, scrawled Lyle's phone number on it, and then thrust it across the table. "Contact Lyle. Talk to him before you go to my father. Give me that much, at least."

I rose. His gaze followed me. If he saw the sadness and fury, he gave no sign of it. "Thank you."

I nodded and spun away. But I'd barely gone two steps when he said, "And Harri?"

I stopped and clenched my fist, fighting the urge to run. Fighting the need to turn around and say all the things I hadn't been able to say all those years ago.

"What?"

"Thank you for allowing Ayasha to be buried on ancestral lands"

I didn't reply. I *couldn't* reply. I just nodded and got the hell out of there.

But I was shaking by the time I got to my car. For several minutes, I did nothing more than breathe deeply in a vague attempt to calm the tempest that roared deep inside. It didn't help, and I once again found myself crying for not only the daughter I'd lost, but for what might have been.

Damn it, why couldn't he have stayed away? Why did he have to come back and raise old ghosts?

Because until those ghosts are confronted, neither of us really can move on.

And that meant, like it or not, we *would* be talking again. Because that inner intuition was right. We needed to confront past events if we wanted a future that was brighter. Or at least, *I* did.

I suspected he did too, even if he'd given very little evidence of it so far. I really couldn't think of any other reason for him to come back to Berren.

I wiped the last of the tears away with the palm of my hands then started up the car and drove home. Kristo's little van was still at the front of my place. I parked just behind it and then climbed out. The TV was once again blasting full bore and, from the sound of it, it was a repeat of one of the weekend's game. Kristo was on his knees next to the front gate, intently studying the section that scraped the concrete.

"I could shave this gate, you know," he said, without looking up. "Otherwise you're going to end up wrecking the hinges."

"What year would you be intending to do it?" I asked, stepping over his crouched form.

"Oh, this year," he said, all seriousness. "Probably in a week or so."

"Okay. Guy's paying you for the front door, by the way."

Kristo nodded, moving the gate back and forth, his frown deepening. "He's giving me first go at the wreckage from the demolition site he's working. It's amazing the stuff they throw out, you know. Most of its still very serviceable."

I'd seen what he considered serviceable, and most of it belonged where it had originally been headed—the tip. I left the gnome crouched on the concrete and walked into the house.

Guy and Keale were sitting either end of the couch, beers in hand. I walked over to the TV and turned the sound down to a more normal level.

"Harri my friend," Guy said, raising his beer in greeting. "How are you this fine day?"

I smiled. Ogres may be loud, they might keep your fridge and pantry empty, but at least they were always happy to see you. "You staying for lunch?"

"But of course."

I glanced at Keale. "How are you feeling?"

"Better now that I have a few of these in me." He shook the beer lightly.

I frowned. "Isn't it a condition of bail that you don't drink?"

"Nah. They didn't mention booze, just the whole no flying outside work hours bit."

I left them watching the game and walked into the kitchen to rustle up something to eat for us all. They wandered in just as I was finishing the last of the sandwiches.

Guy parked on a chair and grabbed several sandwiches. "Keale was saying you don't think his accident was an accident."

I poured myself a coffee then picked out a couple of salmon sandwiches and sat down opposite the two of them. "He also thinks I'm grabbing at straws, but there's just too many coincidences stacking up for my liking."

"Need any help?"

"Maybe." I took a bite of my lunch, and then said, "I don't suppose you know anyone in the removal van business, do you?"

"Why?"

"Because Rebecca's next door neighbor told me she used a removal van with the logo of a truck doing wheelies, and the word *express* on it. I haven't been able to find it in the yellow pages."

"I think Shemp has family in the business, so he might be able to help."

"I take it from that comment," Keale cut in, "That you didn't manage to chase up Rebecca?"

"No. She wasn't at work, and she's vacated the house." I picked up another sandwich and bit into it. "James the bartender told me she reported in sick a few days ago, and hasn't been sighted since."

"James, heh?"

I grinned. "He's lovely, but not my type."

"This," Guy said heavily, "from the woman who was complaining not so long ago that her love life was as sparse as the hairs on Kristo's head."

"I resent that," came Kristo's comment. "Even my hair isn't that sparse!"

"What, my love life has become a neighborhood topic now?"

"I'm afraid so." Keale's solemn expression was somewhat destroyed by the amusement dancing in his dark eyes. "But it's easily fixed. Just find yourself a decent man."

I snorted softly. "Yeah, it's *that* easy."

Guy waved a hand airily. "I'm sure it could be, if you really wanted it bad enough."

"Listen," I said, somewhat exasperated. "We're supposed to be talking about *Keale's* love life, not mine."

"Oh. Yeah. Rebecca." Keale took a swig of beer. "Haven't heard from her, and she didn't leave any messages for me."

"And you have no idea how to contact her?"

"Nope. Dragon ladies like to take the lead, and it's not worth arguing with them. She always contacted me, not the other way around."

So Rebecca was a dead end unless we could find the removal van or rental car. I munched on my sandwich for several minutes. "Did she mention friends, or family, or anything that would give us a clue as to where she might be?"

He shook his head. "She was in season. We had mad sex, not conversation. But I could try the union. She might be a member."

I nodded. It wasn't compulsory for people to belong to unions these days and, as a result, the League of Australian Dragons—like most other unions—had steadily falling numbers. I suspected the current climate of reasonable working conditions made many think the unions were superfluous.

"Do it. We need to find out what happened during those hours you can't remember."

"Why? I wasn't even with her the night I ended up over the city."

"I know. I just want to talk to her."

"*If* there *is* Prevoron in my system, she could hardly have given it to me. As I said, I didn't see her."

I nodded and told him what the nosy neighbor had reported. He frowned. "Well, it couldn't have been me she spotted. As I keep saying, I wasn't there."

And he could keep on saying it, as far as I was concerned. It wouldn't change my mind that there was something rather odd about her abrupt departure.

Guy grabbed another sandwich, then said, "I'm gathering from your expression you suspect Rebecca might have given Keale the Prevoron."

"If there *is* Prevoron," Keale commented dryly. "Hey, don't get me wrong, I'd love there to be a more reasonable explanation other than my own stupidity, but to suspect Rebecca? When she wasn't with me that night?"

I half-shrugged. "I know, but it all just feels wrong. I mean, think about it. You have a night you can't remember and end up smashing into a helicopter, and the very next day, she disappears? Doesn't that seem a little bit odd to either of you?"

"We don't know she's disappeared," Keale stated. "She might have just moved out. Dragons aren't always welcome in neighborhoods, especially during the mating period. In

236

fact, I was a little surprised she'd chosen to remain there—most females retreat to the country during the breeding season."

"Keale, she moved out a week and a half after moving in. That's a bit suss, whichever way you look at it."

"Never trust a woman," Guy said solemnly.

Keale snorted. "This from the ogre who only has to have an ogress look his way, and he's her floormat."

"Have you seen the size of some of them ogresses? You'd be a floormat too, man."

I grinned, and then glanced around as Delilah stomped in. She'd obviously not had a good run on the bus this morning —her hair was all over the place, and there were bits of rolled up lolly paper hanging off the ends like Christmas baubles. "That Kristo still here?"

"Out the front—why?" I asked.

"The bloody mirror in my bathroom is smashed."

"Is it any bloody wonder," Keale muttered.

Guy snorted, then clapped a hand over his mouth when Delilah glared at him. "I'm not laughing," he mumbled between his fingers. "Really, I'm not."

Delilah harrumphed then headed up the hall, shouting Kristo's name as Keale and Guy burst into laughter. The phone chose that moment to ring, so I retreated into the living room to answer it.

"Harri? Darryl here."

I muted the TV so I could hear him better. "How'd you go with Mona's accounts?"

I knew from Kaij that the money hadn't made it into them, but it would have seemed suspicious if I didn't ask. I didn't want him knowing I'd been talking to PIT—he might decide to clam up.

"No luck, money wise," he said. "I got a copy of her statement—her account hasn't been touched in over a week."

"Listen, I have her clientele list here—I don't suppose you can do some snooping, and see if any of them might have suddenly come into a fair bit of cash?"

"I can try. No promises though—most people tend to be tight-lipped when it comes to their activities with sirens."

He gave me his phone number. I quickly scrawled it down, then said, "I bet most wouldn't want to get involved with a police investigation, either. They might prefer talking to you over the police."

"I'm betting they'll talk to you easier than me. And you're easier on the eye, as well."

I smiled at the compliment. "Thanks, but I have to tread a little lightly at the moment."

"Given who could be involved, I can understand that need."

"Yeah. Oh, and the cops are looking for you. If you don't want to talk to them, avoid your office for a while."

"Thanks for the tip. Send me that list, and I'll see what I can do."

"Thanks, Darryl."

I hung up then headed upstairs. The desktops were still bereft of their hard drives, so I hauled out one of the old laptops and spent the rest of the day doing what little paperwork there was and confirming the photographic appointments I had for the rest of the week. It was those appointments that were keeping us afloat at the moment—as Ceri had noted, we really *did* need business to take off soon or we'd be in real financial straits.

Once four o'clock rolled around, I headed downstairs and started preparing for Val's dinner get-together. Keale was asleep on the couch, and Guy was nowhere to be seen. Maybe the beer had run out again.

Ceri came in just as I was putting the last lasagna into the oven. "Need any help?"

"You can keep an eye on the food, but other than that, we're set." I undid my apron and slung it into the laundry. I updated her on everything I'd discovered over the day, and then added, "I also did the accounts. The weepy wife's payment went through."

"Good. I was a bit worried she'd renege given she really *didn't* want the news we gave her." She glanced at her watch. "You'd better go change. Everyone will be arriving at any minute."

I did just that. Guy, not unsurprisingly, was the first to arrive.

"Harri my friend," he said, as he came through the front door. "I've bought some beer."

I raised an eyebrow. Not only had he bought beer, but he'd dressed for the occasion. He was wearing a shirt and a tie

239

rather than his much beloved blue singlet, although the shirt was bright green and the tie purple. Color sense and ogres weren't often on speaking terms. "Why? It's not Christmas yet."

The ogre grinned and grabbed a can before thrusting the rest of the slab at me. "Moe and Curly heard you were making lasagna and invited themselves around."

Just as well I'd made plenty of lasagna. "What about Shemp? I thought those three traveled in a pack?"

"His missus put her foot down, and there ain't no wiggling room when an ogress does that."

I laughed and headed for the kitchen, making room for the beer in the fridge then tossing the empty box into the bin. Keale wandered in, looking tired and limping just a little. He nodded a greeting to Ceri then sat down beside Guy.

"I was thinking about Rebecca—how to find her, I mean."

"And?"

"I remember her mentioning a friend. Lena something. She lived out Lalor way."

"We need a bit more than that to go on," Ceri said.

"No kidding?" Sarcasm edge Keale's tone. "She works at the airport, in the air traffic section."

Ceri and I exchanged a glance. She said, "If Rebecca *is* involved in this, she could have easily gotten hold of the pilot's flight plans."

"The question is," I countered, "would that have left

enough time to drug Keale and prime him to hit the helicopter?"

"Hell, yeah," she said. "That stuff is potent. Within ten minutes of consumption you could get them to whistle Dixie in a pink tutu."

"Now *that* is something I'd like to see," Guy said, raising his can of beer at Keale. The dragon gave him a one-fingered salute.

"How easy is it to get, though?" I asked. "I know small quantities are readily enough available on street corners, but not the amount required to make a dragon malleable."

And if he *had* been drugged, then it was by someone who was familiar with the drug, because if they'd given him too much the side effects would have been evident by now.

"No, but just about any street dealer can tell you where to get it." She hesitated. "I could check with an old source, and see if she knows of any largish sales of the drug recently. If we could track down who sold it, we might be able to uncover the buyer."

"Worth a shot."

She nodded and glanced at Keale. "Did Lyle mention whether or not the test results had come through?"

He shook his head. "He barely spoke to me. Just did what he had to do in court, and rushed off."

To do what? I wondered again uneasily. It seemed odd behavior for someone who'd seemed intent on drinking himself into oblivion until then.

Ceri frowned. "Those results should have been through by now given the high profile of the case."

"That's what I thought." I hesitated, and then added, "I asked Kaij to check whether they've been done or not."

Surprise rippled across her features, but before she could say anything, Guy said, "Kaij? The dark fae who abandoned you, Kaij?"

"Yeah," I said softly. "That one."

"You want me to arranging a good thumping?"

I smiled and touched his arm. "Thanks, but no."

"I will. Anytime. The bastard deserves it."

Yeah, he did—but back then, not now. Ceri said, "When did he arrive back?"

I shrugged. "He's the preternatural squad's investigating officer on Mona's case, though."

She eyed me for a moment, concern evident. "Are you okay?"

I nodded, but was saved from saying anything as the doorbell rang. I rose and walked down the hall, but the door opened before I could get there. Moe and Curly smiled in greeting, handed me a large platter of appetizers, then moseyed on past. Like Guy, they'd dressed up for the occasion, wearing matching red shirts and yellow ties. If nothing else, it was going to be a colorful night. My brother might just find himself being outshone.

Maggie arrived next, parking her broom in the closet before handing me several bottles of homemade wine. "Give it to the ogres," she said with a grin. "It'll ease the risk of wind outbreaks."

"It must be pretty powerful stuff, then."

"Oh, it is. And it even tastes good."

She made her way into the kitchen and joined in the conversation. Val and Bryan were the next to arrive, and while I *had* thought my brother risked being outshone, I really should have known better. The platinum curls had been artfully streaked with pink and gold, and he wore a gossamer shirt that shone with the brilliance of mother of pearl and shimmered with various shades of pink and purple every time he moved. His pants and shoes were metallic gold.

Bryan looked positively staid in comparison, dressed in dark grays and black.

"God," I said, "It's only lasagna, Val. You didn't have to get *that* dressed up."

Val waved a hand at me, fingernails glittering. "Darls, we both know another invitation might not be forthcoming, so I intend to shine while I can."

"Well, you're certainly doing that." I stepped to one side and waved them through. "Though it's a wonder Bryan's not gone blind from the glow of that outfit."

"I was wearing sunglasses until a moment ago," he said, amusement in his voice. He kissed my cheek then added, "But hey, it's nice to see someone totally unafraid to express themselves so...exuberantly."

"That's one word for it." I closed the door and followed them down the hall.

"Fucking hell, it's the neon fairy!" Keale said, his grin wide. "Nice to see you again, old chap."

"Enough with the old, cinder brain," Val retorted, and slapped Keale on the back. "Heard you had a bit of a problem with a helicopter."

"You could say that," he returned, wincing a little and stepping away from Val's reach.

As he filled Val and Bryan in on what had happened, I headed into the kitchen to finish meal preparations. Delilah was the last to arrive and, like everyone else, had taken the time to dress up. She was wearing black leggings and a blue shirt, and her hair was, for once, contained.

"You look nice, Delilah," I said, meaning it.

She patted my hand and smiled. "You need help getting the food ready?"

"That would be great." I waved a hand at the plates and salads. "You can take those over, for a start."

She did, and the food was quickly served up and consumed. Conversation rolled easily along, and everyone seemed to be having a great time—no surprise I guess since everyone except Bryan had known each other for quite a while.

The phone rang as dessert was being served. I handed over dishing out duties to Ceri, then headed into the living room to answer it.

"What the hell have you done?" My father's voice, full of venom.

Fear slithered through me. God, had Kaij questioned him after all, even after I'd told him of my father's threat? I licked my lips, and said, "I have no idea—"

"Don't give me that shit," he cut in. "This has your grubby little fingerprints all over it."

Not Kaij, then, something else. Something bigger. "What has? For fuck's sake, I have no idea-"

"I will get you for this, you bitch—"

"Actually," I cut in, "I'm a bastard. *Your* bastard. And if you don't explain what the hell you're ranting about, I'm hanging up."

"Frank Logan has been murdered," he ground out. "And Gilroy has been arrested for it."

CHAPTER TEN

S hock coiled through me. Frank Logan was *dead?* And Gilroy charged with his murder? "When? How?"

"Not ten minutes ago. The police came to the house and there were damn reporters everywhere. Someone tipped them off, apparently."

"And naturally, you suspect me of being behind it all, because Gilroy is such a saint and hasn't an enemy in the world beside me."

"Do you deny threatening to destroy his reputation?"

"Ruin his reputation, not his whole goddamn life." I ran a hand through my hair. "For fuck's sake, do you really think I'd murder Frank Logan just to set up your precious bloody son?"

The ensuing silence was heavy with antagonism. Obviously, Bramwell *did* believe I was capable of such an act—maybe because *he* was. Which I guess was something of a compliment, given he was more or less implying I was made out of the same sort of steel as him.

"I had nothing to do with Logan's murder, and nothing to do with Gilroy being arrested or accosted by reporters," I said emphatically. "And if you believe otherwise, you're a fucking idiot and I do *not* want to talk to you anymore."

I hit the end button then dropped heavily onto the sofa and swore vehemently. The shit really *had* hit the fan now. But none of it was making sense or adding up. Not Keale's accident, not Mona's death, and certainly not the fact that Gilroy had been arrested for Frank Logan's murder.

I *should* have kept talking to my father and gotten some more details, I guess, but even if temper hadn't gotten the better of me, he probably wouldn't have said much more. Other than vomit more poison, that was.

I glanced up as Val walked into the living room, his expression concerned. "You okay, darls?"

I shook my head. "I'm neck deep in shit and sinking fast."

He sat beside me. "Anything I can do?"

"Yeah, keep acting like a wallflower and go absolutely *nowhere* alone."

"Now I'm really worried. I definitely noted concern in your voice that time."

"That's because Gilroy has just been arrested for the murder of Frank Logan, and my goddamn father is laying the blame for both events at my feet."

"Holy shit," Val said, eyes widening. "Is he insane or what?"

"It's the 'or what' I'm worried about. If he really believes I'm responsible, he'll come after me and everyone I care about."

"But—" Val paused and shook his head. "I guess he never did consider you family, but still, to threaten your own flesh and blood? That's cold."

"He's an elf, Val." And that, really, said it all, especially where I was considered. I was only a half-blood, after all.

Val rubbed his jaw. "Maybe you're the one that needs to keep a low profile. I mean, if you left town until this blows over—"

"If Gilroy is charged, it won't ever blow over," I cut in. "Bramwell will hunt me down and destroy me, no matter where I go."

"I guess." He shook his head. "What are you going to do?"

"The one thing I probably shouldn't—solve this goddamn case." I pushed to my feet. "Could you help Ceri with the hosting duties for a while?"

"Sure, but where are you going?"

"Over to Lyle's." Because if someone was out to destroy everyone who was a client of Mona, he might just be next in line.

"Just be careful, won't you?" Val caught my hand and squeezed it gently. "You may not be much of a sister, but you're all I've got."

"Don't worry little brother," I said, "I intend to be here to ignore and neglect you for many years yet."

"Such a sweet thing to say. You'd better go before I get all teary."

I grinned, then grabbed my coat and headed out. Most of the evening traffic had cleared, so I had a relatively free run across to Lyle's apartment. I parked in the street opposite his building and glanced up as I climbed out of the car. There were no lights on in Lyle's place. No flickering glow to indicate the TV was on.

I locked the car then walked across the road and up the front steps. A row of six intercoms was lined up like soldiers near the main door—I pressed the one marked penthouse and then waited for a response.

Surprisingly, there was one. "Yeah?"

I frowned. The old elf actually sounded sober, so why the hell was he sitting in a dark apartment? "Lyle? It's Harri. Open up."

"Harri, I'm not in the mood for one of your sermons. Go away."

"No. You and I need to talk. Open the damn door, because I will press the buzzer until you do."

He obviously believed me, because the door clicked open. I took the stairs rather than the elevator and by the time I reached the top floor, Lyle's door was also open. I entered and closed it behind me. The shadows pressed close, thick with the smell of alcohol and stale cigarette smoke. He might not have sounded drunk, but empty champagne bottles lined the coffee table. If they were any indication, he should have been out like a light, not staring blankly into the distance and puffing intermittently on the cigarette he held in his right hand. Surrounded by darkness, his face lit only by the glowing end of his cigarette, he looked gaunt, like an old man who was waiting for death's cold touch.

"What the hell are you doing, Lyle?"

He took a long drag on his cigarette then blew the smoke toward the ceiling. "Thinking."

I walked across the room and sat on the arm of the chair opposite him. He didn't look at me, just kept staring upwards at the barely visible smoke-covered ceiling. "About what?"

Lyle shrugged. "Justice."

Unease slithered through me, although I wasn't entirely sure why. "Justice for who?"

"Mona, of course. I heard not long ago on the news that another of the maggots who used her has been found dead."

There was no emotion in his voice, no life. It was as if I was talking to the shell of a man I'd once known, and that sense of unease increased. Something was very, very wrong.

"I gather you're talking about Frank Logan?"

"Yeah. Did you know the bastard threatened her?"

I did, but the question was, how did he? "Why would you think that?"

"Because I asked him."

Oh, *shit*. "When?"

"After we talked to Bramwell and Gilroy. You were the one

who raised the question about James and the money he gave Mona, so I called Frank and asked him about it."

"And?"

"And, James stole it from the family business. I got the impression Frank wasn't exactly sorry that his brother died in that crash."

It sounded like the Logans were as dysfunctional as the Philleckys. "What else did he say?"

"That he'd been dealing with the situation and was totally pissed when James paid her instead. He also said he'd told her not to expect another penny out of their family." He took a long drag on his cigarette and blew the smoke toward the ceiling. "He was the one who'd threatened her the day after the money drops."

"He told you that?" I couldn't help the surprise in my voice. Frank was a politician and should know better than to admit something like that, even to someone he thought trustworthy.

"Not in so many words. But he said he was dealing with the situation, he is a high-profile politician, and it fits exactly with what Mona had said."

"Two and two don't always add up to four. You told me that yourself."

"I'm betting this time, it does. Justice," he added, with a cold smile. "Got to love it."

"Lyle, even the police don't know who killed Mona yet, so it can hardly be justice that both Frank and James Logan have been killed. They might not be the murderers."

Lyle's gaze met mine. Deep in the sapphire depths, anger burned—a dark, all-consuming anger that scared the hell out of me. Anger that like was capable of anything. Truly anything.

"No," he said, "but they used her or abused her, and they deserve their deaths all the same."

"What about Gilroy?"

Lyle snorted. "What about him?"

My eyebrows rose. "What do you mean, what about him? He's been taken in for questioning about Frank Logan's *murder*."

A small smile touched his thin lips. "And justice strikes again."

"Lyle, we both know that Gilroy, for all his faults, hasn't the stomach for murder."

"Maybe." He stubbed out his cigarette, but immediately lit another. The lighter's flame flared across the darkness, a brief sliver that did little to lift the smoky darkness. "But he was willing enough to fuck her, even though he had nothing but contempt for her. Well, he's going to feel some of that contempt himself now, isn't he?"

"He may deserve contempt—" and he certainly had mine —"but we both know he doesn't deserve to have his career destroyed over Frank's murder. He didn't do it."

His gaze rested on mine. "Why are you so sure of that? He's cut from the same cloth as Bramwell—"

"No," I interrupted. "He's not. He hasn't got the same steel in his bones. He's been mollycoddled his entire life. Anytime anything went wrong, it was Bramwell who handled it, not Gilroy."

"So you're saying Bramwell killed her?"

"No, I am not, though he's certainly capable of it." I eyed him warily. "As are you."

"I didn't kill Mona, Harriet. I couldn't. I loved her." He puffed on the cigarette, then said, "You're cut from the same cloth as Bramwell and me, you know. If Gilroy had half your backbone, he would have made one hell of a politician."

I might have the steel, but I didn't have the same cold soul, and for that, I was extremely grateful. "Is that why you're just sitting here? Because you have nothing but contempt for your nephew?"

"I'm sitting here contemplating justice, as I said. And I think *she's* doing a fine job so far."

With more than a little help from a person or persons unknown. "What about Keale?"

Confusion briefly etched his face. "Where does that drunken sod come into any of this?"

"Why haven't you done anything about getting the blood results pushed through?"

"I haven't had the chance." His voice was suddenly testy. "Stop gnawing and let it go."

"No. If he was as drunk as they'd said, he wouldn't have been able to fly."

He snorted. "Blood results don't lie, half-breed. And fly he *did*."

Half-breed. And this time, it *was* an insult. "Keale hitting that helicopter *wasn't* an accident."

"Look, he's going to do time regardless, even if he does have Prevoron in his system, so why the big deal?"

"Because the drug can *kill* him. We at least need to know how much he has in his system."

Lyle shook his head. "All this fuss for a useless, drunken piece of dragon flesh."

"He's a friend, Lyle. And he's not useless. He's a caring, good-hearted—"

"You're a bloody romantic, you are."

Did steel and romanticism go together? Maybe they did, but it still seemed a contradiction—although I'm sure there were plenty of people who would call me just that.

He added, his tone scathing, "When are you going to wake up and smell the roses? You have to look out for yourself, Harriet, because no other bastard will do it for you. Not friends, and certainly not family."

"My friends are there when I need them, Lyle."

"I wouldn't put money on that."

I would. "Look, if Keale was given a safe amount of the drug, it'll be leeching out of his system by now. Another day or so and we won't be able to detect it."

"If I chase it up, will you stop nagging?"

"Yes. But you don't need to. I've actually asked someone else to check, and arrange to get the tests done if they haven't been."

Tension ran across his shoulders. "What, you think I won't do it?"

That's *exactly* what I thought. It was the *why* I had no idea about. Was it simply the unsympathetic—uncaring—nature of an elf coming to the forefront, or was something else going on?

He pushed up from the sofa and staggered into the kitchen. Which was odd, because I wouldn't have thought him drunk, despite all the bottles scattered about. He retrieved another bottle from the fridge and popped the cork. "You want some?"

I shook my head. "I'm driving. And Keale isn't what I came here to talk to you—"

"Then for god's sake spit it out." He sat back down and poured himself a glass of champagne, then leaned back in the chair and watched me. His eyes were narrowed. Wary. For some odd reason, I had the sudden impression of a snake ready to strike. "I'd rather drown my sorrows in peace than have to sit here listening to you nag."

"It's hardly nagging to remind you to do something you said you'd do," I retorted. "And the goddamn reason I'm here is to let you know I think you could be in danger."

He raised an eyebrow. "Me? Why on earth would you think that?"

"It's altogether possible that someone is going after Mona's clients and, if that's the case, your worthless carcass could be next in line."

"Frank Logan wasn't her client."

"No, but he was involved with her thanks to the fact James was being blackmailed by her, and James used Frank's cash to pay her."

He contemplated me for several seconds. "It would also be false to say that I was her client."

"A small detail the murderer might not care about."

"But *I* care." He jerked forward so fiercely that champagne sloshed over the rim of his glass and splattered across his pants. He didn't seem to notice or care. "I didn't just fuck her. I *loved* her."

No, I thought, as I returned his gaze uneasily. This was more than love. This was an addiction that verged on madness.

"Lyle, I really think you should get away for a few days. At least until I can sort this mess out."

"You don't have to, you know."

I blinked. "What?"

He waved his free hand. "Sort it out. You don't have to."

I frowned. "Why not?"

"I've been sitting here for a while now, and I've come to realize it doesn't really matter. Mona's dead. Nothing going to bring her back, so what is the point of trying to find the killer?"

"Because he's still out there. Because he may have killed five people and might kill more." My frown deepened. "Hell, Lyle, you've been around enough felons to know that crime sprees tend to escalate every time the perpetrator thinks they've gotten away with it."

"That's presuming Mona is the key. She might not be."

"This all started with her. She's the link. We just to need to find out how, and I think we'll find our murderer."

He downed his champagne and poured another. "I'm not paying you to go on."

"I don't care. I was never working for the money, anyway." It was handy, true, but I'd helped him out often enough in the past, and no money had ever exchanged hands then.

"Well, that's just stupid. If you're reduced to taking wedding photos, you can certainly use the cash."

"Life is more than just cash, Lyle."

"That's where you're wrong. You can buy the world if you have enough of it."

"I don't want the world."

"Neither did I." Lyle's voice soft, and gaze suddenly distant. "I just wanted Mona. They'll pay, Harriet. They'll all pay eventually."

It was fair to say I was getting a little confused by the differing messages he seemed to be giving. One minute he wanted an end to the investigation, the next he was out for revenge. I hoped it was the booze speaking, hoped he didn't actually intend to go after anyone, because if the anger I kept glimpsing were any indication, retribution would be fast and bloody. And he wouldn't care who he unleashed on —not even family.

"I thought you said it didn't matter anymore?"

He blinked. "It doesn't. But we all have to answer for our sins eventually, even if it is when we arrive on the evergreen fields."

I snorted softly. "It's more likely to be the gates of hell if we're talking about you, old man."

"Aint' that the truth," he murmured.

I frowned. "Look, you dragged me into this. You can hardly complain when I want to see it through."

"You're putting yourself in the line of fire, Harriet." His voice was flat, filled with an odd intensity that sent a shiver down my spine. It was almost as if he were warning me.

Which he *was*, but it somehow seemed to be *more* than just that. It was the sort of warning one antagonist might give another.

A snake ready to strike indeed.

A chill ran up my arms, but I resisted the urge to rub them. "Right now, we need to get you out of the line of fire."

Lyle's smile was bitter. "No one's after me, Harriet. You can be assured of that."

"Why? Because you're an old fool too busy drowning his sorrows in alcohol?"

"Maybe."

Frustration swirled through me. "Look, it's not going to hurt to make yourself scarce for a few days, is it? You can chase insobriety in a hotel room as well as you can here."

Lyle lit another cigarette then regarded me over the glowing tip for several seconds. "This place is safe. We have security monitoring twenty-four seven. Any trouble, and we only have to press a buzzer and they'll come running. You won't get that in a hotel."

I gave up. And maybe he was right. Maybe he *was* as safe here as anywhere else. "Just be careful who you let in the door, then."

"I will." He took a puff. "You heading home?"

"No. I thought I might contact my old boss and see what he can tell me about Gilroy's arrest."

"You really *don't* believe he did it, do you?"

"It's all just a little too convenient, Lyle." I rose. "I learned long ago to trust instinct, and right now, it's telling me this whole mess is stinking higher than fresh dog crap."

"Let the police deal with it. That's what they're there for."

And where was *that* sentiment when he'd first hired me to find her? "Are you sure you'll be-"

"Yes," he growled. "Stop fussing, Harriet."

"Fine. I'll talk to you tomorrow."

He nodded. "Is Keale staying at your place?"

I paused. "Yeah, why?"

"Keep an eye on him. It won't look good if he gets himself in more trouble before his case comes up."

259

"He'll be fine."

I headed for the door. Lyle remained where he was, a hunched, lonely figure surrounded by the smoky darkness. And once again I had the notion that something was very wrong. Something that was more than just natural grief over a loved one's death.

But what?

That was the question I couldn't answer—but it was one I was beginning to suspect I needed to.

Once back out on the street, I grabbed my phone and rang my old boss. He didn't answer, so either he was out of range or he couldn't hear it ring. I glanced at my watch. Greg was a man of habit; if he stuck to form, he'd be at Mystix's, a small restaurant and bar just down from the paper's offices. If I hurried, I could still catch him there.

I unlocked the car and then hesitated, instinct making me look up at Lyle's windows. He was standing there, watching me. I frowned and wondered how wise it was to leave him alone. Yet, short of hog-tying him and hauling him away, what choice did I have? I shook my head, climbed into the car, and headed into the city.

Even though it was Tuesday night, Mystix's was overflowing. Rock music blared over the hum of conversation, and the air was rich with the scent of the homemade bread and pizzas Mystix's was famous for.

I made my way through the crowd, every now again greeting a familiar face from my days at the paper. Greg's large form was parked at one of the tables near the rear of the bar, close to the kitchen doors. It was the only way to ensure the food was piping hot, Greg used to say, although I'd never once been given cold food in all the times I'd come here.

"Harri," he said, pushing the paper he'd been reading to one side. "Haven't seen you around these parts for a while."

I ordered a lemon-lime and bitters from a passing waitress, then pulled out the chair and sat down opposite him. "It's not a social call, I'm afraid."

"Didn't think it would be. Nice job on those photos, by the way. We sold quite a few more papers with them on the front."

"Which is why I sent them to you."

He nodded. "You always did have a good eye for that sort of stuff. If you ever want to come back, you're more than welcome."

"Thanks, but I'm not that desperate yet."

He laughed, an action that sent ripples rolling across the sea of flesh that was his stomach. "More's the shame. So, what can I do for you?"

"I came to pick your brain about Gilroy Phillecky's arrest."

"Ah." Greg's gaze narrowed as he leaned back in his chair and shoved his hands into his jacket pockets. "You wouldn't happen to be related, would you? I mean, the Philleckys are a big clan, so it's not a given but—"

"I'm his half-sister," I cut in. "What do you know about Gilroy's arrest?"

Greg shrugged. "Not much. The police received a tip-off

about the weapon used in Logan's murder. A registration search showed it belonged to Gilroy."

I frowned. "That doesn't seem enough to arrest him on."

"No, but the address given was Gilroy's apartment, and his prints were all over the gun."

"I'm guessing they'll be testing for gunshot residue." And I'd bet they wouldn't find any. The waitress appeared with my drink. I dug out some cash to pay for it, and then added, "Do you know what Gilroy said?"

"His father released a statement not long ago. Apparently, Gilroy came home, discovered the gun on the coffee table, and picked it up to investigate. The cops appeared not long after that."

It was a stupid thing to do, but also a very natural one. "Do you believe him?"

Greg's eyes narrowed slightly. "The question is, do you? You're related, after all."

"I'm the daughter no one speaks about," I said, voice dry. "I don't know them, and they certainly don't know me. But yeah, I'm inclined to believe him, if only because a politician as smooth as Gilroy could come up with a far better story than that."

A small smile touched his lips. "I tend to think the same, although his prints being on the gun is pretty damning."

"Not if he has a watertight alibi." And I suspect he would.

Greg studied me for a moment, and then said, "Given what you said about your status in the family unit, I'd have thought you wouldn't care either way what happened to your half-brother."

"I don't."

"Then why the interest?"

"Because I believe Frank Logan's murder is linked to at least one other."

Interest flared in Greg's brown eyes. The newshound scented a good story. "Care to share?"

I smiled. "Maybe. What else can you tell me about Frank's murder?"

"He was killed by a single shot to the back of the head. Close range, so not pretty, according to my source."

"At home?"

Greg nodded. "No sign of forced entry, and no evidence of any sort of struggle. He knew his murderer, that much is certain."

And trusted him enough to turn his back on him. "No one else in the house? No known appointments?"

"That I can't say. I know it was the housekeeper who found him. She'd been out buying supplies for dinner."

"What about the security tapes? They show anything?"

He smiled. "I'm a newshound, not a bloody cop. I can only give you what my source is willing to share, and right now, that's not much."

"Damn." I took a sip of my drink and wondered if it was worth the heartache to ask Kaij about them. No, I thought. Definitely not. Not for Gilroy's sake, anyway. "So really, we have nothing more than the gun linking Gilroy to the murder?"

"A gun with his prints all over it."

"Gilroy's been set up. I'm almost positive on it."

Greg gave me his best shark smile. "Tell your lovely old boss all, my dear."

I snorted. "My lovely old boss can go to hell. I have no intention of saying anything to anyone until I can prove my theories. Doing anything else just might get me as dead as Logan."

Greg raised his eyebrows. "Really? Then I *insist* you give the story to me when you can. I have a feeling it could be a good one."

"You have no idea *how* good." I hesitated, and then said more soberly, "To that end, can I send you some information for safe keeping?"

"What sort of information?"

"The sort that must only be opened if I'm dead or incapacitated."

He raised his eyebrows. "What the hell are you investigating that you're worried about dying?"

"A fucking good story, as I said." I smiled. "So, can I send it to you?"

"You can, but I'm surprised you'd trust me not to open it."

"Do you promise that you won't?

"Yes, but curiosity has been known to kill the occasional cat."

"I'd keep that warning in mind if you think about opening before it's necessary."

"Good grief, now I'm *really* intrigued."

I half smiled. "Is there anything else you can tell me about Gilroy's arrest?"

"Well, they did find a partial print that doesn't seem to belong to any of Logan's family or staff, but they're still running tests."

Meaning the partial print hadn't been Gilroy's. "So have they actually charged him?"

"No. Officially, he's still helping with their inquiries."

Complete with an armada of lawyers by his side, I was betting. "I was told you newshounds arrived at Gilroy's the same time as the cops did—that true?"

"Yes."

"So the paper got a phone call?"

"Not the paper—me."

That raised my eyebrows. "Why you? I mean, no disrespect Boss, but you haven't been in the field for years. You're not a name anyone who didn't know the paper's structure would recognize."

"I thought it was a little odd, too." He contemplated me with a pleased sort of smile.

Meaning, I thought with amusement, he'd done something he shouldn't have. "Line trace?"

His smile grew. "You know as well as I do that sort of thing is highly illegal."

"It's also illegal for anyone but the police to record a conversation without first informing all parties, but that's not stopping you now, is it?"

He laughed and pulled his hands out of his pockets. A small recorder was nestled in his right palm. He placed it on the table, but didn't turn it off. "Just want to make sure I get my facts right when I print this story of yours."

"*If* you print this story of mine," I said. "Now, we were talking about a line trace."

"Ah yes." He paused for a moment. "The trace wasn't successful. He hung up before it was complete."

"Did you manage to pin down a general location?"

"It came from somewhere in Brighton." He shrugged. "I suspect whoever it was called from an old phone box, because there was a hell of an echo."

Darryl's mystery woman had called from a phone box, too. The coincidences just kept on mounting.

"There're not that many phone boxes left in use these days, so it shouldn't be too had to uncover a location." Not that it would do us all that much good now. Whatever prints had been left would probably be smudged to hell by subsequent users. "What did the person actually say?"

"That if I wanted to see Hartwell Gilroy Phillecky arrested

for the murder of Frank Logan, head over this Brighton address."

I raised an eyebrow. "He said Hartwell?"

"Yeah." Greg frowned. "Why?"

"Because Hartwell is his Elven name, and it's only known—and used—by family or those close to the family. Gilroy is the name he uses publicly."

"So you're basically saying that whoever made the call is an elf, and either a family member or a close friend."

"Yes." And the only person I could think of who'd revel in seeing Gilroy so disgraced was the man I'd just left.

But I couldn't imagine Lyle going to such lengths—not when it came to his nephew, anyway. Sure, he was pissed off at Gilroy's attitude when it came to Mona, but that didn't warrant murder. Not even the most irrational mind could think that it did. Besides, blood looked after blood—at least when it came to full-blooded Elves. Us half-breeds could definitely take a long jump off a short pier as far as the Elven community was concerned.

Greg leaned back in his chair, his expression suddenly curious. "Given your outcast position, what do you call your brother?"

"Brother." I grinned. "It really pisses him off."

He snorted. "Good to see you're still stirring the pot, Harri."

When it came to my family, there was little else I could do. And at least pot stirring annoyed them as much as their refusal to acknowledge my existence annoyed me.

Although really, you'd think that, given I was almost thirty, I would have gotten over it all by now.

"You can't think of anything else?"

"Well, a source in the squad suggested cigarette butts had been found outside Frank's house, but they're not sure if they're connected." He paused, studying me intently. "I have a feeling you know more about this case than I do."

"Maybe." I smiled and glanced at my watch. "Let me know if you hear any interesting gossip, though."

"I will. You off?"

I nodded. "I have a dinner party to get back to."

"Just remember, my sweet, the story is mine."

"If I piece it together, most definitely." But first, I had to survive it. "Thanks for the help, Greg."

He nodded and picked up his paper again. I made my way back to the car and headed home.

It took me about ten minutes to realize I was being followed. I studied the rearview mirror for several seconds, and then changed lanes. Two sets of headlights back, another car did the same. I might have considered it little more than a quirk of traffic, except for the fact that the car had been echoing my movements for a good ten minutes.

Which made me wonder if they wanted to be seen. I mean, anyone who'd watched enough cop movies knew better than to mirror movements exactly.

I did a left into Smith Street, then slowed down and watched. A white Holden swept around the corner, and then the brake lights flashed as the car came to an abrupt halt outside the Seven-Eleven store. No one climbed out of the car to go inside, however.

Maybe they thought I was the type of driver who didn't pay attention to such things, and normally they'd be right. But after Goliath's attack, I'd learned the hard way that paying attention was a good thing.

I put my foot down. My old car hesitated—as if in shock—then surged forward with an almost throaty roar. I swept through amber lights at Langridge Street, saw the Holden sweep through the red, barely missing a turning tram in the process. The two of us roared down a thankfully empty Smith Street, the Holden steadily gaining ground—not surprising given my old car's glory days had long ago pass her by.

I swung left at Johnson Street, my tires squealing, sending pedestrians scattering as I fought to keep the car in a straight line. Then I planted my foot on the accelerator again and took off. The Holden echoed my movements a couple of heartbeats later, but he wasn't quite as lucky at keeping the nose of the car straight, and its rear end hit the side of another car before it took up the chase again. It gave me a few precious seconds space.

I swung left, did a right into a one-way street, then turned off my headlights and parked under the canopy of an over-grown tree.

And that's precisely where I stayed for the next twenty minutes.

Once my heartbeat had come down to a more normal rate, and I was reasonably sure that my tail had given up, I made my way home. I didn't see the Holden again—although maybe that was because they'd finally gotten a clue and figured out how to tail someone properly.

There were no lights on in my house, but the TV was, meaning everyone but the ogres had made their way home. Guilt swirled through me—it had been my dinner party, after all.

I made a mental note to hold another one—more to make it up to Val than anyone else—then locked up my car and headed around to the front door. A shiny new lock greeted me, but thankfully, it wasn't actually locked because I didn't have a key for the thing.

The dueling sound of snores coming from both the spare bedroom and the living room greeted me as I walked down the hall. Keale had obviously gone to bed, but Moe and Curly were sprawled over the sofas, bare feet dangling over the ends, and Guy was on the floor. I continued on and found Ceri in the kitchen unpacking the dishwasher.

"You didn't have to do that," I said, as I threw my keys and bag on the nearby counter. "But I appreciate it all the same."

She half-shrugged. "There was nothing else to do given we're not exactly rushed off our feet with work at the moment."

"True. You want a coffee?"

She nodded as she put the last of the plates away, then dried her hands on an old tea towel and walked across to the table. "So, family problems all sorted out?"

I snorted. "Hardly. Someone murdered Frank Logan and

set Gilroy up to take the fall. The only person I can think of right now who is mad enough to even *attempt* something like that is Lyle. But-"

"But you don't want to believe he's capable of something like that," Ceri finished for me.

I passed her a coffee then sat down. "Oh, I know he's capable of murder. He's an elf *and* a Phillecky, after all."

"You're a Phillecky," she noted dryly. "That doesn't automatically make you a murderer."

"Well, no, but I'm only half elf. There is a difference."

"Only in the minds of elves. To the rest of the world, you're an elf—only friendlier."

I smiled. "What I meant is, elves don't view killing in the same light the rest of us do. If it's more efficient to kill a rival than deal with them, then kill they will. Besides, I'm definitely *not* a Phillecky in their eyes, even if I bear the name."

"For which we all say a prayer of thanks every day." She grinned. "Particularly the ogres, who would be shadows of themselves without the use of your fridge."

I laughed. "*That* is sadly true."

She took a sip of coffee then leaned back in her chair. "If you believe Lyle is more than capable of murder, why don't you want to believe he killed Frank Logan?"

"It's not so much the murder, but rather the fact Gilroy was set up to take the fall." I took a drink then wrinkled my nose and reached for the sugar. "I might not be family, but Gilroy *is*, and even Lyle respects the blood bond."

"Even if his family has, over the years, tried to get him committed?"

"Even if."

She studied me for a moment. "What about Mona? Could he have also murdered her?"

I was shaking my head before she'd even finished. "If there's one thing I truly believe in this whole fucking mess, it's that Lyle honestly loved Mona."

"You can love someone and still kill them, you know." There was a grim edge in her voice. "I saw it time and again when I was a cop."

"Lyle didn't do it."

It was almost stubbornly said, and Ceri smiled. "Is that family loyalty speaking, or instinct?"

I hesitated. "Probably a bit of both, if I'm at all honest."

"Well, let's do what we used to do in homicide, and look at all the other possibilities. Who else, besides our dead suitors, had a reason to murder her?"

I snorted softly. "Well, there's a little black book filled with images of the men who'd answered her call, and if she was attempting to blackmail some or all of them as well the Logans and Gilroy, that would certainly provide a number of suspects."

She raised her eyebrows. "And have you handed this book over to Kaij? It should be in his possession if you want this case solved."

"Yeah, I know." I half shrugged. "I just—"

"Didn't want to drop family into it, even if that family deserves jack-shit from you when it comes to loyalty or respect."

"Basically, yes."

She shook her head, her expression bemused. "So who else is there?"

"Well, if it's no-one in the black book, there's only Darryl, her driver."

"And is he capable?"

"More than capable. He didn't do it though—if only because I'm sure he would have had more sense than to dispose of the body so thoughtlessly."

"Is the fact that she was dumped in the bay any clue?"

I frowned. "I guess it *does* suggest that whoever disposed of her might have cared enough to give her the sea burial." In siren lore, being buried under the earth or cremated was akin to sentencing your soul to an eternity of hell. The sea was their mother, their birthplace, and it was the sea to whom they returned at the journey's end. And anyone who knew anything about sirens would be more than a little aware of this. "But there are better ways of hiding a body, even in the sea. I mean, she didn't even appear to be weighted."

"Which is no doubt why she washed up."

I nodded. "And *that* speaks to someone who was reacting emotionally rather than logically. More attempting to give her a proper burial rather than getting rid of evidence."

"Which, again, points to Lyle."

"It's not Lyle. It's *not*."

And yet, I knew deep down, he *had* to be a suspect. It made sense, especially given his recent behavior. I took another sip of coffee, then played the devil's advocate and said, "Let's just say he *did* murder Mona. Why then employ us to find the killer?"

"It's more than possible he's blanked out the event. Physical or emotionally traumatic events can lead to a condition called dissociative amnesia, which helps a person cope by allowing them to temporarily forget details of the event." She shrugged. "Sufferers often suppress memories of the event until they are ready to handle them, which, unfortunately, doesn't always occur."

I grimaced. "I still can't imagine—"

"You may not want to," she interrupted softly. "But if you want this case solved, you may just have to."

"I know, but—"

"Look at the facts, and just the facts." She raised her hand and began ticking points off on her fingers. "One, Lyle believed James Logan had been threatening Mona; James Logan is subsequently killed in a helicopter crash with a drugged up dragon. Two, Lyle discovers that Frank Logan was responsible for beating her up, and that Gilroy had answered her call but had zero respect for her. One day later, Frank is dead and Gilroy set up for the crime. Three, Lyle, through you, had easy access to a dragon with a very bad drink-flying record. Four, he's a very high-profile lawyer working with legal aid, and would have no trouble getting in to see Frank Logan. And finally, five; given that he is now working for legal aid, he has the contacts, if not the knowledge himself, to know where to get Prevoron."

When it was all laid out like that, there certainly was enough evidence to suggest that Lyle, at the very least, should be on the suspect list. And hell, maybe he *was* on Kaij's list.

"We don't know yet that Keale *was* drugged."

"That still doesn't alter the truth of points one to four." She hesitated. "Cigarette butts were found at the scene, weren't they?"

"No," I said, answering what she was inferring not what she actually asked.

I could feel her gaze on me, but I didn't look up. I couldn't. I didn't want to believe, didn't want to *see*.

"When you saw him this evening, what would you say his state of mind was?"

An image of Lyle's hunched figure flashed through my mind. Disturbed and withdrawn were apt enough descriptions. "He's just lost someone he loved. It's natural that he's not actually rationally."

Yet was it natural to be sitting in darkness gloating about justice being done? And how was it justice for five people to be dead, and three of them unconnected to Mona in any way?

Ceri reached across the table and clasped my hand. "You may not want to believe," she said, voice gentle. "But you really *do* have to consider the possibility that Lyle might be behind this whole damn mess."

275

"No," I repeated, but with less force this time. The seed had been planted, and there was no escaping it now. It would haunt me until I uncovered the truth.

"And *if* he is behind it all," she continued. "You might be in danger yourself."

"He won't come after me."

"Why?" She leaned back and arched an eyebrow. "If he's set up his nephew—a full blood kin—to take the fall for a murder he didn't commit, what makes you think he'd have any problems dealing with you should you become too much of a problem?"

"He won't come after me." I had to believe *that*, if nothing else. I might not be a full blood relative, but surely all our years of friendship had to mean *something*.

But I remembered the spite in his voice when he'd called me half-breed earlier tonight, and shivered.

She sighed softly. "You place an awful lot of faith in your family and friends, Harri. Even the ones who don't seem to deserve it."

"I have to, because, in the end, that's all I have." I glanced at the clock and echoed her sigh. It was after one—way past time for me to be hitting the sack. "I'll worry about it all in the morning."

"Which is my cue to head upstairs and play FreeCell. Which, by the way, is the only thing we can play on our old laptop since your damn father swiped the desktops. When are you going to get them back?"

I snorted softly. "Given he thinks I'm responsible for setting up Gilroy, probably never."

"Your father is an idiot," Guy said, as he walked into the room. "And you're out of beer, by the way."

"A disaster," I said dryly. "Especially at one in the morning."

"Hey, an ogre is entitled to a nightcap, isn't he?"

I shook my head, wondering why medical science had never untaken a study of ogre constitutions, because they certainly never seemed to blow over the limit in any alcohol test, no matter how much they'd been drinking. I walked across the room and grabbed one of the shiny new keys from the hooks behind the door. "I'm off to bed and Ceri is going up to the office. Use the key. I don't want the lock busted again."

His grin was one of sheer delight. "My own key? Now *that* is true friendship."

"No, it's an attempt to save myself some money on broken locks and doors. And if you don't go now, you won't get your beer. They close at two."

"I am the wind," he said, and dropped a fart as he left.

"*That*," Ceri said severely. "Was disgusting."

I couldn't say anything. I was too busy not breathing. I waved to Ceri and headed for my bedroom. I was half undressed when someone knocked at the door. Wondering if we finally had another customer, I walked over to the front window to check them out. It certainly couldn't be Guy—he rarely knocked and besides, he now had a key. I pushed aside the curtains, but couldn't see any unfamiliar cars parked out the front. And if they were standing near the door, they weren't visible from this angle.

Whoever it was knocked again. It sounded more impatient this time.

"You want me to get that?" Ceri yelled from upstairs.

"No." I grabbed my sweater, pulling it on as I opened the front door. "I'm still awa—"

The rest of the sentence froze in the back of my throat. It wasn't a friend, but it *was* someone I knew.

Goliath.

And this time, he'd bought a friend.

A very *large* friend.

CHAPTER ELEVEN

I'd barely even registered that fact when Goliath's fist buried itself into my stomach and sent me flying back down the hallway. I crashed into the wall hard enough to dent the plaster and fell to the floor in a heap, struggling to breathe and fighting blackness.

There was a scramble of movement from the living room, and then Moe and Curly appeared in the doorway. They took one look at me then launched themselves at Goliath and his mountainous mate. There was a collision of arms, legs, heads, and plaster, and the whole house shook.

"Fucking hell, what's going on—" Ceri appeared at the top of the stairs and her face went white. "Run, Harri. I'll call the cops."

Great idea, I thought. Except my legs didn't want to support my weight and I couldn't seem to get any air into my lungs. Somehow, I forced myself onto my hands and knees. The hallway did a three-sixty degree dance around me and my stomach suddenly seemed intent on viewing my tonsils.

Goliath was the first one free from the tangle and he clomped towards me, the floor vibrating under his footsteps. "You broke my head," he growled. "For that you *pay*."

Meaning my father *hadn't* sent this bastard here again; Goliath simply wanted revenge. *Great.* I struggled to my feet, my breath hissing through clenched teeth. Air screamed behind me and I ducked instinctively. The blow that would have smashed my head into the wall hit the plaster instead, sending debris and dust flying everywhere.

Moe reappeared, tackling Goliath hard and forcing him to his knees. The troll roared and smacked backward with an elbow, mashing Moe's nose and sending blood and snot flying everywhere. He hung on though, ignoring the blows, slowing the troll's movement toward me but not stopping him.

I staggered into the kitchen, my gaze searching the counters for a weapon. *Any* weapon would do, but it had better be something big, like the shovel. Something I *didn't* have to get close with to use. A knife was definitely out—the bastard had arms like a gorilla and would catch me long before I got anywhere near enough to use it.

Another roar echoed. Moe, not the troll. God, how the hell was Keale sleeping through all this?

Footsteps echoed behind me—troll steps. They were too heavy to be Moe's or Curly's. I cursed and dove for the nearest remotely dangerous thing—the toaster. I ripped the power cord free from the wall then spun as the troll came into the kitchen. I swung the toaster over my head and hammer threw it at the troll. He didn't see it soon enough, and the appliance hit him square in the face, shattering his nose and smearing blood everywhere. He roared again, took two quick steps toward me, and lashed out. I ducked, but nowhere near fast enough. The blow caught my left side and sent me spinning into the dishwasher.

Moe and Curly reappeared; they grabbed the troll and dragged him backward. Goliath lashed backward with a booted foot, catching Moe in the balls and dropping him like a stone. Curly wrapped an arm around the troll's neck and punched him in the face with his free hand. The troll reached back, grabbed a fistful of hair, and yanked down. The ogre yelped as the hair was torn from his head, but kept on punching. The second troll appeared, grabbed the back of Curly's shirt, and yanked him away Goliath. Curly swung and punched the other troll in the face. As the two of them exchanged blows, Goliath came at me.

Fabulous.

I pushed upright. Pain shot through my side, a red-hot agony that tore a gasp from my throat. The troll grinned, his beady eyes alight with anticipation.

"Now *you* pay," he growled.

"Not so fast, buddy," Ceri said, appearing out of the shadowed hallway. "One move, and I'll shoot."

The troll spun and studied her for a moment, then his gaze dropped to the weapon in Ceri's hand. It was a taser, but one of the ones designed to cater for non-humans. The troll sneered and I didn't actually blame him. I don't think the manufacturers had someone Goliath's size in mind when they were developing their product.

"Try it," he said, and spread his massive arms wide, presenting her with his entire chest.

She fired. The twin projectiles flew unerringly and lodged into his chest. The troll's muscles jumped erratically, but it had little other effect. It certainly *didn't* bring him down.

Ceri swore, then threw the weapon to one side and took several steps before launching herself feet first at the troll. She was a big woman, with a body mass that was heavier than a regular human's thanks to her gargoyle heritage, but she made as little impact on the troll as the ogres did. Goliath laughed and reached for her as she flipped elegantly back to her feet. She ducked, smashed her fist against the side of his head, and then danced out of the way.

"What the fuck...?" Guy said from the back doorway. His gaze took in Ceri, the troll, and me, then he flipped the slab of beer he was carrying from his shoulder and, in a two-handed grip, smashed it across the troll's head.

Beer and cans exploded everywhere. The troll staggered sideways several steps, but all too quickly caught his balance.

"Don't touch the head!" he roared, and swung a fist wildly at Guy. It hit the nearby cupboard instead, disintegrating the old door and sending bits of crockery everywhere. If we kept fighting in here, I wasn't going to have a house left.

"Guy, outside," I gasped.

The ogre didn't hesitate, just charged the troll and hit him full tilt, roaring in effort as he picked the monster up and staggered toward the back door. The troll swore, punched, and kicked, but Guy ignored everything and staggered out the back door and down the steps.

I followed and grabbed the shovel that still leaned against the stair rail. I raised it above my head, but there was absolutely no way I could unleash a blow because there were arms and legs going everywhere and it was hard to tell which belonged to the ogre and which to the troll.

"Fuck," Ceri said, "Is there *any* stopping this bastard?"

"Hit his head with something hard. Worked last time."

She snorted, but jumped down the stairs and raced across to the small rockery near the back fence. I went down at a somewhat slower pace then headed right.

Goliath saw me. He growled low in his throat, then grabbed a fistful of Guy's shirt, thrust upwards with his legs, and flipped the ogre over his head. Guy hit the turf headfirst and slid hard into the fence. Wood splintered. He didn't move.

Goliath jumped to his feet. Blood poured from his nose, staining yellowed teeth when he smiled.

"Just you and me now," he said.

"Not quite," Ceri said, and threw a rock at him.

The troll spun then ducked, the speed of the movement belying his bulk. The rock sailed over his head and barely missed my toes as I swung the shovel with all my might. He ducked again and the shovel sailed over his head. The force I'd put behind the blow unbalanced me, and I staggered sideways for several steps before I could catch my balance.

Out of the corner of my eye, I saw the troll's fist go back. I swore again and threw myself out of the way, hitting the ground with enough force that my breath whooshed from my lungs and the shovel went flying. As I scrambled desperately after it, a boot bigger than the sky came at my head. I wrapped a hand around the shovel's grip then rolled out of the way. The ground trembled as the troll's booted foot hit the space where my head had been only seconds before.

Another rock sailed through the darkness and crashed into Goliath's shoulders. He roared, spun around, and charged. Ceri yelped, but before she could run, Guy came out of nowhere and hit the troll side on, sending him flying towards the fence. He hit with enough force to splinter wood, but before he could react, a shadow appeared over the top of the fence and held a knife that gleamed with soft blue fire against the troll's neck.

"Please," a soft, all-too-familiar voice said. "Just give me *one* reason to use this blade."

The troll wasn't stupid. He froze.

I closed my eyes and took a deep, shuddery breath.

Kaij.

Talk about an opportune moment to arrive.

"Everyone okay?" His gaze was on me as he said it, a heat I felt rather than saw, and one that pooled somewhere deep in my stomach.

But I didn't look up, didn't respond. Now that it was all over, pain and shock had leaped into focus, and it was all I could do not to throw up.

"No, my good tie has grass stains all over it," Guy growled. "Not to mention the fact I had to smash an entire slab of beer over that idiot's head, and *that* was a damn waste of good alcohol."

"I'm sure you'll survive the loss." There was a dry edge in Kaij's voice. "Ceri, you want to find something to tie this bastard up with? Harri, are you okay?"

"Fine," I muttered. "Just don't ask me to move for the next year and everything will be okay."

Guy walked over and squatted beside me. "You want me to carry you inside?"

"That," I said heavily. "Depends entirely on whether Moe and Curly have managed to contain the second troll."

"I'll go check."

"Good idea."

Guy disappeared. I watched Ceri and Kaij hog-tie Goliath with some fencing wire and tried not to breathe too deeply. The ogre reappeared. "The second troll is down. Moe and Curly have him gagged and bound."

"Good. I'll accept the offer of being carried inside, then."

He slipped his arms around me, lifted me as easily as a feather, and gently carried me into the house. The second troll's wrists had been bound with the toaster cord and his ankles with the ironing cord. Moe and Curly were in the process of picking up beer cans, but from the look of it, had only managed to salvage a half dozen.

Guy deposited me onto a chair and then studied the remaining cans with a woebegone expression. "Is that all you could save?"

Moe nodded. His face was a swollen, bloody mess. Curly had faired a little better—he had a bald spot where Goliath had ripped out his hair, and one side of his jaw was bruised and swollen, but other than that, he seemed okay.

"Man," Guy said, "These bastards have to *pay*."

"I'm sure they will." I hesitated, suddenly remembering the car that had followed me. I might have lost it, but the last thing I needed right now was another surprise visitor. "Can you do me a favor?"

"Sure—what?"

"Take a walk around the block, and see if there's a white Holden with rear right panel damage parked anywhere nearby."

Guy frowned. "Sure, but why?"

"Because I spotted someone following me when I was coming home, and I doubt it was Goliath." He was already familiar with where I lived, after all.

"And if we find said car?"

"If the driver is there, maybe you could question him? Gently."

Guy grinned and cracked his knuckles. "Gentle is my middle name. Come on boys, we have work to do and beer to replace."

As they walked out, Kaij came in. His gaze met mine and, just for an instant, fury glittered in the green depths. But then, he'd never condoned violence of any sort against women. He and my father had that in common, if nothing else.

"Where are the ogres going?"

"To get more beer." My reply was a short and sharp as his. "You know where Guy lives if you want to talk to them."

"I hardly need to question him at home when he still spends the majority of his time here."

I raised an eyebrow at his tone and leaned back in the chair —a bad move, given my stomach muscles were as bruised and sore as my side. What I needed was a long soak in a hot bath, but given the current rate of house invasions, that probably wasn't a wise move right now.

"Which is just as well given the police are apparently incapable of keeping Goliath locked up."

"Breaking and entering is not the sort of crime that warrants immediate locking up. He was charged then bailed."

He dragged out a chair and sat down opposite me. His expression gave little away, but the anger I'd glimpsed so very briefly simmered not far below the surface. The force of it burned through me.

"He actually did a little more than break and enter. He also assaulted—I still have the damn bruises to show for it."

"Trust me, neither he *nor* his mate will be released this time. Not until this whole fucking mess is sorted out." He paused. "Though I'm seriously impressed you managed to take the bastard down the first time when five of you couldn't the second."

"There were two of them this time," I pointed out. "Besides, he didn't expect me to put up a fight the first time. He was prepared this time."

"It's still an impressive feat." He eyed me for a second, and once again I sensed the anger that burned just below the cool exterior. "What the *hell* is going on, Harri? Why is your father so determined to come after you? What do you know that we don't?"

"Given I don't know what you know, I can't honestly say." I glanced past him as Ceri came through the door. She raised an eyebrow, her expression challenging. She wanted me to be honest with him, and while that might be the totally sensible option, it wasn't one I was willing to take just yet. Not until I was absolutely, *totally* sure Lyle was behind it all. I couldn't—wouldn't—give him up to Kaij otherwise.

"Do you think your father is behind this second attack?"

"No. Goliath wanted payback." I half smiled. "A sapling sized elf got the better of him. That's not something he could let lie."

"Except for the fact that trolls generally don't resort to violence unless they're paid for it. If it wasn't your father who sent him here, then it has to have been either your brother or one of the other Elven bastards you're related to."

Which maybe included the *only* Elven relative I'd trusted up until now. I shoved the thought aside, not wanting to give Kiaj any hint of my suspicions. He'd always been able to read the source behind emotions better than me.

Which was what had made his walking away all that much harder to accept. He'd known what I was going through, and he'd left regardless.

Something flickered in his eyes—an emotion that moved too

fast to define. I would have liked to think it was regret, but too much time had passed to honestly believe it.

I reached for one of the remaining beers and popped it open. It probably wasn't the brightest thing to do right now, but screw it. Between the aches in my body and the force that was my ex sitting opposite me, I need the additional courage boost.

I drank some beer then said, "The only thing I know that you probably don't is the fact that Mona was keeping a little black book of all her clients. Only instead of names and numbers, she had pictures. Lots of pictures. Some of them very compromising."

"And where did you find this little black book given her apartment is a crime scene and you shouldn't have entered?"

"It wasn't a crime scene when I went there. She was missing at that stage, not dead. Lyle gave me the key."

His look suggested he didn't entirely believe me, but all he said was, "Where is the book now?"

"Upstairs." I glanced at Ceri. "It's in the floor safe, if you wouldn't mind getting it."

She nodded and walked out. Kaij studied me for a moment, then said, "You told your father about the book, didn't you?"

I grimaced. "Stupid, I know, but I thought Gilroy deserved the right of reply before I made the book's existence public knowledge."

"But in delaying informing us, you've perhaps let a killer go free. Didn't it occur to you that *any* of the men in that book could have murdered her?"

"It occurred."

He snorted and shook his head, his expression one of disgust. "And you don't care."

"It's not that I don't care, it's just that I don't believe—" I stopped, and his gaze narrowed.

"You don't believe *what*?"

That someone else in that book did it. But I was saved from answering by Ceri's return. She handed him the book then glanced at me and said, "Painkiller?"

"Yeah." Though mixing alcohol and medicine was probably an even less than bright idea. I met Kaij's gaze again. "Did you ask about Keale's blood tests?"

He raised an eyebrow. "Answer my question, and I might just answer yours."

Frustration swirled through me, but I guess fair was fair. Which still didn't mean I was about to be totally honest. "All I was going to say was that I don't believe she was murdered by someone in that book."

"Is Gilroy in that book? Was James Logan?"

"Yes."

He frowned. "So you think her murder was a random event?"

I continued to meet his gaze steadily. "Yes."

His disbelief swirled deep inside. But it didn't matter. All I needed was time enough—space enough—to find out whether or not Lyle was behind it all. "Your turn."

He hesitated, then said, a little reluctantly, "They never tested for Prevoron."

"Why not?"

"Because his alcohol reading was so damn high they thought it unnecessary."

And maybe it was, but it still needed to be checked. There was always a chance—however minute it might seem at the moment—that my suspicions were right.

"And?"

"And," he continued, voice harsh, "while I think it will be a waste of everyone's time, he will be contacted first thing tomorrow to arrange a suitable time for it to be done."

I just had to hope there'd still be enough evidence of the drug left in his system to be detectable by then. Presuming, of course, he had been drugged. "Thanks. I owe you one."

"You owe me nothing," he said, voice still harsh. "Except complete and utter honesty. And we both know I'm as likely to get that as I am to see pigs fly."

I didn't say anything. I couldn't, because where this case was concerned, he was right and we both knew it.

Ceri placed a couple of pills and a glass of water in front of me, then plucked the beer from my fingers and glared at Kaij. "Look, can't these questions wait until tomorrow? She really needs to get some rest."

His gaze briefly swept my upper body. Gold glittered deep

in the green depths—a sure sign of emotions barely controlled. Whether it was just anger, or something stronger, I couldn't say. He was controlling himself too tightly for me to get any true grip on his deeper emotions.

"Tomorrow, then," he said softly. "But I want some answers, Harri, or I'll drag you down to headquarters like I *should* have done in the first place."

"Fair enough," I replied, with a casualness I certainly didn't feel. "Tomorrow then."

His gaze rested on mine for a few seconds longer, then he rose abruptly. But halfway to the door, he stopped and turned. "I've ordered a watch to be kept on you and the house."

Which explained his sudden appearance, I thought, studying him through slightly narrowed eyes. He'd been coming here to tell me. "That's not necess—"

"It fucking is," he snapped back. Then he took a deep breath, said something under his breath, and walked out.

Ceri released a breath. "Wow, he certainly hasn't lost any of his intensity, has he?"

"No." I took the painkillers, and then glanced around as the ogres walked back into the room. "Anything?"

Guy shook his head. "Plenty of white Holdens, but none with recent rear panel damage." His expression suddenly brightened. "We did, however, find Goliath's van. It had some very lovely leather seats in it."

"Had?" Ceri asked, voice amused.

Guy nodded. "Lovely black ones. Like armchairs to sit in, they are. Perfect for watching the TV from."

"You are not bringing stolen car seats into my house," I said.

"Harri my friend, they are *not* stolen. They are Goliath's contribution to the beer I had to replace and the damage he did here."

"Well, you can keep them at *your* place. I do not want them here."

Guy shook his head, his expression one of resignation. "You have no sense of style, Harri."

"And hardly enough space in the living room for three ogres let alone two big car seats."

"We could move the—"

"No." I pushed wearily to my feet. "Now, if you don't mind, I need to go collapse into bed."

"You should," Guy said, expression suddenly concerned. "You look like crap."

"And you have to look bad if an ogre is telling you that," Ceri said blandly. She made a shooing motion with her hands. "You three, out. You can haunt the fridge and TV tomorrow."

He frowned. "You don't want us to stick around, just in case the unwanted come calling?"

I hesitated and then shook my head. "Thanks, but Kaij has ordered someone to keep watch on the house. If Goliath or anyone else *does* attempt a break in, they'll stop them."

Only that someone had been ordered to keep a watch on me as much as the house. And that meant from now on, I'd have a tail—an official one.

Which was going to put a cramp on my investigations—something Kaij had no doubt intended.

"Then we'll shoo, as ordered. Good night, friends Harri and Ceri."

The three of them left. Ceri locked up the house and I somehow managed to stay awake long enough to send those files to Greg before I collapsed into bed and fell fast asleep.

The phone woke me hours later. I forced an eye open, noted somewhat blearily the sun pouring in through the windows, and then groped for my cell.

"Hello?"

"Harri?"

"Yeah." I rolled onto my back, and instantly a dozen little men armed with sharp pokers began assaulting my body. I bit back a hiss and added, "Who's this?"

"Darryl. I've found a drug dealer you might want to talk to."

That certainly got my attention. "Does he happen to handle Prevoron?"

"Considering the word on the street is that he pocketed two hundred and fifty grand recently in a Prevoron sale, I'd say yes. And seeing we're missing about the same about of cash, I thought it was worth mentioning."

It certainly was. "Where is he now?"

"Home, safe and snug in his bed. You want to pay him a visit?"

I hesitated. The way I was feeling right now, a vicious teddy bear could knock me over. I doubted I'd provide much threat to a drug dealer and I really wasn't up to sweet-talking anyone. "You wouldn't happen to be free this morning, would you?"

"Certainly am. Swing by the gym opposite the Stoke House to pick me up, and we'll go from there."

I glanced at the clock. It was barely seven—no wonder I still felt like shit. Although after the beating I'd taken last night, I doubted if even twelve hours sleep would have been enough. "I'll be there in half an hour. And thanks for the tip-off."

"Hey, I want the bastard who killed Mona as much as your relative does."

I believed Darryl when he said that. I was no longer so sure when it came to Lyle.

I hung up, scrubbed a hand across gritty feeling eyes, then forced aching muscles into action and walked across to the windows. I pulled the left side slightly open, wincing at the brightness as I peered out. A nondescript blue car was parked just down the road. I knew all the neighborhood cars —this wasn't one of them. My watcher was in place.

Which meant I had two options—let them follow me, or sneak out the back and see if I could borrow Delilah's car. Hell, she'd borrowed enough things from me—time for a little quid pro quo.

I grabbed a quick shower then dressed in my usual jeans

and a loose T-shirt and headed out the back door. The back-yard bore the bruises of last night's fight, the rockery half destroyed and more bushes crushed. I wasn't much of a gardener, but I *had* put a fair bit of effort into getting this one half-decent, and it was really annoying to see it wrecked.

My father definitely owed me—not that I was ever likely to be compensated.

Delilah walked into her kitchen the same time I did. "Har-ri," she said, blinking in surprise. She was still in her PJ's, but her hair had at least been combed, so she'd been up for a while. "What the hell are you doing here at this hour?"

"I wanted to borrow your car for a couple of hours, if you weren't planning to use it this morning."

She glanced at her watch and then shrugged. "I've got lunch with the family at midday, but if you're late back, it doesn't matter."

"I won't be late."

She nodded, then walked across to the table, dug her keys out of the purse hanging off one of the chairs and tossed them to me. "Ignore the rubbish. Haven't had a chance to clean it out yet."

"Thanks, Delilah."

I headed out. Her car—a cute little Mini Cooper—was parked just several doors down from her house, and it was, as she warned, filled with an assortment of takeaway wrap-ping, empty drink cans, and a mountain of old receipts. Not that my car was usually much better—the only difference was that I didn't have the takeaway rubbish.

The traffic was light thanks to the early hour, so it didn't take me that long to get down to Sandridge. Darryl was waiting on the steps leading up to the gym, a gym bag slung over one shoulder and wearing pale blue bike shorts that left very little to the imagination.

"Mixed circuit class," he said, as he climbed into the car. "Good for stamina, and not bad scenery for the eyes, either."

If all the women in the class wore shorts as short as Darryl, I could see why. "Where are we headed?"

"He lives on Duke Street."

I raised my eyebrows. "Isn't that close to the police station?"

The dwarf snorted. "Yeah. He practically sells it under their noses."

I glanced at the rearview mirror, and then pulled back out into the traffic. It didn't take us that long to get across to Duke Street, and I parked in the first space I spotted.

"It's the red-brick building, third floor," Darryl said, as he shut the door.

"I'm betting they haven't got elevators, either," I grumbled.

He glanced at me, eyes narrowing. "Now that you mention it, you are looking a little worse for wear this morning. Tough night?"

"An encounter with a troll nicknamed Goliath."

"Huh." His gaze swept me. "I take it you didn't tackle the bastard alone."

"Nope." The building's glass front door wasn't security

protected or even locked. I pushed it open. "It still took six of us to bring him down."

"And was he pissed off at you for any reason?"

"It has been suggested someone doesn't like my current line of inquiries."

"Which is always a good indication that the current line of inquiries is the right one."

I guess there was that. We headed up the stairs. I made it up the first flight okay, but by the second flight, the little men in my side were getting busy with the hot pokers again. By the third, sweat had broken out across my brow and it felt like my stomach was about to get reacquainted with my throat.

Maybe I *should* have gone to the hospital again.

Darryl came back down the stairs. "You okay? You're looking rather gray."

I waved a hand rather weakly. "I copped several punches from Goliath. I suspect ribs have been broken."

"Nothing much they can do about those," he commented, sympathy in his voice. "Except wrap them and tell you to rest up."

"Yeah." I dragged myself up the few remaining steps and took a deep, relieved breath at the top—not a good move considering the ribs. I pressed a hand against my side then said, "Which door does our target hide behind?"

"This one." He walked down the hall to three-four, kicked the door open, then, with remarkable speed, ran inside.

I followed at more sedate pace. The flat was small, with a

kitchen-cum-living room that was only a little bigger than my bedroom. Two doors led off, one closed, the other open. It was the latter one that Darryl had disappeared into.

"Now, now," he said from inside the room. "Don't be attempting to dive out that window so fast."

He reappeared a second later, dragging a thin, naked man behind him. The dealer looked to be little more than twenty, with rat-tail hair and sallow, pocked marked skin.

"I ain't done nothing," he yelled. "You can't arrest me when I ain't done nothing."

"Who said we were cops?" I crossed my arms—which hurt like hell but hopefully lent an air of nonchalance—and regarded him steadily. "We're just two people who need a little chat with you."

Darryl dumped him in the middle of the living room floor then stepped back. The dealer didn't bother shifting from his prone position, nor did he attempt to cover-up. Maybe he was used to being dragged naked out of bed by strangers. Or maybe he was just proud of the goods—though I had no idea why. I'd seen bigger parcels on ants.

His gaze ran from me to Darryl then back again. "You're not cops? Then what the fuck gives you the right to break into-"

The rest of his sentence was lost to a yelp as Darryl clipped him over the ear. "Language. We have a lady present."

The dealer sneered but he didn't actually voice the retort I could practically see on his lips—no doubt because he knew Darryl was ready to clip him over the ear again. "What do you want, then?"

"The word on the street is that you made a rather large Prevoron sale recently," I said.

"Then the word on the street is wrong." He shrugged, the movement casual despite the tension I could sense in him. "I only sell small amounts to humans, for recreational purposes. I never carry enough to get a dragon high."

Darryl clipped him over the ear again. "We like liars even less than we like dealers."

Obviously, I thought with some amusement, I'd been relegated the 'good cop' roll. Which was probably just as well given how crappy I was feeling.

"All right, all *right!*" The dealer rubbed his ear. "So maybe I do make the occasional larger sale. If the money is right."

"Then tell us about the recent sale."

He glanced sideways at Darryl then, with a resigned note in his voice, said, "I was asked to get two-hundred and fifty grand worth of Prevoron. I mean, that's a lot of money, you know?"

"How much Prevoron is it, though?"

He shrugged. "A couple of vials. Enough to get a couple of dragons high on, if that's your fancy."

It wasn't, and I clung to the hope that it hadn't been Lyle's. Or Keale's—although given he couldn't rustle up a thousand dollars let alone two hundred and fifty grand, it was doubtful he was the purchaser. "Is it enough to kill them?"

He shrugged. "Two vials might, if it was administered to just one dragon, and the dragon in question was small.

Generally, though, that amount would just get them as high as kites and make them very malleable."

"Who was the buyer?"

"Hey, I don't ask names, you know?"

"But you could see him, couldn't you?"

"Well, it was dark-" He yelped as Darryl clipped him again. "Jesus man, ease up. I was just going to say it was dark, but I could see he was an elf, you know? Saw the outline of the ears as he lit a smoke."

Which put the one person I *didn't* want there squarely in the line of suspicion. *Fuck.* "Young, old, what?"

"Oldish, though it's hard to tell with you lot. He was wearing a large coat, so couldn't see much of his build."

"Anything else?"

The dealer sniffed. "What do you want, blood? We made a deal, he gave me the money, end of story."

"Did you happen to see the car he was driving?"

The dealer hesitated. Darryl raised his palm again.

"It was some little red thing," the dealer said quickly. "Can't tell you the make or number plate because I wasn't close enough."

I closed my eyes in brief relief. I'd expected him to say BMW—the make Lyle drove. But just because it was a different car didn't mean Lyle was off the hook. Not by a long shot—after all, there weren't that many elves who actually smoked.

"What happened to the money?" Darryl asked.

"Hey, I've spent most of it, on bills and stuff, you know?"

Anyone who spent two hundred and fifty grand in less than a week was either a fool or a liar, and I was betting on the latter.

Darryl obviously came to the same conclusion. "Where is it? Tell us now, or tell the police. Your choice."

The dealer muttered something undoubtedly unpleasant, then said, "It's under the bed. What's left of it, anyway."

Darryl glanced up at me, one eyebrow raised. I shrugged at the unasked question. In the end, the money wasn't important—but this dealer didn't deserve to hang on to it either, and Keale just might need it to pay for his defense if Lyle was the instigator of that crash.

"Where under the bed? Mattress or safe?"

"Safe. But you can't take it. I mean, a deal was done fair and square."

"Tough." I glanced at Darryl, and added in explanation, "The recipient of that Prevoron could use it to pay for his defense."

Darryl grabbed the other man by the scruff of the neck and hauled him none too gently to his feet. "Right then," he said, pushing the dealer toward the bedroom. "Let's go fetch it for the lady."

The dealer muttered more obscenities, but he had little choice and he knew it. And it wasn't like he could report our theft to the cops. They came back a few minutes later, and Darryl tossed me an old red duffel bag. "There's about one hundred and seventy odd grand in there. That should more than pay for your friend's defense."

And perhaps some of the damage to my house. I wasn't above using dirty money, especially when it came from the Phillecky family coffers. It wasn't like they'd contributed greatly toward my upbringing.

I slung the bag over my shoulder and said, "Is there anything else we should know?"

The dealer shook his head. If his expression was anything to go by, I'd be a dead woman if he ever met me in a dark alley. But then, it wasn't like I spent much time in dark alleys.

"Then we'll leave. Thanks for your help."

He snorted. Darryl forced him onto his knees then patted his shoulder. "Be a good lad and don't move for the next ten minutes. Otherwise, the cops might just be informed that they have a major drug dealer on their doorstep."

We headed out. The lock was broken, so Darryl just pulled the door closed then followed me down the stairs. "Is that money really for the Prevoron recipient?"

I glanced over my shoulder. "You've heard about the dragon crashing into the helicopter?"

His eyes widened. "That's who got it?"

I nodded. "He's a friend, and the man I asked to represent him just happens to be Lyle Phillecky."

Darryl whistled softly. "Who just happens to fit the description we were just given."

I nodded. "I'm not totally convinced it was him, though."

"Not convinced, or not wanting to believe?" he asked, rather shrewdly.

Damn it, the man didn't even know me and he was guessing right. Was it really that obvious?

Yeah, I thought, it was. It's just that I didn't want to believe the one Elven relative I actually liked could do this to my friends and me.

But then, he was an elf. Why in the hell would I expect anything else?

"More the latter." I shrugged, the movement casual when I was feeling anything but casual about the whole matter. "But I think he might have gone a little crazy when he heard about Mona being beaten. Frank Logan was supposed to have been on that helicopter."

"An elf doesn't have to be crazy to believe that the death of two or three innocents is justifiable if it leads to the death of one enemy."

"No." I winced as the bag bumped against my side, and switched it over. "He doesn't drive a red car though."

Darryl snorted. "Like it's hard to borrow or rent a car."

"And he wouldn't do anything that could be traced back to him. He's too canny."

"If he's unstable, he may not be thinking with his usual clarity."

"That's true." I opened the car, threw the money bag onto the back seat, and then got in.

"And if that is the case, it might just be worthwhile to keep an eye on him. Maybe he's intending to go after everyone who was involved with Mona."

"Presuming it was a client who killed Mona, and not a random event."

"You don't believe that any more than I do."

"No." And yet, who had? Not Gilroy, I was sure of that. My father was certainly capable, and yet he wouldn't have paid her if murder was his intention. Which again left me with Lyle. And yet, I couldn't believe he would have inflicted such violence on her—murder her, yes. But rape? Strangulation? That didn't seem right.

"I agree that a tail might be a good idea, but I can't do it myself right now. And I can't afford to hire you—but there is a large bag filled with money sitting in the back of the car. Would you have the time to do it?"

"Sure. I'd do it for nothing, but hey, seeing it's drug money." He twisted around and helped himself to one thick stack of bills. "I'll have to go home to change first. I'm a bit obvious in these bike shorts."

I grinned. "Obvious is certainly a good way to describe them."

"Hey, if you've got it, flaunt it." He tucked the money into the gym bag at his feet. "It'll take about half an hour to shower and change before I could head anywhere though."

I grabbed a bit of paper rubbish sitting in the cup holder and scrawled Lyle's address on the back of it. "He seems intent on drinking himself into oblivion of late, so I shouldn't imagine he'd be up and about too early."

"Elves do a lot of things they shouldn't be able to," he said, voice holding the slightest trace of bitterness.

I raised my eyebrows in surprise. Obviously, elves and he did not have a happy past, but I knew better than to question him. Besides the fact I sensed he wouldn't answer, it wasn't the time or place to satisfy curiosity.

I started the car then said, "Where are you staying at the moment?"

"Not far from the gym. Just drop me off there, and I'll jog over."

I did that, but as he opened the door to get out, he paused and glanced back at me. "Remember, no matter who is behind her murder, if you go after them, I want a part of it."

"No worries. But if you want to do something for her, then make sure she gets a proper burial."

"I will. She deserves that, after everything she's gone through."

Yes, she did. Especially if the man she was going to stop her song for was also the man behind her murder.

I pushed the thought from my mind and swung back into the traffic. I didn't head home, though, but rather to Lyle's.

We needed answers and we needed them fast, and that meant I had to do the one thing I really didn't want to do.

I had to poke the snake.

CHAPTER TWELVE

I parked just down the road from Lyle's apartment building, then locked up and walked back. It was after eight on a Monday morning, so there were plenty of people out and about on the street, and yet, rather weirdly, I felt more than a little alone.

And more than a little uneasy.

My gaze rose. The penthouse's blinds were closed. Maybe he was asleep. Maybe he was still sitting in the dark, brooding and plotting.

I flexed my fingers in an effort to ease the growing tension, then walked up the steps and pressed the penthouse's intercom button. He didn't respond. I kept pressing, because if he was there, sooner or later he'd answer. He knew me well enough to know I wouldn't give up—and if he was up there, I had no doubt he'd know it was me at the end of the buzzer.

But after five minutes, there was still no response. I punched the intercom in frustration, then made my way back to the car. But as I took a final glance up at the pent-house, trepidation stirred anew. Something was wrong. *Very* wrong.

Acting on instinct rather than any logical reasoning, I dug out my cell phone and dialed my father. Jose answered the call and put me through again.

"Why the hell are you calling? To gloat?" Bramwell said, without preamble. "If so, enjoy it while you can. Gilroy will neither be charged with this crime nor destroyed by it."

Why the hell did I bother? It was tempting, very tempting, to just hang up on the bastard, but I'd never be able to look my mother in the eye again if I did. I might not care for him, but she still did.

"If you value the life of your precious son, you might want to shut up and listen to what I have to say."

He snorted. "And why would think you have anything I might want to hear?"

Well, he was still on the phone, for a start. "Listen, father of mine, I believe Gilroy was set up and I don't think the person who did it is finished with either of you yet."

"Considering you're the one most likely to be behind it, I'm taking *that* as a threat."

"Neither you nor Gilroy are so important to me that I'd go to such lengths to destroy you both. I don't need revenge when the mere fact I exist is more than enough to blight your precious little world."

That was one statement he didn't bother refuting.

"The problem is," I continued, voice not as cool and

controlled as I would have liked. "That I think the person behind the set-up is the one person we would never normally suspect."

"And just who might that be, given we walk in very different worlds?"

I snorted. "Don't play dumb, father. There's only one person who fits that particular description, and you know it."

"Lyle is my *brother*. He might not be all that we would wish, but he would not do this to Gilroy. You, on the other hand—"

"*Think* about what I'm saying rather than reacting for a change, asshole," I cut in, more heatedly than was probably wise. "Lyle isn't in a stable frame of mind at the moment—you must have seen that yourself. And we both know he's more than capable of setting something like this up—he's a Phillecky, after all."

Bramwell was silent for a moment. "And what proof do you have of this?"

"Nothing concrete." I hesitated, but decided against telling him what I'd learned from Greg. "It's more things he's said."

"I will not dishonor my brother with questions on this matter based on little more than your suspicions and a few unguarded comments he might have made."

And yet he was willing to believe *me* capable of doing this based on a whole lot less. But then, I *wasn't* family. "Fine. I've done what my mother would have expected of me, and given you the information. What you do with it is your problem."

"Your mother understands the bond of blood. She would never have accused Lyle of such deeds."

"Mom might understand the bond of blood, but she's also under no illusions as to what answering a siren's call long term can do to some men."

She'd lived long enough to see the madness take hold on more than one occasion. And maybe, if she'd been down here, she would have been able to tell me if such madness had taken Lyle.

But she wasn't, and I could only go on intuition. However much I might not want to believe it, I also could not ignore it.

And neither should my father.

"Lyle would not do such a thing to family. Blood is all."

"Except all blood *isn't* equal, is father dearest?" I retorted. "Fine, then. Just don't say I didn't warn you if the shit hits the fan."

"You can be assured of that," he said, voice like ice. "And would you kindly refrain from ringing me in the future?"

"Believe me, I'm only ringing now because it's what Mom would have wanted."

"Goodbye, Harriet," he said and hung up.

I barely resisted the temptation to throw the goddamn phone across the road. Only the knowledge that I couldn't afford to replace it if I damaged it stopped me—although I *did* have a bag filled with cash sitting in the back seat, so technically I guess I *could* replace it.

I threw it on the passenger seat instead, then started up the car and headed home, returning the keys to Delilah before sneaking back into my house via the back door.

Keale, Guy, and Moe were sitting in the living room watching Get Smart repeats, all three laughing so hard that tears streamed down their faces. I shook my head in amusement and closed the door before retreating to my bedroom. After hiding the bag amongst the mess at the bottom of my closet, I stripped off and climbed into bed.

Dusk had invaded the room by the time I woke. I stretched, remembered the sore side when the men with pokers got busy again, and carefully climbed out of bed. A hot shower and fresh clothes didn't do a great deal to make me feel better, and I was feeling a little less than pleasant as I made my way down to the kitchen, my footsteps echoing in the silence.

"Harri my friend," Guy said, from the bowels of the living room. "Ten minutes later and you would have missed the food."

I paused in the doorway. Half a dozen pizza boxes had been piled haphazardly onto the coffee table, and he, Keale and Moe were making serious inroads into demolishing everything. No wonder the house had been silent.

Then I took one look at all the muck on the top of the pizzas and shuddered. When an ogre asked for a pizza with the lot, they meant the *lot*. I didn't mind seafood, but certainly not when it was combined with ham, pepperoni, salami, chicken, egg, pineapple, peppers, spinach, and tomatoes, as well as a wild assortment of cheese.

"Thanks, but I'll think I'll have something a little more sedate."

"Hey, this pizza covers all the basic food groups—meat, dairy, and grain. What more could you want?"

"Good taste," I muttered and continued on into the kitchen.

Guy snorted. "There's nothing finer than pizza. Except maybe your lasagna." He followed me into the kitchen. "Asked around about that truck today."

"And?" I opened the fridge door to see what had escaped the ogre raids. I discovered some tuna that smelled reasonably fresh and decided that would do.

"Got a couple possibilities. We could check them out once you've eaten. They're basically back-yarders—they only do it as a sideline to raise some extra cash."

I pulled out the frying pan, shoved it on the stove, and then looked around. "You've got their addresses?"

He nodded. "One's in Vermont, the other in Keilor North."

Talk about hiking from one side of the Berren to the other. Still, it wasn't like I had any real work waiting for me—not unless Ceri had managed to drum up some business after I'd gone to bed last night. The pan began to smoke, so I dropped the tuna steak into it then placed some bread into the toaster.

"You available to go out there tonight?"

"Certainly am."

"Go where?" Keale asked, as he wandered into the kitchen, pizza box in hand.

"To chase down a lead on the removal van Rebecca hired." I flipped the tuna. "Did Kaij ring you about blood tests today?"

He nodded. "I got the impression he thinks it's as big a waste of time as I do, but he got me in straight away."

"It's hardly a waste of time if it saves you from going to jail."

"Maybe, but it doesn't negate the fact I killed four people, Harri. Nothing will."

"No, but it will negate the sentence." I raised an eyebrow. "Or do you want to be locked up for the rest of your life?"

He snorted. "Of course not. It's just that—"

"Keale," I said, pulling the frying pan off the gas. "If someone drugged you in order to make you hit that helicopter, then they're responsible for the crash, not you. You're just the weapon used."

"And he was one hell of a weapon," Guy commented, snagging a piece of pizza from the box Keale held.

Keale gave him a sour look. "A weapon that killed four people."

Guy slapped him on the shoulder. "You can't be responsible for what you can't help. It's just a fact of life. Like farts, really."

"Only an ogre could equate death with farts," Keale muttered, and then glanced at me. "You want company chasing down this lead?"

"Yes, but you're staying here with Moe. You need to keep your head down and out of any sort of trouble right now."

"Staying here doesn't seem like it's a guarantee of avoiding trouble. Guy told me what happened last night."

"And how you slept through it I have no idea." I buttered the toast, spread some tomato relish over it, and then put the tuna steak in between the two of them. "Guy, is Moe okay to stay here until we return?"

"Sure. Curly will be here soon, too—he had to stop to get some beer."

I raised my eyebrows. "How does he order anything if he doesn't speak?"

"Self-service, of course."

"But they do have voices, don't they?"

Guy grinned. "Yeah, but five years ago they decided to have a contest to see who could remain silent the longest. There are five slabs riding on it."

Only an ogre would carry on a daft bet like that for this long. "Can they talk when they're alone?"

"Nope. Not at all. The first one to break buys the beer."

"What about Shemp? Isn't he married?"

"Yeah, but not talking is the best way to get on the good side of an ogress, I tell you."

I snorted softly. "They must be fun phone conversationalists."

"Talk your ear off, they can," Guy said. "You just have to learn to read the finer nuances of their silence."

"Ah-huh." I dug my credentials and wallet out of my handbag, then grabbed my sandwich and said, "You ready to go?"

"Sure am." He snagged the last bit of pizza then waved me ahead of him.

"Be careful," Keale said. "And remember, if you happen to find Rebecca, don't antagonize her. She may be going off the boil but she'll still be as touchy as hell."

"Only a male would equate not being in season to going off the boil."

He grinned. "Hey, in this case, it's nothing but the truth."

I shook my head and left. My watcher was still present but that was okay. Kaij knew about my suspicions when it came to Keale; it was the ones I had about Lyle I didn't want him aware of just yet.

Once we were in my car, I grabbed the Melway Street Directory from the back seat and handed it to Guy. "Tell me where I'm heading."

"Drive across to Canterbury Road. I'll direct from there."

"Might help if you hold the street directory the right way around."

He grinned and turned it right side up. "Harri, you have no sense of adventure."

I snorted and started the car. The last time Guy had let his sense of adventure get the better of good judgment, we'd ended up in Dandenong. Which wasn't a bad thing unless you were actually headed for Healesville—the opposite direction.

Despite the remnants of peak hour still hanging around, it

didn't take us that long to get across to Vermont. Guy directed me through a maze of side streets and eventually told me to slow down. My gaze flicked to the rear vision mirror. Down the other end of the street, a car I presumed was Kaij's tail pulled to a stop. They were good—I hadn't actually spotted them much on the journey over there, despite knowing they were somewhere behind us.

"It's number nine, if my information is right," the ogre said, peering out through the windscreen.

Number nine, it turned out, was down the other end of the street, and there was a big white truck parked in the driveway. I maneuvered the car so the headlights hit the truck's side—the words "Mark's Express Removals' were plastered on the side, but there wasn't a little truck doing wheelies to be seen anywhere.

"Not the right one," I said.

"Well, fuck them," Guy muttered. "Keilor North here we come."

I did a U-turn and headed back the way we'd come. It took almost an hour to get across to Keilor thanks to the road-works on the Calder Freeway. As we neared Keilor North, Guy flicked the internal light on and squinted at the directory. "Take the next left."

"You sure? That's the speedway exit, isn't it?"

"Yeah, but it heads back towards Sydenham. The house we want is just off the Sydenham end of Calder Park Drive."

"You're the navigator." I swung left.

"Scary thought, isn't it?" He grinned.

Only if he got us lost again. Which he hadn't. We found the house we were looking for pretty quickly, and the truck we wanted was parked in the vacant lot beside the house.

I stopped. "I'll go question them. You'd better stay put."

"You don't think I could charm the information out of them?" he said, and let rip with a fart of such power I practically fell out of the car to get away from it.

Guy's laughter followed me as I walked up the steps to the front door. I pressed the doorbell and waited.

After a few seconds, footsteps echoed, then a middle-aged woman opened the door and raised an eyebrow. "Can I help you?"

"I hope so." I dragged out my PI credentials and showed them to her. "I'm trying to track down a woman named Rebecca. I believe you helped shift her furniture a few days ago."

The woman looked me up and down, and then sniffed. She didn't look impressed and I couldn't say I blamed her. Between the bruises, the cut on my head, the faded jeans and baggy sweater, I probably didn't give a great impression.

"Is she in trouble or anything?"

"No. But we think she may have been a witness to an accident my client was involved in, and we need to talk to her."

"If it involves the police, why aren't they chasing them down?"

Good question, I thought. "Because the police have better things to do than waste time chasing down a woman who may or may not have witnessed an accident."

She looked me up and down again. Not exactly believing my story, but not disbelieving it, either. Some siren charm wouldn't have gone astray right now, but even if I could get it to work on females, she didn't actually look the type who'd be charmed.

"How did you find us, then?"

"Her neighbor in Research gave us the name of your company."

"*That* tart," she muttered. "She was out the front, watching everything we did, taking notes, like she expected us to steal something vital."

And thank God she had, otherwise I might have never gotten even this close to finding Rebecca. "Would you be able to give me the address you took her goods to?"

The woman's gaze narrowed. "I'm running a business here. I don't give anything away for free."

I sighed and dug out my wallet. "I've only got twenty on me."

"That'll do." She snatched the note from my fingers. "Wait here."

She disappeared down the hallway, her footsteps echoing on the polished floorboards. I waited as directed and, after a few minutes, she reappeared and handed me a torn off sheet of yellow notepaper.

"We took her stuff to a place in Greenvale. Near the school it was."

"Anyone else living there?"

The woman shrugged. "Didn't see anyone."

"Thanks for the help, then."

"No probs."

She closed the door, and I headed back to the car—only to discover Guy had not been idle while I'd been questioning the woman. The air was thick enough to carve.

"Any luck?" he asked, as I climbed back in.

"Yes." I hastily wound down the window. "And can you please restrain yourself in restricted areas?"

He grinned. "As my grandmother used to say, wherever you be, let your wind go free."

"Your grandmother obviously *never* had to sit in a car with you."

"It ain't that bad. Not yet, anyway. So you've got the she-dragon's address?"

"Well, I've got the address of where they dumped the furniture. Whether that's her address or not is anyone's guess at this stage."

"I don't think the problem is going to be finding her," Guy commented. "I think it'll be convincing her to help us. I don't like our chances, you know."

Neither did I. But if the drug test didn't reveal anything, then Rebecca might be Keale's only real chance. We had to at least try.

Her house was a large, double fronted brick veneer with a two-car garage and a manicured garden. It wasn't as big as some of the neighboring houses, but it certainly couldn't be termed small by any means. My house would fit into it twice over, and there'd still be room for a dance floor.

"How are we going to play this?" Guy's expression was dubious.

"We don't know yet if this is her place, or if she's even home." After all, there were no lights on. "That's the first thing we need to find out."

"But if she *is* there?" He glanced at me. "If she jumps us, we're dead."

"Females are smaller than males. She can't take the two of us out at the same time. As long as we keep some distance between us, we should be fine."

And if something *did* happen, then at least our follower would witness it.

"Keeping our head down won't help if she decides to make us toast," he grumbled.

"Think positive. Maybe she doesn't like toast."

Guy didn't appear comforted by *that*. To be honest, neither was I. I climbed out of the car, then hesitated, and left not only my keys on the seat but also my cell phone. Guy didn't generally carry a cell phone around, and if something went wrong—if Rebecca *did* attack me—then at least he had some way of marshaling help.

We headed up the driveway. The street light at the front of the property washed the lawn with brightness, yet the porch itself was crowded with shadows. Guy hung back while I walked up to the front door and pressed the bell. Inside, music played, the bass hard and heavy. Techno—an unusual choice for a dragon, as their hearing tended to be sensitive. Most seemed to prefer easy listening. Grandma stuff, as Guy called it.

I pressed the doorbell again. The music suddenly cut out and footsteps approached. As the door opened, the porch light came on, making me blink against the sudden brightness.

"Yes?" a woman asked, her voice low and somewhat sultry. It was the sort of voice that could have made her a fortune on the phone sex lines. "How may I help you?"

She was tall, at least three or four inches above my own five six, with sharp features and hair the color of icebergs—white, with a shimmery blue heart. Her eyes were an incandescent blue. Beautiful, and yet also alien.

And oddly, I was suddenly reminded of Numar's description of the woman he'd met—a stunning blonde with beautiful blue eyes.

"How can I help you?"

I flashed my ID, and then said, "I'm looking for Rebecca Price."

"That's me. What can I do for you?"

"We need to talk to you about Keale Finch."

"We?"

She stepped forward enough to spot Guy and something flared in her eyes. Something that stirred fear deep inside.

"I'm sorry," she said softly, "But I do not know who you are

321

talking about."

I resisted the urge to back away, and said, "Rebecca, we know that's a lie. You talk to us, or you talk to the police. Your choice."

Her gaze swept from me to Guy, but her cool expression didn't change. "By all means, then, come in."

I glanced at Guy. He didn't look any more pleased about stepping into a dragon's den than I felt, but there was little other choice. We needed answers, and this was our only way of getting them.

She led us into her living room. The furniture was expensive looking, antiques and leather filling the space. She sat down on one of the voluminous chairs, and then motioned us toward the sofa. I sat. Guy remained standing behind me.

A cool smile touched her lips. "What do you wish to know?"

I studied her for a moment, then decided I might as well jump in feet first, even if we had absolutely nothing more than unsubstantiated suspicions. "We know you were the one who gave Keale Prevoron. We want to know who your accomplice was."

She raised a pale eyebrow. "You're making a pretty dangerous statement considering where you currently sit."

Trepidation shivered through me. Though neither her expression nor position had changed, she suddenly seemed more on edge, more ready to attack. Guy felt it too, if the tension suddenly radiating off him was anything to go by.

"If you don't help us," I said, meeting her gaze and seeing

that flare get deeper, "then it's a statement the police will be hearing."

"And it is also one you cannot prove."

Meaning she *had* been involved in drugging Keale? "Blood tests have been done, and we both know they will reveal the presence of Prevoron. They will also pinpoint the administration date."

"Which will prove nothing, as Keale himself will confirm that our date had been called off that night. Besides, I wouldn't be sure that the drug test will reveal *anything* more than alcohol."

"Alcohol you drip fed into his system after the administration of the drug." It was another guess, but I suspected it was a correct one.

She raised her eyebrows, denying nothing, admitting nothing. I continued on, keeping my voice flat, unemotional. I had a bad feeling that if I didn't, she'd explode—quite literally—into dragon form. "We also have a witness who will testify an elf was with you the night the drug was administered. That same elf was seen purchasing Prevoron. It's enough, I believe, for the police to begin investigations."

"They cannot investigate if they do not have the information. And they cannot get the information if you are dead."

I smiled, but there was very little humor in it. "We are not foolish enough to have come here without ensuring someone not only knows where we are, but why we are here."

And I was suddenly very glad Kaij had insisted on me having a tail.

"Why should I divulge any information? You can suspect my part in this alleged drugging event all you wish, but there *is* no proof. If there was, the police would be here rather than yourselves."

She had *that* right. I studied her for a moment, and, for the second time that night, wished I could call on my siren magic.

"Rebecca, the man we suspect to be your partner in this has already killed several people. We believe he's tying up ends and you may well be the next on his list."

"Oh, he's welcome to try, but I shall eat him before he does."

It was a none-too-subtle reminder of what she was. Not that we needed reminding. I changed tact yet again. "I want the person behind this whole plot, not the administrator of the drug. But as I said before, I'm more than happy to go to the police if the latter does not give me the former."

She smiled. There was nothing remotely pleasant or human about it. "I would not do that if I were you."

The phone rang shrilly into the silence that followed her comment. She rose, the movement unhurried and graceful. "Please excuse me while I answer that."

She walked from the room, and I released the breath I hadn't even realized I'd been holding.

"Man," Guy said, wiping a hand across his forehead. "That's one cold reptile. I think a quick retreat is called for here. She isn't going to tell us anything."

"Probably not, but we have to at least try to convince her it's in her best interest to help us."

"And how do you propose to do that? I can tell you now, the Phillecky charm is not doing the job."

"Well, it won't because she's female. But if we leave, Keale's prison bait. We need more than just the fact he's been drugged to get him off the hook."

"And if we don't leave, we're dragon bait," Guy muttered. "I'm telling you, she's got that look in her eye."

"I know. But I'm not leaving just yet."

"Fucking hell," he muttered. "Are you trying to send me *gray*?"

"Considering you're bald, that would be quite a feat."

"I've got hair where it counts, Harri my friend, but I'm telling you, gray is not a good look down there."

I restrained my grin and looked around as Rebecca walked back into the room. There was something about the way she moved, something about the sharpness of her gaze, that had the hairs on the back of my neck rising.

"Now," she said softly, as she sat down. "Where were we?"

I met her gaze calmly enough, but the need to move, to get the hell away from her, was becoming so intense my feet itched and my pulse raced. "What would it take to convince you to help us?"

Slowly, deliberately, she looked us both up and down. Sizing up her next meal, I thought, with an internal shiver. "Certainly more than you two have."

"I guess that's it then," Guy said, his voice a little too loud and jovial. "We'd best get going."

I rose. "Keale never did you any harm, Rebecca. He deserves better than this."

And better than you, I wanted to add, but I wasn't about to poke this particular reptile any more than I already had.

"You were foolish to come here in the first place," she said, that gleam in her eye growing. "You must have known it would be of little use."

I shrugged. "Keale's our friend."

"And friends look after each other," she said, nodding. "A noble, if somewhat archaic, sentiment."

I suddenly wondered just how old she was. A dragon's life-span far outstretched even that of elves; given the way she spoke, Rebecca probably had at least a hundred years behind her, if not more.

"We'll be seeing you, Rebecca."

She rose gracefully to her feet. "I doubt it."

I paused. Guy groaned, but I ignored him and met her gaze squarely. "Believe me, one way or another, you will help us clear Keale."

So much for not poking the angry reptile.

She raised a silver eyebrow. "I do like a woman who can look death in the eye so fearlessly."

There wasn't much I wanted to say to that, so I turned and followed Guy down the hall to the front door. Rebecca followed us out onto the porch.

"Goodbye, Rebecca." I paused and met her gaze again. "Or would that be Mandy?"

She merely smiled. "Goodbye Harri."

I'd actually taken two steps before I realized what she said. I stopped abruptly, my stomach sinking as I turned around. There were only three ways she could have known my name—one, she was a speed-reader, and had somehow caught my name as I'd briefly flashed my credentials. Two, she'd overheard Guy's whisper, or three, whoever was on the other end of that call had told her.

I knew, as I met her gaze, it wasn't either of the first two options.

"Who was on the phone, Rebecca?"

Her smile was almost sweet. "My accomplice."

"Oh man," Guy muttered. "This is not good."

I didn't move. I didn't dare. If I did, she'd change, I had no doubt about that. I watched her eyes, knowing from Keale that the dragon would rise there first. It would give us a few seconds warning; time enough to run, to feel fear, but not time enough to save ourselves.

"What did he want?"

"You."

The incandescent blue of her eyes went black and the air began to shimmer with energy. The beast was rising.

"Guy, run!"

I turned and did exactly that. I didn't get far. One moment I was running, next there was a huge gust of wind that sent me tumbling but before I could scramble to my feet let alone look around, I was being swept into the air.

"Harri!" Guy screamed.

A rock bit through the air close to Rebecca's right wing. She shifted direction abruptly, and I heard the hiss of steam rise in her throat.

"Oh no, you don't," I said, and kicked her belly with all my might.

Dragon's had thick hides, but it was enough to put her off flaming, enough to give Guy time to run for cover. She hissed, her head snaking around. Steam trickled from her nose and for a moment I thought she was intended to crisp me right there and then.

Then the madness left her eyes. She surged upward, her wings creaking as she headed for the stars. I tried to move, tried to get free before we got too high, but her talons were wrapped so tightly around me that my arms were pinned to my sides and it felt like my cracked ribs were being driven into my chest. I could barely even breathe let alone wriggle free.

I looked down and saw the ground far below us. Too late to get free now—I'd kill myself. Although that would probably be a better death than the one Rebecca had planned. Movement caught my eye—Guy was an ant running toward a matchbox car.

She shifted position, leveling off, and suddenly all I could see was the silver hide of her underbelly. Her wings rose and fell effortlessly and the wind was icy, tearing at my clothes and freezing my skin. Moonlight and stars seemed to surround us, so bright it could have been day. I wondered if she'd been ordered to find somewhere isolated to drop me, or whether she simply intended to eat me. Probably the former, I thought, somewhat vaguely. There wasn't a whole lot of fat on me, after all, so I'd probably be awfully grisly.

We'd been flying for some time when I heard the trumpeting. It was an angry sound that seemed to shudder through every fiber of the silver creature who held me so tightly. The tempo of her wings increased, and the air roared, slapping against me so hard my cheeks flapped. I would have screamed if I'd had the breath.

Again the trumpet sounded, closer this time. Rebecca bellowed in response, an angry sound that shook her body and sawed at my ears. She swerved to the left, snapping my head back, then dove so fast bile rose in my throat. Then we were climbing again, her wings straining, body vibrating with effort.

Abruptly, she swerved right. Something big and red shot past us and bank sharply, wings gleaming with molten fire against the cold light of the moon.

Keale, I thought distantly.

Then, more sharply, *Keale!*

But how? His wing had still been in plaster last time I'd seen him.

A heavy rumble came from deep inside Rebecca's gut. The hiss in her throat rose again, then she opened her mouth and spewed fire into the night. A cloud of ash and smoke and heat flew back into me, searing my skin and choking my lungs. I coughed, tears suddenly streaming down my face as I tried desperately to see if Keale was okay.

I spotted him to our right, driving upwards, the flames licking at his tail, scorching where they touched. He kept rising, going beyond my sight but not hers. She screamed and surged forward, her silvery wings almost a blur. The wind seemed to echo her scream, and it was an almost human sound. Maybe it was. Maybe it was *me* screaming. I couldn't say. I could barely even see let alone hear.

She swerved to the left. Keale appeared, his tail lashing out like a whip, striking one wing and tearing membrane. She screamed again and shook her head in fury. The moonlight danced across her ice-colored scales and, just for a moment, it looked like her skin was littered with diamonds.

Again she made that strange noise in her throat, then flames arced through the sky, almost seeming to follow Keale as he did a belly roll and dove. He reappeared underneath us, his tail once again lashing out. This time it struck her reptilian head and she trumpeted her fury. Droplets of black blood began to splatter across my face and body.

She was finally hurt.

Fire rained from the sky above. Rebecca swerved then dove. The snaking lines of streetlights leaped up to greet us, and bile rose in my throat. Then we were rising again, slower than before, Rebecca's gasps for breath shuddering through her entire body.

Another wall of fire appeared in front of us. She screamed and dove under it. Heat and ash sizzled across my skin and a scream tore up my throat but was released unheard. There was too much noise surrounding us for any sound I made to make an impact.

Keale reappeared above us. He shadowed Rebecca's movements for several wing dips then surged forward and dove directly in front of her, forcing her to swerve and dive away. He was trying to force her down, I realized suddenly, and wondered how the hell that was going to help me. Caught between her claws as I was, I'd be squashed the minute we hit the ground.

He appeared yet again, his tail flicking out as he arrowed past, catching Rebecca in the head once more. This time, the flow of blood was stronger, soaking my clothes and filling my nose with its rancid scent.

If the dragons didn't kill me, that smell damn well could.

But Rebecca didn't scream, didn't respond in any way. But there was a hint of desperation in the way she hurtled forward.

Keale swooped in from the left. Rebecca dove underneath him, then snaked her head around, spewing fire across his scales. Keale's tail lashed back and forth, then he rose swiftly, body rolling as he disappeared from my sight.

Rebecca dropped, her body shuddering, as if she'd been hit. Red wings shadowed silver in flight, rising and falling as one. Rebecca bellowed, a sound that became a grunt of pain.

Then the talons that had held me so tightly no longer did so.

I was free.

And hurtling toward a shimmering blackness far below.

CHAPTER THIRTEEN

I seemed to be floating, neither conscious nor unconscious, but caught somewhere in between. The ache of my ribs was distant, muted, and the air no longer screamed. It was silent out here in this wet blackness, yet it was not the silence of death.

Wet.

My mind suddenly focused on that one word.

Why was I wet?

I shifted my arms and felt a familiar ripple across my fingertips.

Water. I was in the water.

I licked my lips and tasted salt. Not just any water, then, but the sea.

I was home.

Or at least, as home as a half-breed siren ever could ever get in the gentle bosom of the ocean.

That was why I'd survived the fall. Hitting the water so hard and fast would normally have killed me just as surely as it would have had I hit the ground. But sirens were born of the sea; it was in their soul, in their blood, and while that blood was diluted in me, there must have been enough for the sea to recognize. She'd caught me, healed me, and kept me safe.

As she would have done to Mona, had Mona still been alive when she'd been dumped here.

I opened my eyes. Dragons no longer fought amongst the stars and I wondered briefly what had happened to them. I hoped Keale was all right. Hoped he wasn't too badly burned.

I closed my eyes again and drifted away, safe in the tender grip of the ocean. When consciousness returned, it was to the sound of voices and the realization I was no longer in the water.

"She should be in the hospital." The voice was cool, controlled, and male.

Kaij, I realized. What the hell was he doing here—wherever here was?

"Darls, she's my sister. Trust me when I say the last place she'd want to be right now is in the hospital."

Val was here, too? What the hell was going on? And where the hell were we?

"She doesn't need the hospital," another, more feminine voice said. It took me a moment to realize it was Maggie. God, was the whole damn circus here? "Other than bruises and a couple of broken ribs, she's fine."

"She should be damn dead, falling from that height," Kaij muttered, and just for a moment, I'd swear there was relief in his voice.

It was that, more than anything, that forced my eyes open. Above me, trees waved, and moonlight danced coldly through their dark green tresses. I lay on my back below them, but my head resting on what felt like warm steel.

I shifted my head slightly, looking up and back. Kaij's gaze met mine, the green depths remote.

"How are you feeling?" he asked, voice holding as little warmth as his expression.

"Cold, wet, but otherwise, no worse off than before I was snatched by a dragon." I paused, then added, with a touch more acidity than I meant, "Why are you here?"

His expression closed over even more—and I hadn't thought *that* was possible. "My men called me and told me you'd been snatched by Rebecca. Guy then informed them that Keale had gone after her. I had both dragons radar tracked until they landed."

"So how did you get here, and where the hell are we?"

"I flew, and we're in Point Nepean national park."

Meaning I'd come down near the heads of Port Phillip Bay. Then I blinked. "You *flew*?"

"Helicopter, not wings." The slightest trace of a smile touched his lips, and it was a sharp reminder that he hadn't always been so cold in his dealings with me. "That's the other branch of the fae family, remember?"

"Oh. Yeah." I paused, watching that slight smile fade and mourning its loss "What happened to Keale and Rebecca?"

"Keale forced her down not far from here. Val wrapped a containment shield around her, but Keale and Guy are keeping watch until I have the chance to question her."

"You haven't yet?" *That* surprised me. I'd have thought it would have been the first thing he'd do.

"No."

Because he wanted to see if I was okay first. He never actually said the words, but I felt the force of them shimmer deep inside all the same. He might be distant, he might be a part of my past and would never be anything more now, but some small part of him still cared enough to not want to see me hurt.

And damn if that realization didn't go some way to warming the chill from my flesh.

"I want to be in on the questioning," I said bluntly. "The bitch owes me some answers after everything she's put me through."

"I figured you'd probably say that." There was a hint of resignation in his voice. "Which is part of the reason I'm still here. Are you up to moving yet?"

"She's not going anywhere until she strips out of those wet clothes," Val stated. "With all the shit going down at the moment, she can *not* afford to catch a cold."

"You bought clothes?" I asked, surprised. "How did you know I'd need them?"

335

"Felt the impact, darls, and sensed you were in the water." He studied me for a moment, expression as serious as I'd ever seen it. "I thought I'd lost you, Harri, and it made me more determined than ever that you and I will never again make like strangers. Like it or not, I am now in your life for good."

I smiled. "I wasn't the one who went off in a huff the last time."

"*That* is beside the point."

I laughed, then winced and gripped my side, even though it didn't hurt quite as much as it had before Rebecca grabbed me. "Maggie, you haven't got something for the ribs, have you?"

"I've put some numbing salve on, but it takes about ten minutes to kick in." She glanced at her watch. "You should be right in four."

"I have *no* intention of laying still for that long. Someone help me up."

Maggie—sans nose wart—and Val offered me their hands, and hauled me gently but effortlessly to my feet. Kaij rose behind me, one hand pressed against my spine, as if he expected me to fall back down again. I didn't, although the night took several mad dashes around me.

"Right," I said, when I felt stable enough to move. "Clothes."

Val presented me with a plastic bag. "They're Bryan's, I'm afraid. I didn't have time to get anything else, as I had to catch a broom taxi to get here."

I frowned. "Why didn't you just magic yourself here?"

"Restrictions, remember? It took a bit to provide Keale's wing with a temporary fix, so I was saving my remaining store of daily magic for whatever I might find here. Just as well, considering what is here is one hell of a pissed off female dragon."

I glanced at Maggie. "So you provided the broom? You're game."

She snorted. "Yes. And he will *not* be heading back that way unless he can refrain from whooping 'Ride 'Em Cowboy' the entire time."

Val grinned. "What can I say? It was exciting."

"And you can excite yourself on someone *else's* broom to get home, laddie."

"You, Maggie Tremaine, are almost as boring as my sister."

"Which is probably why I like her so much. You need a hand stripping those wet clothes off, Harri?"

"Probably." I paused and glanced over my shoulder at Kaij. "Turn around."

His expression was deadpan. "It's not like I haven't seen you naked before."

"That was when we were together, and a long time ago."

He made a disparaging sound, then crossed his arms and turned around. But if lean, muscular backs had a language, then his said 'pissed off'. Good, I thought, a little uncharitably given he was here with me and not questioning Rebecca like he probably should have been.

I stripped off my wet clothes with a little help from Maggie

337

and Val, and then carefully pulled on Bryan's shirt and jeans. They were miles too big, but they were at least warm and dry. I rolled up the sleeves while Val did the same to the bottom of the jeans, then he produced a pair of the most garish pink slip-on shoes I've ever seen. "These *can't* be Bryan's."

He raised his eyebrows, "What, you think Bryan can't do bright?"

"You're all the *bright* anyone would need, so no."

He chuckled. "I'll take that as a compliment. And you're right."

I slipped them on and turned around. "Okay, let's go question our dragon."

Kaij led the way, moving out of the clearing and following a winding path through the trees. The rest of us followed in single file, me with one hand still pressed against my side. Despite Maggie's promise, the salve hadn't yet kicked in, and walking hurt.

We heard Rebecca long before we saw her—the air was thick with hissed expletives. As we came out into a second clearing, her head came around and she belched fire. The flames shot forward, only to stop abruptly and crawl upwards, as if along an invisible wall. Val's shield. Keale and Guy stood over the other side of the shield. Guy leaned against the bonnet of my car drinking a can of what had to be beer given he rarely touched anything else, and Keale studied Rebecca with a somewhat grim expression. There were scorch marks along his tail and flank, and a cut near his forearm, but other than that, he seemed to come out of it relatively unharmed

"Harri my friend," Guy said, raising his can in greeting. "Good to see you up and about."

"Thanks for rousting everyone, Guy."

He grinned. "Least I could do. Besides, whose fridge would I raid if the ice bitch had made a meal of you? My own?"

"Heaven forbid," I said, voice dry.

Keale's head snaked around. "S'arri? S'kay?"

"Yes. And thanks for breaking bail to rescue me."

The dragon shrugged—an awkward movement on a beast so large. "S'kay. You's s'elping me."

My gaze moved past him. Rebecca sat on all fours, her tail flicking back and forth and the moonlight dancing off her silver scales. There were two deep cuts just above her eyes, and another along one wing, but both had stopped bleeding some time ago, if the minimal scent of blood was anything to go by.

Kaij stopped a few steps behind the shimmer of the containment shield. I stopped beside him.

"You's," Rebecca hissed, her blue-black eyes glowing with alien fire. "S'ould 'ave ate you when I's had s'hance."

"It's fortunate that you didn't," Kaij commented, before I could, "Because then you would have been up for six murder charges rather than five."

Her gaze snapped to his. "I's no s'ucking kill anyone. You's talk s'it."

Kaij took his badge from his pocket and showed it to her. "I may talk shit, but I'm also with PIT. If you're the person responsible for drugging Keale Finch, then you're ultimately responsible for the deaths he caused when he crashed into that helicopter."

I have to hand it to Kaij—he sounded very convincing, almost as if he actually believed every word he'd just said.

"I's s'illed no one."

"Then you deny giving him the drug?" I said—obviously to the chagrin of the man standing beside me, if the annoyance that washed through my mind was anything to go by.

"S'eny s'illing. Saying s'othing else."

"Then I guess we have no choice but to charge you." Kaij shook his head. "Hope you enjoy being locked up while your partner walks around free."

"S'all not gets me on no s'uking cell."

I half-smiled. Her words were an echo of what Keale had said only a couple of days ago—only he'd been referring to a truck, not a prison cell.

"Then give us a name, Rebecca," Kaij said, and this time there was an edge in his voice that the wise would *not* ignore.

Rebecca continued to flick her tail back and forth as she contemplated the two of us. It was the sort of look a spider might give a fly—but if she thought Kaij would make an easy meal, then she was in for a rude awaking. Not that she'd get the opportunity to eat either of us anytime in the near future.

"Name," Kaij snapped. "Or I walk and you get the full murder rap."

Still she said nothing. Tension wound through my limbs. I wanted the answer—wanted to know once and for all who'd employed Rebecca to drug Keale—and yet, at the same time, I didn't. Because I already knew what the answer would be.

Eventually, just when the tension running through my limbs was so fierce it felt like I'd surely snap, she spat, "S'yle. S'yle S'lecky."

Damn it, *no.*

I closed my eyes against the sudden sting of tears. I might have been expecting it, but damn it, hearing the confirmation, knowing he'd been playing me—using me—all along hurt more than it really should have.

"Lyle Phillecky?" Kaij cast a sharp look at me—something I felt rather than saw, because I just couldn't look at him.

"Yes." Her tail flicked. "I's paid to s'rug. S'othing else. S'othing to do s'ith s'rash."

"That's hardly true, Rebecca, when you're the one who got hold of the helicopter's flight plans through the friend that worked at the control tower." A fact we actually had no proof of, but one I'm sure would be easy enough to prove. "If you think he's not setting you up to take the fall for all these murders, you're a fool."

"Being an accessory to drugging and false imprisonment is a far lesser charge than being an accessory to murder, Rebecca," Kaij added coldly. "Cooperate fully, testify against Lyle to clear Keale's name of intent, and I'll see you get a lenient sentence."

She didn't immediately say anything, but she had little in the way of options and we all knew it.

She obviously came to the same conclusion, because she reluctantly said, "S'kay."

"Good." He hesitated and glanced briefly at me. "As a matter of interest, just what were you going to do with Harri?"

"S'old to gets rid of her."

"Meaning kill her, or just get her out of the way?"

"Second."

Relief swam through me. He hadn't intended to kill me. That was something, I guess.

"Why?" Kaij asked. "What did he intend to do once she was gone?"

Rebecca shrugged. "S'idn't say."

The image of Lyle sitting in the darkness spouting pretty lines about justice ran through my mind, and fear crawled down my spine.

"This isn't good," I said softly.

"No," Kaij agreed. "I'll put out an APB on him."

"I'm betting you won't find him. Not before he does whatever it is he plans to do."

"Any idea what that is?"

"No-" I stopped as a phone rang.

Guy pushed away from the car, walked around to the back

door, retrieved the phone I'd left sitting there then tossed it over the shield. Kaij caught it one handed then gave it to me.

I hit the receive button. "Hello?"

"Harri? Daryl here."

Oh shit. Here it comes. "What's happened?"

"Your mad Elven uncle has just gone and purchased himself a gun."

The fear, it seemed, had been justified. I rubbed my head wearily. "I thought you had to get a bloody license before you could purchase a gun?"

"Not on the streets, not if you know the right people. Your elf is a lawyer, and he mixes with a lot of low life's these days."

Like the kid who'd sold him the Prevoron. "Where is he now?"

"Driving."

"Aimlessly? Or does he seem to have a purpose?"

"He obviously has a purpose, love, if he's bought himself a gun. He's currently on Punt Road."

"Heading toward the city, or away from it?"

"Toward."

My gut sunk. He was heading toward my father's. With a gun. I was as sure of that as I was the fact that the sun would rise tomorrow. "You don't have to keep following him. I know where he's going."

"You sure? It's no skin off my nose to keep going."

"Thanks, but there's only one place he could be heading given where he currently is."

"Well, he's just turned onto Toorak road."

I closed my eyes. "And in a second, he'll turn into Rocklea Road. Don't follow him."

"If you're sure." He paused. "He just turned as predicted. You'll keep me posted on events, won't you?"

"I will. And thanks, Darryl."

"Darryl?" Kaij said grimly, as I hung up. "This the same Darryl that you didn't know how to get in contact with?"

I opened my mouth to answer, but the phone saved me the effort. I glanced down at the number and felt sick to the core. It was Lyle.

I hit the answer button yet again, and met Kaij's gaze as I said, as evenly as I could, "Hi, Lyle."

Kaij immediately stepped away, dragged his cell phone out of his pocket, and began dialing. Lyle said, "I'd guess that me ringing you is something of a surprise."

He sounded...well, normal. Just like he had, every other time that he'd rung. He did not sound like someone who'd murdered at least five people and who'd gone more than a little out of his mind. I swallowed heavily, and said, "And why would you think that?

"Because the people I hired to keep you secured until certain events were finalized have not been in contact to say that you were safely delivered," he said. "And *that* no doubt means Rebecca is now in your hands and singing her little heart out."

"Oh god, Lyle, *why*?" The question was almost wrenched out of me.

"You know why." There was no emotion in his voice, no life. "It had to be done, Harriet. They all had to pay."

"Keale didn't know Mona, three of those people on the helicopter didn't know Mona, so how is it right—"

"Enough," he said. "If you want answers, Harriet, come see me."

A chill ran through me. He no longer wanted me out of the way. He wanted me dead. As dead as Bramwell. As dead as Gilroy.

Oh god, oh *god*.

"Why? It's not like you're going to tell me anything I can't guess, Lyle."

"That doesn't matter. Nothing really matters, except justice for the dead." He paused, then added, "And if I see or even suspect you've contacted the cops, your father is dead meat."

And with that, he hung up.

"Fuck," I said, and this time I *did* throw the phone. It hit the containment shield and bounced sideways, almost hitting Kaij in the shins. He bent, picked it up, and tossed it back at me.

"What's the mad bastard done this time?" Val asked, concern in his voice.

"He's bought a gun and he's intending to use it."

He raised an eyebrow. "Against Gilroy? Can't honestly say I'd be sad to see that."

"Well, no, but as much as I hate what he represents, Gilroy doesn't deserve to die simply because he was involved with Mona and had a less than stellar opinion of her."

"Given he has a less than stellar opinion of the entire world, that is probably true." A wicked smile touched his lips. "I still wouldn't mind seeing him at least winged, darls. Both he and that bastard father of yours deserve that, at the very least, for their treatment of you."

"Right," Kaij said, striding towards us. His gaze, when it met mine, was resolute. "You and I will take the helicopter back to the city, and from there—"

"Lyle will kill both my brother and father if he so much as *thinks* there are cops nearby."

He crossed his arms and glared at me. "You are not going anywhere near him without a wire and some form of backup close to hand."

"Kaij—"

"*No.* You either do this my way, or we simply storm the place and take him out. Your choice."

"Taking him out isn't going to get answers," I snapped. "All it will get is people dead."

"Considering we're talking about the Phillecky clan, I personally don't think that's a bad thing."

I clenched my fingers against the sharp surge of anger. "*I'm* a Phillecky, in case you've forgotten that." I paused. "Or was I actually included in that little statement?"

"Uh, people," Val interrupted. "Mad elf with a gun, intending to kill—remember him?"

Just for a moment, I had. I cast him a somewhat shamefaced look, then took a deep breath that didn't actually hurt for a change, and said, "Okay, we'll do your way. Just remember to tell everyone to keep out of sight."

"We have done this once or twice before, Harri," he said, voice cool once more.

And I hadn't. I swallowed heavily then said, "What about Rebecca?"

"We can't get a big enough truck up here, but I've ordered reinforcements. But until they get here, Val, are you able to stick around, just in case the shield needs a boost?"

"Sure thing. Just don't get my sister dead, or I might get a little pissed-off."

"I'll look after her."

Val snorted. "Like you did the last time she needed your help? That's not a very comforting thought, you know."

"Val," I warned softly.

He gave me a 'he deserves it' sort of look, but restrained from saying anything else.

"Guy, Keale," Kaij said, obviously deciding to ignore Val's comments. "You able to stick around also?"

Both gave affirmatives. Maggie said, "I'll head home. There's nothing much I can do here that Val can't."

I touched her arm and gave it a squeeze. "Thanks for flying out here."

She patted my hand. "No problems. And sorry about the way this has all turned out. I did rather like that old bastard."

So had I. I took another deep breath, then glanced at Kaij and raised an eyebrow.

"This way." He walked to the left of the containment shield and into the trees.

Darkness enveloped us, and the only sound to be heard was the soft crunch of leaves and twigs under my feet. Kaij, like most fae, walked light.

After a while, the moonlight began to break through the canopy above us, giving the leaves a silver shimmer and glinting brightly off the knife hilt at Kaij's waist. I wondered briefly what had happened to its mate—had he finished it? Had he given it to someone else?

He probably had by now. Ten years was a long time to be without anyone special in your life. Hell, I should know.

The familiar crash of waves upon a shore began to flow across the night, and it was soon followed by a soft whirring noise. We walked for another five minutes or so, and came out onto the beach. The helicopter sat on the sand like some gigantic metal blackbird, its rotor blades picking up speed as we approached. I climbed in, buckled up, and put on the headset.

"Ready?" the pilot asked, his voice loud in my ear as he glanced around.

Kaij gave him the thumbs up. I gripped the sides of the seat tightly, my stomach somewhere in my throat. I'd never been in one of these things before and, to be honest, I think I would have preferred to be on Maggie's broom or even dragon back. Helicopters had never seemed particularly safe to me.

We lifted skyward and banked to the right, heading for the bright glow of city lights. We'd barely seemed to be in the air for more than a few minutes before we were descending again. A yellow cab waited to the right of the helipad, its headlights washing brightness across the luminous X in the middle of the pad.

Once we'd landed, Kaij opened the door, helped me out, and then touched his fingers to my back to guide me across to the car.

"Everything set, Sam?"

Sam—a big man with arms the size of tree trunks and a hint of tusk-like teeth—nodded. "We have six in place. Infra-red says there's four inside the house."

"Lyle Phillecky one of them?"

He handed Kaij what looked like a sports watch. "From what we can ascertain, yes."

"Good. Tell the team we're on our way."

"Yes, sir."

Kaij glanced at me. "Ready to go?"

"Yes." I climbed in and buckled up. Once we were under-way, I added, "Why a cab?"

"Because we couldn't get a car to match yours at such short notice. A cab will raise fewer eyebrows than you arriving in an unknown car."

"Lyle's not likely to be hanging around a window to see what I arrive in."

"I wouldn't bet on it."

Actually, neither would I. He might have gone bat-shit crazy, but his brain seemed to be working just fine. I rubbed my arms to ward off an increasing chill that had nothing to do with the cold of the night and stared out the window. The shops and houses were little more than a blur as we sped past, though I doubted that would have changed even if we had been going slowly.

All too quickly, we were nearing my father's. Kaij slowed then pulled into the nearest empty parking spot, a couple of houses down from my father's.

"This," he said, holding up the watch he'd been given earlier, "is what we call the Enforcer. It looks like a regular watch, but it's capable of recording several hours of conver-sation and is sensitive enough to even pick up phone conver-sations."

"I doubt that's going to be an issue inside."

"No." He paused and strapped the watch onto my left wrist, his touch light but warm against my skin. He pressed two of the buttons, and then said, "Okay, it's now recording."

I frowned. "How will you hear what's going on if this just records our conversation?"

"We have long distance devices in place but this recording will be clearer when the case goes to trial. We can't risk placing a wire on you, because Lyle might just be looking out for it."

Maybe. Maybe not. He'd remarked often enough on my loyalty to my father to believe that I wouldn't do anything now to jeopardize him in any way. "Won't Lyle recognize it if it's something you use all the time?"

"No, because we don't use it all the time and certainly not on the sorts of cases he's been involved with lately."

I hoped like hell he was right. "How much do you need me to get?"

"Everything you can without endangering yourself."

No mention of endangering my Elven kin, I noticed. "Will recording it on the watch hold up in court?"

"Yes. We don't have to advise suspects they're being recorded if it's a private conversation."

I knew that already, but I just wanted confirmation. Wanted to delay what was coming.

"Is that it?" My gaze met his, searching for reassurance, searching for strength. I found the latter, not the former.

"Just be careful." He touched another button on the other side of the watch. "If it looks as if it's about to go pear-shaped, press this. We'll be in there in seconds."

I swallowed heavily and gripped the door handle. "Don't kill him."

"No. He has to pay for what he has done, Harri. Killing him is too soft an option."

I nodded, then threw the door open. Once I was out, he added softly, "And Harri?"

I bent, meeting his gaze again. "What?"

His green eyes glinted with cool gold fire in the shadows of the cab. "You were never a Phillecky in my eyes."

You were better than that. Better than all of them combined. Once again, he never said the words, but they echoed deep inside of me all the same. I blinked back the sudden sting of tears, then nodded, slammed the door shut, and walked quickly back up the street to my father's.

Damn him, I thought. Damn him to *hell* for saying that, and for coming back into my life and raising memories and emotions that should have been little more than dust.

Although maybe *I* should be damning myself for not being able to control myself a little more tightly around him.

The large, wrought iron gates into my father's house were open, an invitation I wished I didn't have to accept. As I walked up the driveway, my footsteps echoing lightly on the smooth concrete, I glanced up and studied the windows. There were no lights on up there, no shadows lurking at the side of the drapery. Which didn't mean Lyle wasn't aware of my arrival. I had a feeling he was aware of everything that had gone on—except, perhaps, for his part in Mona's death.

And maybe that should be the angle I take. If Ceri was

right, and he had blanked out just what he'd done, then I had to make him see. Make him *remember*.

I took a slow deep breath that did little to calm the churning in my stomach, then stepped up to the front door and pressed the intercom.

"How may I help you?" came Jose's polished response.

"It's Harri. Here to see Bramwell."

"I believe he's expecting you. Please proceed upstairs as before, Ms. Harriet."

The door clicked open. I blinked at the sudden brightness of the interior then headed inside as ordered, the bright pink of my shoes the only cheery spot in this otherwise austere white world.

My steps became slower as I climbed the stairs, and my heart was beating so fast it felt like it was going to tear out of my chest. I paused at the top, my gaze on the study door, trying to gain some measure of calm before I entered. I might as well have tried to hold back the tide.

I walked down and knocked.

"Come on in, Harriet, and join the party," Lyle said, his voice close and practically jovial.

I opened the door and went in.

And found myself eyeballing the wrong end of a gun.

CHAPTER FOURTEEN

Lyle pressed the barrel lightly to my forehead, the metal cold against my skin. I didn't move, didn't react in any way. I simply stared at the only elf I'd ever really trusted or liked.

"So is this how it ends?" I asked softly. "You shooting me in cold blood?"

He blinked, and the bright edge of madness in his eyes retreated a little. "No, this isn't how it ends. I merely wish to check that you've done as I asked. Raise your arms, Harriet."

I did. He lowered the gun and patted me down quickly and efficiently, then grunted and stepped back. "Okay, please have a seat."

I walked forward and, for the first time, saw my father and Gilroy. "How the hell did you get out, Gilroy? I thought the cops had arrested you?"

Gilroy looked me up and down, and sniffed. It was a

disdainful sound. Neither he nor my father looked overly worried about the current situation. Obviously, neither of them were aware just how far over the edge Lyle had jumped.

"They held me for questioning, nothing more."

"I thought they had your fingerprints on the murder weapon?"

"They did, simply because I picked up the thing. I did not, however, fire it. Nor did I kill Frank."

"Officially," Lyle snapped, "Gilroy has been released on his own recognizance, pending further investigation."

I sat down on the arm of the sofa. The sofa itself looked too low and soft—I doubted I'd be able to get out of it in a hurry if I needed to.

"So where was Rebecca meant to take me, Lyle?"

"A little place I have up in East Warburton."

Bramwell's eyes narrowed suddenly. "You were taking her onto ancestral land?"

"Not only that," I said, somewhat cheerfully, "He'd invited a couple of thugs onto it to keep me hostage while he came here to kill you both."

Bramwell's gaze ran from me to Lyle and back again. He still wasn't seeing the true gravity of the situation. "Lyle knows better—"

"Lyle," he said heavily. "Is getting mighty sick of the 'holier-than-thou' attitude of the Phillecky's."

"You're a Phillecky," Bramwell said, voice cold. "Now enough of this—"

Lyle took two steps, raised the gun, and smashed it across my father's face. His head snapped sideways, and blood spattered across the pristine carpet.

"Enough, brother dearest," Lyle said, shoving his face into Bramwell's. "You will speak when I tell you to, not before."

For the first time, I saw understanding flare in Bramwell's eyes. He saw the madness. Saw how deep it was.

When it was all too damn late, I thought bitterly.

"Why decide to bring me here, then, Lyle," I said, keeping my voice conversational. "I mean, you could have disappeared the minute Rebecca snatched me. Why do this? Why risk this?"

He retreated from Bramwell but didn't sit down. Instead, he stood in the middle of the room, a thin stick of humanity primed and ready to go off. "You're here for what you *didn't* do, Harriet."

"And what would that be, Lyle? Catch Mona's killer? Because we both know I was never going to do that."

Something flickered in his eyes. Something uneasy. Dark. "You didn't tell me about Gilroy's involvement with Mona, and wouldn't have told me that Bramwell was in that damn car if I hadn't insisted on accompanying you. That's not the way it works, Harriet."

"Neither is setting a dragon on me. She could have very easily have killed me, you know."

356

He shrugged. "I would have sung you onto the evergreen fields had that happened, half-breed. I promise you."

I snorted. "Thanks, but I'm not exactly comforted by that thought."

"You should be. It's more than I'll do for these bastards." He waved the gun in Bramwell and Gilroy's direction, and both men stiffened. Although there was little sign of emotion on my father's battered face, Gilroy's façade had begun to crack.

"She's going to testify that you paid her to inject Keale with Prevoron, setting him up to hit that helicopter, and thereby kill Frank Logan."

"Frank Logan wasn't in the helicopter," he said calmly. "Besides, who are the courts going to believe? A lawyer with years of pro bono work behind him, or an ice dragon with a somewhat checkered past?"

"Frank Logan *would* have been on that helicopter had it not been for a fortunate last minute phone call. But Rebecca isn't our only witness. We also have the testimony of the dealer you bought the Prevoron from."

He smiled bitterly. "You always were too clever for your own good, Harriet."

Which wasn't an admission, not by a long shot. "Obviously not, because I have no idea why you'd go to such lengths to kill Logan. Or how Numar comes into it."

"Numar was a blind lead. He was meant to be nothing more than a witness to the fact Keale had been drinking heavily."

"Which neither of them actually had. Rebecca seduced and

357

knocked Numar out, then drip-fed alcohol into his system." It was another guess, but it was also the only real explanation for not only the amount of alcohol Numar had inside of him, but the inability of either man to remember the events of that night. Hell, for all we knew, Numar also had Prevoron in his system—Lyle had purchased two vials after all, and it would certainly explain Numar's inexplicable ability to remember the precise time the woman he'd known as Mandy had left. "She did the same to Keale after you'd primed him with Prevoron."

The darkness came back into Lyle's eyes. A tremor ran down my spine. That darkness was capable of anything. Literally anything.

"Tell me, Harriet, how would you have felt if you'd come home one day and found your brother beaten and bloody?"

My gaze flickered to Bramwell. "Angry. No, furious."

Lyle nodded. "I was so furious I was shaking. She lost the baby on the way to the hospital, and I couldn't bear it, half-breed, I really couldn't. Once she was out of danger, I made her tell me who'd done it."

She lost the baby. He'd known. Despite all his statements to the contrary, he'd *known* she was pregnant. But it was the other part of that statement that caught my attention. He'd forced her to tell him. Had he used a bit more force than he'd intended?

"So why not confront Frank head on, or go to the police. Why make up some elaborate scheme to make them pay."

The darkness shifted, swirled. Became haunted with pain. "Because it would have come to nothing. She didn't want to press charges, and I couldn't without her testimony. But I couldn't let it go, either."

"So, you hatched a scheme to drug a dragon and induce him to hit the helicopter Logan was supposed to be in, thereby making his death seem an accident. But why Keale?"

He walked across to the desk and pulled the office chair around to the front. The aim of his gun never strayed far Gilroy's heart.

"It was simply a matter of convenience." Lyle shrugged and sat down. "As you noted, it had to look like an accident, and no one would think to question the actions of a dragon with a history of drink flying as long as a troll's arm."

"No one except me."

He sighed, and it held a sad note. "I kept trying to put you off, but you just wouldn't listen. You shouldn't have been so persistent, Harriet. I would have made sure he only got a couple of years."

"If you'd gotten the dose of the Prevoron wrong, Lyle, it could have killed him."

"But I didn't get it wrong. I couldn't, because an autopsy would have revealed its presence if I had." He lit a cigarette and studied me over the end of it. "You're awfully nosy all of a sudden, Harriet. Why?

I smiled, though it held little humor. "We both know there's only one person who's going to walk out of this room alive, Lyle. I just want some answers before you sing me onto the fields."

"Then why come here in the first place if you were aware of

what I intended? You are many things, but you are not the suicidal type."

I snorted softly. "I live in hope that you'll do the right thing, Lyle. Even now."

He nodded and took a drag of his cigarette. "I wouldn't hold your breath waiting for that, Harriet."

I wasn't. Not anymore. "Then tell me about Frank. He wasn't involved with Mona. Killing him because he beat her up seems a bit excessive, especially considering she was blackmailing James."

"And me," Gilroy said coldly.

Lyle glanced his way and, just for an instant, his finger hovered over the gun's trigger. I tensed, and then heaved a silent sigh of relief when Lyle relaxed.

I glanced at Gilroy. Sweat had broken out across his forehead. He knew how close he'd come.

"Frank had to die because he didn't *just* beat her. He raped her. Apparently, she tried to sing him into submission, and it had the opposite effect."

Which could very easily happen if the man called was in a highly emotional state such as anger. Mona must have been terrified to have even attempted it.

I studied him for a moment, then frowned. Something in what he'd said didn't sit right. Or maybe it was simply the way he seemed to be looking inwards rather than outwards, at us. Seeing something in his mind, not his immediate surrounds. Yet I had no doubt he'd react—and violently—if one of us so much as twitched.

"Mona told you this?"

"Yes. And he took the missing memory card. It had both James and Gilroy on it, she said." He blew smoke toward the ceiling. "He had to die, you see that, don't you?"

No, I didn't, and the mere fact Lyle saw it that way showed how far he had slipped. Once upon a time he would have been happy with busting Frank Logan's butt through the legal system, because if Frank *had* raped Mona in a fit of rage, there would have been DNA evidence.

"But why set Gilroy up for it?"

Lyle shrugged. "You heard what he said about her. He had as little respect for her as Frank did."

"So you set him up to take the fall for the murder, only it hasn't quite worked out that way, has it?"

He smiled and shook his head. "Ah, Harriet, you have more brains in your head than these two put together."

"Neither Bramwell nor Gilroy has access to the information you and I have, Lyle."

"Perhaps." He stubbed the cigarette out on the edge of the desk.

Bramwell's eyes narrowed, but he didn't say anything. My father wasn't stupid, despite Lyle's comments to the contrary.

"Meaning?" Gilroy snapped. "If we are to meet our end tonight, then we also deserve a full explanation."

"Did I ask you to speak?" Lyle said, then, before I could react, lowered the gun and shot him.

The bullet tore through Gilroy's kneecap, spraying blood and bone everywhere before it smashed into the wall behind him. Gilroy went down screaming.

No one came running and, after a moment, I realized why. The shot had been close to silent. There must be a silencer on the gun, meaning no one else inside the house would have heard it.

Kaij and his team outside *would*, of course, and I had my fingers crossed that they wouldn't react immediately. Not yet, not until I'd gotten *all* the answers.

Bramwell rose abruptly. Lyle immediately leveled the gun on his heart and he stopped. "Do not move, brother dearest, or you will be next."

"This is insane—"

"Perhaps," Lyle agreed. "But nevertheless, you *will* sit."

I shifted fractionally, and the gun's barrel jerked in response. I suddenly realized Lyle was waiting to be jumped—that he expected it, *wanted* it. Perhaps, somewhere in the shadows of madness, he thought he could claim self-defense and walk away a free man.

I cast a warning look at my father. For once, he seemed to understand exactly what I was saying, even if I used no words.

Maybe I should not speak to him more often.

"What about Mona?" I asked, as calmly as I could.

His gaze flicked to me. "What about her?"

"Didn't this whole mess start out with trying to find her murderer? What happened to that idea?"

He didn't immediately answer, just pulled out another cigarette and lit it. He sucked on it for several minutes, blowing the smoke toward the ceiling. I wondered what he was thinking. *If* he was thinking.

"Frank killed her," he said eventually.

"No," I said. "He didn't. You said yourself that he beat and raped her, but she was alive when Frank left her. She went to the hospital, remember, and that's where she lost the baby."

"Then it must have been one of these two. We both know they're capable of it."

"Yes, they are, but neither of them would have risked being seen paying ransom money to a siren if they'd intended to kill her all along."

More smoke drifted toward the ceiling. "Then it must have been one of her other clients. She had to be blackmailing more than just Gilroy and James."

"Perhaps she was, but we both know that none of them killed her, Lyle."

His gaze leveled on mine, and again I saw that darkness. But beneath it, shadows of pain and remorse stirred. "What do you mean?"

I tensed, ready to move should that gun waver in my direction the merest inch.

"I mean," I said softly, with just the slight touch of siren magic—enough that it might help calm him down, but not enough that he would sense it. "You left out one suspect, Lyle. You left out yourself."

He laughed—a harsh, unpleasant sound. "I didn't kill her, Harriet. I *loved* her."

"And yet, the minute she was out of the hospital, you forced her to tell you who'd beaten and raped her. *Forced* her, your words, not mine."

"But I didn't mean-"

"When did you find out the baby wasn't yours, Lyle?" I cut in ruthlessly. "In the hospital, or when you'd beaten the information out of her?"

"I didn't beat her," he muttered. "I loved her. I didn't do it."

He was trying to convince himself more than us. Ceri was right—he *had* blocked out those events.

"You loved her, but you hated what she did. You hated the fact other man continued to answer her call."

"I was going to take her away. I was going to marry her."

"You're already married, Lyle. And you were never going to get divorced, because you had no intentions of splitting your property in the settlement."

"The bitch is not getting her hands on *anything* of mine," he said, voice dark and low. "She's not."

"Why do you think Mona was blackmailing James and Gilroy? Why do you think she wanted money?"

He stubbed the cigarette out on the desk again, his movements sharp, angry. "I guess she wanted money of her own to go away with."

"Yeah," I said. "But not with you. She was running from you, Lyle, wasn't she?"

He ran his free hand across her eyes. "I loved her. Everything I've done, I've done for her."

It was an almost desperate sound. The wall was coming down.

"For her, or for you?" A hint of anger crept into my voice, despite my best effort to remain calm. Lyle had destroyed, or attempted to destroy, so many lives, and all in the name of his so-called love for a siren. "If you were so in love, why couldn't you accept who she was, and what she did, instead of trying to mold her into something she could never be? If you were so in love, why did she feel it was safer to run than tell you the child she carried was not yours?"

For a moment, he simply stared at me, face white, eyes wide. Shock. Then the darkness swirled in, and with it came the madness.

I saw the decision to kill before he even raised the gun. I threw myself sideways, but after everything that had happened over the last couple of days, I simply wasn't fast enough. The bullet hit tore into my shoulder and all I felt was pain. Red-hot pain. I screamed as I went down, heard a second soft retort, then that gun was in my face.

"Damn it, half-breed, I *loved* her. Don't you dare tell me I killed her."

I gripped my shoulder, but blood pulsed through my fingers

365

and there was a roaring inside my head that almost consumed me. But if I blacked out now, I'd be dead.

Kaij, I thought, and somehow pressed that button, *get here fast.*

"You killed her, Lyle." The words little more than a hiss of air through clenched teeth. "You beat the information out of her, and then you raped her. Mona tried to use her song on you, not Frank, didn't she?"

"No," Lyle said, almost desperately. "No."

"You hired me to find her killer, Lyle. You wanted revenge. This whole sad mess was all about getting justice for the woman you loved. Well, I *found* her killer. What are you going to do, now that you know who it truly was?"

For the longest minute of my life, I simply stared at him. And for the first time in a long while, I saw true clarity in his gaze.

"I'm sorry, Harriet," he said softly, "For everything."

He raised the gun. I surged forward, a scream wrenched from my lips that was both pain and denial. But I was too late. Far too late. Lyle pulled the trigger, splattering blood and bone and brain matter across my father's pristine carpet as his body fell backward.

He was dead.

It was over.

I closed my eyes and let unconsciousness take me.

EPILOGUE

"Hey, Harri, you want another beer?" Guy said, poking his head into the living room.

"You mean there's some left?"

A pained expression crossed the ogre's face. "I've only been here an hour, and Moe and Curly haven't arrived yet. Of *course* there's some left."

"Then I'll have one." I hesitated, hearing footsteps out in the hall, and leaned back to see who it was.

Keale appeared, carrying a slab over one shoulder and a newspaper under the other. "Footy started yet?"

"Five minutes. What did the new lawyer say?"

He grimaced, handed the beer over to Guy, and then sat down rather gingerly. Five days had passed since he'd forced Rebecca out of the skies, but the burns had been deeper than they'd looked. "He said Lyle's confession, along with Rebecca's, should help convince the judge of extenuating circumstances. Especially since Kaij will put a good word in for me-"

"Kaij said he'd do that?" I cut in, surprised.

"Yeah." He eyed me for a moment. "You haven't talked to him?"

"No." I hadn't even seen him. Neither during the three days I'd been in the hospital, or two days out of it. Oh, plenty of other police officers, and even the occasional PIT officer had come in to take statements, but not Kaij. Not once. Not even to see if I was okay.

To say it pissed me off would be something of an understatement. I mean, I hadn't really expected any deep show of sentiment, but hell, would it have killed him to come in and say 'Hello, how's the shoulder?'

Obviously, the answer was yes.

"Odd," Keale said. "He did ask after you. I thought he—"

"Did the lawyer say anything else?" I cut in, really not wanting to discuss or think about Kaij any further.

He grimaced. "The fact is, I did hit the helicopter, and I did kill people. He reckons that, at the very least, I'll be put on a long-term community service sentence, and lose my flying license, except for set times when I'm working. I'll have to attend a drug and alcohol course, as well."

"All of which will be better than prison."

He nodded. "Have you seen the front of the Herald-Sun?"

"No." Nor did I really want to. The day after Lyle's death—once I'd been patched up and was fairly sensible—I'd given

Greg his exclusive. The story was quickly syndicated across the country, dragging Lyle's name into the mud and clearing Gilroy in the process—although it *had* brought his liaison with a siren out into the open.

But, as he'd predicted so smugly, it really hadn't done much to dent his popularity. In fact, it had probably *increased* it by making him seem more 'human'.

My father was happy. Gilroy was happy. Greg was happy.

I wasn't.

I'd lost a friend. A friend who'd also been a relative. And whatever else Lyle had become, whatever he'd done during the last few days of his life, that's what I would remember. Not the madness, but the man who had occasionally treated me as kin.

"You might want to." Keale took the newspaper out from under his arm and handed it across.

I unfolded it. There, on the front page, was Lyle being carried through the golden trees of the Phillecky clan's retreat. Bramwell and Gilroy were at the head of the procession, putting Elven sensibilities before everything else, as always.

No one had told me about the funeral. No one had invited me onto the ancestral lands to sing his soul onto the evergreen fields.

Some things never changed it seemed.

I threw the paper to one side. I intended to say goodbye to Lyle in my own way. With Darryl's help, I'd give Mona a proper siren burial. That, more than anything else, would set Lyle's soul at rest. He *had* loved her, at least until love had turned to madness and aggression.

More footsteps echoed, then Moe and Curly appeared, carrying another slab of beer and a stack of pizzas. Curly slid one off the top and handed it to me with a grin, then put the rest on the coffee table. I opened the box warily and was surprised to see seafood. Just seafood and cheese, and none of the other muck they preferred. The ogres were definitely spoiling me.

Guy reappeared, carrying beer. He handed a can out to everyone then chucked the newspaper on the floor and sat beside me. "See that Elven brother of yours got his pic in the paper again."

"Yeah. Lyle's funeral."

"You didn't want to go?" he asked.

"I wasn't invited."

"Harri my friend, when has that ever stopped you from doing anything?"

I grinned. "Well, almost never, but this is different."

"How?"

"It's family. I'm not."

"Their loss, man." He snagged one of the pizza boxes and opened it up. The aroma of pineapple and meat filled the air. He inhaled deeply, sighed in contentment, then said, "You heard from them at all? I mean, you saved your brother's life, not to mention his political career. I would have thought they'd be falling all over you with gratitude."

I snorted. "I don't think gratitude is in my father's vocabulary."

Guy shook his head. "Elves. They suck, don't they?"

"In the case of the Phillecky clan, they certainly—"

The rest of my sentence was cut off by a roar from Keale. The umpire had bounced the football. The sermon had begun.

I grinned and settled back to eat my pizza. I didn't need to hear from my father or half-brother. I didn't need their thanks or their acknowledgment.

With friends like these, I was richer than either of them ever would be.

ABOUT THE AUTHOR

Keri Arthur, author of the New York Times bestselling Riley Jenson Guardian series, has now written more than thirty-nine novels. She's received several nominations in the Best Contemporary Paranormal category of the Romantic Times Reviewers Choice Awards and has won RT's Career Achievement Award for urban fantasy. She lives with her daughter and two old dogs in Melbourne, Australia.

for more information:

www.keriarthur.com

kez@keriarthur.com

ALSO BY KERI ARTHUR

IN SERIES ORDER

City of Light (Outcast Series, 1)

Winter Halo (Outcast Series, 2)

Fireborn (Souls of Fire Series, 1)

Wicked Embers (Souls of Fire Series, 2)

Flameout (Souls of Fire Series, 3)

Ashes Reborn (Souls of Fire Series, 4)

Darkness Unbound (Dark Angels Series, 1)

Darkness Rising (Dark Angels Series, 2)

Darkness Devours (Dark Angels Series, 3)

Darkness Hunts (Dark Angels Series, 4)

Darkness Unmasked (Dark Angels Series, 5)

Darkness Splintered (Dark Angels Series, 6)

Darkness Falls (Dark Angels Series, 7)

Full Moon Rising (Riley Jenson Series, 1)

Kissing Sin (Riley Jenson Series, book 2)

Tempting Evil (Riley Jenson Series, 3)

Dangerous Games (Riley Jenson Series, 4)

Embraced by Darkness (Riley Jenson Series, 5)

The Darkest Kiss (Riley Jenson Series, 6)

Deadly Desire (Riley Jenson Series, 7)

Bound to Shadows (Riley Jenson Series, 8)

Moon Sworn (Riley Jenson Series, 9)

Destiny Kills (Myth & Magic Series, 1)

Mercy Burns (Myth & Magic Series, 2)

Circle of Fire (Damask Circle Series, 1)

Circle of Death (Damask Circle Series, 2)

Circle of Desire (Damask Circle Series, 3)

Beneath a Rising Moon (Ripple Creek Series, 1)

Beneath a Darkening Moon (Ripple Creek Series, 2)

Memory Zero (Spook Squad Series, 1)

Generation 18 (Spook Squad Series, 2)

Penumbra (Spook Squad Series, 3)

Dancing with the Devil (Nikki & Michael Series, 1)

Hearts in Darkness (Nikki & Michael Series, 2)

Chasing the Shadows (Nikki & Michael Series, 3)

Kiss the Night Goodbye (Nikki & Michael series, 4)

Lifemate Connections: Eryn (Novella)

Made in the USA
San Bernardino, CA
09 December 2017